THE LOST TARPON

THE LOST TARPON

AND OTHER SHORT STORIES

PHILIP HIRSH

MARINER PUBLISHING

3608
.I75
L6
2012

Copyright © 2012 by Philip Hirsh

1 3 5 7 9 10 8 6 4 2

Library of Congress Control Number: 2012934608

The Lost Tarpon: And Other Short Stories
Philip Hirsh

p. cm.
1. Fiction: Short Stories (single author)
2. Fiction: General
3. Fiction: Psychological

I. Hirsh, Philip, 1938– II. Title.
ISBN 13: 978-0-9849214-2-3 (softcover : alk. paper)

Edited by Judy Rogers
Cover Design by Ross Frazier
Book Design by Emilie Davis

Mariner Publishing
An imprint of
Mariner Media, Inc.
131 West 21st Street
Buena Vista, VA 24416
Tel: 540-264-0021
www.marinermedia.com

Printed in the United States of America

This book is printed on acid-free paper meeting the requirements of the American Standard for Permanence of Paper for Printed Library Materials.

THE BEST STORIES COME FROM
OUR WORST IMPULSES.

—PENROSE PLUME-ARCHER

Index of Stories

A PERFECT MURDER

Nearly 17,000 murders are committed in this country every year, over 500 in Los Angeles alone—sixty-two percent result in arrest, and slightly under a quarter of those lead to any form of conviction and punishment. Given such bleak statistics you might readily conclude that getting away with murder is actually pretty easy, especially if you're willing to invest a little time in planning. If justice reaches but one in nine, it would seem only bunglers get caught; by inference, a carefully concocted scheme ought to make the odds of success temptingly good.

But before you decide it's safe to go after your boss with moth poison, take a closer look at the stats. Of all homicides, fewer than five percent are in any way planned. Most killing is impulsive, driven by sudden rage fueled in the vast majority of cases by alcohol and/or drugs. Pure idiotic jealousy and boundary-pissing account for most of the remaining non-substance related murders.

That leaves very little room for calculated revenge or money-inspired killing. In those two specific categories, eighty percent fail. Even the twenty percent who aren't caught can't be credited with perfection since they almost always escape because of someone else's incompetence, not because they were so damn clever in the first place.

There are two other myths to be explored before we get into the story of Peter Odell. One is the "perpetrator profile" trumpeted on television. If you would believe it, a killer's identity (with address and phone number) can be found simply by punching the facts of the crime into a computer program. *Voilà!* He's a twenty-two-year-old hog farmer with a penchant for classical music, a collection of animal porn, and a sister who owns a red pencil box. Piece of cake.

The other, more important, myth is that homicide detectives solve crimes. They don't. If you need proof, just tune in to any of the popular true-crime television shows. It isn't tire tracks or pubic hair that catch killers, it's pure dumb luck, usually in the form of a tip from a disgruntled girlfriend or neighbor who, two years after the crime, suddenly remembers seeing Bob throw a body bag into the town dumpster.

That brings me to Peter Odell and, for a moment, back to the profile issue. While most of us would concede that killers don't necessarily look the part, we still—in defiance of logic—think there *ought* to be something that would give them away. Ted Bundy and Jeffrey Dahmer were *too* good looking. Richard Speck looked too twisted *not* to be a mass murderer. Wayne Gacy just *looked* like a murderous pedophile in his clown suit. And who would pick up Aileen Wuornos at 2:00 a.m. on a Florida turnpike? Even as ordinary as John Hinckley appeared, you only had to look at his pasty complexion and empty, mirthless smile to grasp the connection between killing Ronald Reagan and winning Jody Foster's eternal love.

It's human nature to be frightened by the possibility of living next door to Henry Lee Lucas or Leonard Lake, and comforting to entertain the delusion we might spot something in our neighbor's look or behavior that would signal danger in time to find a new apartment—but don't count on it.

If you are one of the tiny fraction of potential murderers who plan to get away with your crime, think again. True, you can usually count on inept law enforcement, but coincidence, bad luck, snoopy neighbors, or an overdue library book will nail you every time. But there are exceptions, like the story of Peter Odell, the tale of a murder planned and executed with extraordinary perfection by someone you would not imagine capable of such an act.

At the point in time just before Peter concocted his perfect murder scheme, he was truly the invisible man living as banal and uninteresting a life as can be imagined. Peter grew up in Elizabeth, New Jersey, in an anonymous middle class community of 1920 look-alike homes on small lots surrounded by uninteresting, but generally non-belligerent, blue-collar neighbors. Peter's father, Butch, was a machinist, member of the Elizabeth Boosters Club, a weekend fisherman, and by any measure, a family man. Delia Odell was a stay-at-home mom (except during WWII when she worked in a tank factory), and sometimes-member of the

PTA. Butch was drafted in 1942 when his first son, Raymond, was six months old. Peter arrived while his father was serving in a supply depot in England.

The war years were scary times for the Odells, as they were for millions of others with a parent, spouse, or child off fighting in battle. It helped that theirs was a small family and Butch was the only near relative in the service. Delia was very close to her only sibling, her sister, Mary, and the two spent as much time as possible together. Martin, Mary's husband, worked in the same machine shop as Butch, but the two were not as close as their wives. Martin, incidentally, only had one kidney so he wasn't drafted.

Happily for the Odells, Butch came home from Europe unscratched, went back to his old job, and life as usual returned to Locklear Avenue.

The family attended All Souls Methodist church, Delia participated in the Lady's Circle, and little Peter and Raymond occasionally attended Sunday school. The boys went to public school, played baseball with friends in Locklear Park, bumped along with middling grades, and were never in any serious trouble in school. After graduation, Raymond got a job with the city sanitation department, took an apartment with two friends, and seemed to be on course in a steady job with the promise of a pension in a few short decades.

Peter decided (with some prodding from his mother) to give higher education a try and enrolled in a local community college. That was the fall of 1960—the point when the first whiff of trouble drifted into the Odell household.

Butch Odell had a 10th grade education and was decidedly ambivalent about the virtue of college for his son. Like Raymond, he had gone from school into a good job without college, so why couldn't Peter do the same? Worse yet, Butch was footing the tuition, and while a modest sum, it still took a bite out of the family budget. On top of that, Peter was living at home and making no visible effort to get a job.

In the middle of the growing crisis, Butch's brother-in-law was struck in the face by a piece of steel, lost an eye, and was out of work. The Odells stepped up with what meager funds they had left, and for a while it looked like they might lose their home. Peter was still an unemployed college student, he and his father were hardly on speaking terms, and Raymond—in spite of his good job—seemed mysteriously unable to contribute.

Fortunately for Martin and Mary, a lawyer successfully sued the machine shop owner and Martin collected an enormous award said to be close to a million dollars. He and Mary moved to Pompano Beach, Florida, bought a home on a canal and a fishing boat, and settled down to a comfortable, one-eyed early retirement. While thankful for support from the Odells, there was no offer to repay any of their accumulated debt. Delia, as always, was forgiving, thankful her brother-in-law only lost an eye.

"It could have been worse," she used to say.

No, it couldn't, Butch fumed to himself. In fact, from his perspective it was considerably worse. For starters, even though Butch had nothing to do with Martin's accident and successful lawsuit, his boss seemed to blame him. He didn't get any more promotions, didn't feel welcome at company picnics, and always seemed to be given the toughest and most tedious work.

And things at home weren't much better. Raymond was caught selling drugs from the sanitation truck, and narrowly missed doing time by getting diverted into a drug treatment program. At his own expense, of course. And that translated into Butch's expense. Pay up or your son goes to the slammer.

Delia went to work rather than see Peter be pitched out of the house and have to give up college, but Peter only lasted another six months. Butch mistakenly opened a letter from the dean telling Peter he was on academic probation for poor attendance in his one course.

"*One course!?*" Butch screamed. "I'm paying for *three* goddamn courses!!"

It turned out Peter felt the pressure of three courses was simply too much to handle, had dropped back to one and was saving the rest of the money for later when he would resume a more rigorous schedule. Unfortunately, the funds had somehow become depleted. And that was the end of both Peter Odell's academic career and his comfortable living arrangement.

Peter moved into the Patterson YMCA and got a position with Carl's Used Cars in Newark. Delia remained supportive of her sons, though she was depressed by Raymond's inability to stay clean for more than a month or two at a time. Butch basically terminated his relationship with both boys, became a closet drinker, and within ten years was dying of cirrhosis of the liver.

Peter eked out a living selling used cars, and when sales were slow he sold vacuums door-to-door and worked as a short-order cook in a local Greek restaurant, all the while dreaming of the Big One, the idea that would make him rich. He always knew it was right there at his fingertips, he just couldn't quite grab it. He was a reasonably good salesman, could sometimes put together several car deals back-to-back and earn enough to try a new scheme. But inevitably he failed and wound up back at another car lot. I say "another" because when Peter was hot on the trail of a new idea he had a way of burning his bridges, leaving a trail of unappreciative former employers in the embers.

Nor was Peter particularly successful with women. He liked women, to be sure, but his relationships typically fizzled out after only a few dates. In high school, the girls generally didn't notice him. He wasn't on any athletic team and certainly wasn't an academic standout. Worse, he didn't even have a car. His mother encouraged him to date girls in the neighborhood, but her idea of a "date" was to invite a young lady to walk to the Odell house to watch TV and eat cookies in the family room under the watchful eye of Mom and Dad.

Raymond had a car, earned with money from his summer job as a life guard at the YMCA outdoor pool. Peter felt that summers were to be enjoyed, not ruined by the distracting burden of steady employment. He did, however, hatch a few schemes to make money, though none worked out the way he planned. His nearest miss was selling used golf balls scooped out of the pond on the Elizabeth Country Club golf course. Every fall the management drained the pond (grandly named "Lake Elizabeth") and recovered hundreds of balls to recycle into their driving range.

Peter saw an opportunity. At night he sneaked onto the course with a bucket, waded into the shallow bog feeling for golf balls with his feet. He could fill a bucket in a few hours. At home he cleaned the balls, packaged them in plastic bags, and sold them at the public course in nearby Rahway. He could make as much as fifty dollars from a bucket of rescued balls, but he disliked wading around in the pond muck so his trips were only as frequent as his need for money.

Unfortunately for Peter, the manager of the driving range noticed a lot of foot prints around the pond and figured out that someone was pilfering his golf balls. He was a patient man willing to spend many nights waiting for the thief to show up. He finally nabbed Peter and turned him over to the Elizabeth police. He was charged with trespass, put on probation, and that was the end of it.

His next caper was better thought out. At that point, Peter was between his junior and senior years in high school, and his parents—especially his father—were putting a lot pressure on him to get a summer job. A real one.

The challenge, from Peter's perspective, was to find something that would get his father off his back and make decent money yet not require him to lift heavy objects, be forced to get up too early, or work into his evening social hours. He also wanted to avoid any interaction with the police because he was still on probation from the golf ball scam.

The answer came to Peter during an especially satisfying bowel movement one Sunday morning while his parents were at church. He composed a flyer advertising himself as an experienced Handyman (with a capital "H") available by appointment between the hours of 9:00 a.m. and 5:00 p.m. He put the flyers in neighborhood mail boxes and sat back to wait for business.

And business came. Peter raked leaves, weeded flower beds, and hauled junk off to the dump (in the trunk of his mother's car). Foolishly, his patrons assumed Peter to be trustworthy; after all, he was the son of church-going neighbors, had a bright smile and cheerful manner. What they didn't realize was that while they were away from home, their trusty Handyman was rummaging for treasure. For Peter, it was exciting to snoop through his employer's underwear drawers, closets, and medicine cabinets. He quickly realized three things about most of his neighbors.

First, they all had hiding places for cash and jewelry. Tempting, but too obvious. People know what they hide, missing items are instantly noticed, and by simple deduction Peter would be the stand-out suspect.

Second, many of the husbands have another hiding place where they keep their porn, old love letters, and condom supply. Nothing to steal there, and Peter was not ready to graduate into the blackmail business.

Finally, the medicine cabinets. Everyone had drugs, lots of them, some with street value. Peter knew he couldn't steal cash or jewels without risking immediate discovery, but pills were a different matter. He could take a few Miltown tablets out of a bottle with virtually no risk. Who counts pills? So Peter began to collect pharmaceuticals: a few Nembutals here, some Equanil there, and maybe on a good day some Demerol or Tuinals. And turning his booty into cash was as easy as having Raymond sell them on the street, splitting the profits fifty-fifty.

Like the golf ball con, this one came apart over laziness and lack of vigil. He was surprised one day by a customer who returned home unexpectedly, catching Peter coming down the stairs. Peter said he was only using the bathroom, but the neighbor wasn't buying it. He fired Peter and made it his duty to warn all of his neighbors about Peter. Business immediately died and Peter had to journey further from home to get any jobs. It all became too complicated for Peter and he simply gave up, though he continued to absent himself from home during the day to reassure his parents he was still hard at work.

The following summer—after graduation from high school and before community college—Peter got a real job: a "prep boy" at a local used car lot. He cleaned up the cars, made sure any leaking oil was quickly sopped up, and when customers looked over a car he was often heard to say things like "Best damn car on the lot" or "Damn! I had my eye on that baby for myself."

Peter learned the used car trade, and quite clearly had a knack for selling. Finally! A career possibility, one he returned to whenever another scheme failed. Indeed, after his college career hit the rocks Peter worked more-or-less consistently in the used car business. Over the next ten years he bounced around from lot to lot, occasionally getting a position with a new car dealer, but he couldn't keep up with more seasoned salesmen and inevitably returned to selling used cars.

That brings us up to 1970, when Sally Shafer entered Peter's life. At home, Butch was drinking himself to death, Raymond was still struggling to stay clean (meaning he was doing his best to stick to selling drugs, not using them), and Delia was busy pretending all was well. She stayed in daily contact with Uncle Martin and Aunt Mary who were in Florida enjoying their retirement.

Sally Shafer was the dispatch operator for an ambulance company, graduate of community college, and a devout Catholic. She was full-bodied though by no means fat, and her freckled face, perpetual smile, and endless good humor long made her a favorite with teachers, neighbors, and employers. Popular as she was with the older crowd, she was not a hot ticket in dating circles. In fact, she made it through three years of high school without a single date. She went to her senior prom with her geeky cousin, Jeff, a junior, and was only asked to dance once: by Peter Odell. That magical moment was forever stamped in her mind, an omen, a sign from God Himself that she was a real woman. All previous doubts were erased, and henceforth she fastened her hopes on Peter Odell.

Peter, of course, was oblivious to his messianic role. After all, he had danced with her only because Cousin Jeff had begged him, promising in exchange to steal a copy of the Algebra final from the principal's office where he had an after-hours cleaning job.

Peter got the exam and Sally got her promise of a better life. The fact Peter paid no attention to her after the prom made no difference. The faithful don't require proof; in fact, the less proof the stronger the faith.

Doubt generates anxiety but certainty soothes the faithful mind. Sally knew it was only a matter of time until God sent Peter a vision, complete with wedding gown and several baby showers.

And finally the moment arrived. Sally's father ran into Peter while shopping for a used car. When Peter realized who his customer was, he gushed over his fond memories of Sally and asked if he might pay a call to the Shafer home. Mr. Shafer was delighted to think someone might actually be interested in his daughter, quickly agreed to buy the car, and invited Peter to dinner.

It's a small price for a good sale, Peter thought, and he dutifully arrived for Sunday dinner with the Shafers. As a group, the Shafers didn't bubble over with dinner conversation, so Peter had the floor to himself. He was becoming increasingly skilled at the fine art of glib conversation, self-inflating stories, and good old-fashioned flattery. When the subject of religion came up Peter didn't miss a beat, let it slip he was giving serious thought to converting to Catholicism.

"I think if you're going to take Our Savior's Promise seriously, you owe it to yourself," (pause for effect—lower the voice) "and your future family, to practice the True Faith." Sally nearly fainted.

Peter moved on.

"Nothing against All Souls Methodist, but I just don't feel the, well, *connection* I need there. It's hard to put into words," he added. There was immediate agreement around the table.

So the courtship began, and before long Peter was studying the Baltimore Catechism, enjoying regular meals with the Shafers, sharing with them the plans he had for the future. He and Sally saw each other regularly, and cautiously engaged in what was known as "petting" in those days. Peter sensed that anything beyond a kiss and a quick, seemingly innocent brush across Sally's ample breasts was forbidden. Sally was saving it all for her wedding knight.

Peter didn't mind, and what Sally took for respect and purity was actually something entirely different. Peter had a long-time relationship with a hooker, Hazel, who worked at the House of Mirrors, a Newark brothel, and whenever he had the money, he visited her place of employment for a satisfying "Around the World," the house specialty. Her name, by the way, changed depending on a customer's taste—Frau Hazel der Whippe, Nurse Hazel, Naughty Hazel, Latex Hazel, Officer Hazel. You get the idea.

Before long, wedding plans were being made, the Shafers and senior Odells were becoming fast friends, though in truth the relationship was more between Delia and the Shafers. Butch was sloshed most of the time and rarely came out of the basement for social engagements. Delia made excuses, but the Shafers didn't seem to care; after all, this was about the "youngsters" and their future together.

Peter and Sally were married in Saint Thomas the Martyr Cathedral in Elizabeth, Father Flynn presiding over a lengthy (and extremely expensive) Marriage Mass and Communion Service. Just to top it all off, Sally's parents hired Newark's leading for-rent tenor who presented an inspiring rendition of *Ave Maria* between Father Flynn's extensive Homily and equally protracted Communion. Father Flynn was delighted to announce at the reception (after a few glasses of Taylor's best champagne) that over a quart of Blessed Wine was sipped by the faithful at the communion rail. Not a record, mind you, but damned impressive.

The Odells honeymooned in Atlantic City. After a splendid dinner at Salty Dick's, they repaired to the Honeymoon Suite where Sally gladly surrendered her virginity. She required treatment for a urinary tract infection in the local ER two days later, but it was a small price to pay for the bliss she found in Peter's arms. In fact, quite contrary to what you might have guessed, the Odell marriage was pretty good, at least for the first five years. Peter went to work at his father-in-law's auto parts store, quickly rising to assistant manager, and on a day-to-day level, he and Sally were quite happy.

Sally became pregnant within a month, and delivered Rose Angel Odell nine months later—on her mother's birthday. Though Baby Rose was colicky, and an expert at projectile vomiting, everyone agreed she was a perfect baby and looked just like her grandmother. Peter wasn't really keen on the diaper thing, but Sally didn't mind. "Just like a man," she said. The two grandmothers agreed.

Little Reginald Porter Odell and Regina Mary Odell arrived a year apart. With three kids under five all demanding new sneakers at the same time, Peter decided it was time to take action and had a vasectomy. He had the procedure done in New York City, explaining to the urologist that he was a bachelor with no intention of marrying and thought it would be "more responsible" if he had himself neutered. The doctor praised Peter's morality and quickly snipped his *vas deferens*.

Peter explained his swollen balls to Sally as an accident at work, and bravely spared the family budget the expense of a doctor visit. Sally bought it, of course, eased the pain with warm compresses, and his condition quickly resolved. She hoped the injury would not compromise their ability to have more children. Peter assured her it would not, but cautioned that children were a Blessing from Above, and if it didn't happen, it should not be questioned.

Sally agreed on the surface but every night she prayed to the Blessed Virgin that Peter would want to have sex, and if they did, that she would become pregnant. Peter was less inclined sexually, and when they talked about it, he blamed work and the stress of raising a family. He made no mention of his frequent visits to the House of Mirrors.

Another problem for the Odells was Peter's increasing distance from his benefactor, Mr. Shafer, who was growing tired of Peter's frequent business errors. At first it was just little stuff—missing inventory, coming in late, charging personal expenses to the business—but when the IRS ordered a review of the business' taxes for 1976, Mr. Shafer was in for a shock. The auditors questioned a series of unsecured loans by the company to Peter, loans that were not even collecting interest. There was a huge uproar over it, but for Sally's sake, Mr. Shafer quietly paid the taxes and fines, then gave Peter three months to find a new line of work.

Fortunately, Mr. Shafer hired Sally to work in the company, basically replacing Peter. He paid her generously knowing that without her salary the Odells would implode. If it could be arranged so only Peter would suffer, Mr. Shafer would have been delighted, but he had to think of Sally and the kids, so he swallowed hard, content in the knowledge that in a few short months he would no longer have to deal with Peter at work.

Peter realized he had to do something dramatic—and fast—or his dream world would collapse. He immediately took himself to Florida to visit Uncle Martin and Aunt Mary. He was terribly apologetic over not keeping in touch, but the rigors of business and a large family were overwhelming. Martin and Mary understood completely, and were delighted to learn about a new business prospect Peter was working on, and happy to become what Peter called his "Start-up Investors." The details of the new business were a bit vague, but Mary and Delia were certain this was going to be the Big One for Peter.

"He's such a dear," Mary said to her sister on the phone, "And so brave to be thinking about his family's welfare when his own father is so ill." Butch was, in fact, only weeks away from the fatal rupture of an esophageal vein caused by one last enormous drinking binge.

"It's like having a bleeding hemorrhoid in your throat," the sympathetic ER doctor explained to Mary.

Butch's last words, by the way, were, "Fuck it."

Martin and Mary came up for the funeral, Peter was solicitous, but asked that they not discuss his business plans with the Shafers. "I haven't told Mr. Shafer I'm leaving yet. *Timing*—it's everything in business." A few days after the funeral Delia announced she would be selling the house and moving to Florida to live with Martin and Mary. The money from the sale of the house would be used to build on an extra bedroom and add a swimming pool between the patio and the canal.

"Won't it be wonderful?" she gushed to Peter. "We'll all be together, and you, Sally, and the kids can visit any time you want!" Peter and Raymond were deeply depressed over the idea of all that money taking flight, but there was nothing more to do but say how happy they were. "Dad would have wanted it this way."

No doubt. Especially if it would have been the end of Peter's hopes for financial rescue. But in spite of being in a tight spot—the tightest of his life—Peter decided to seize the moment, told Sally he was off on a secret mission to meet new investors, and armed with a chunk of Martin and Mary's investment, disappeared for a few days to think things over.

And what better place for contemplation than the House of Mirrors? He started off with a double trip Around the World with a new girl and ended up in the arms of his favorite, Hazel.

Peter was very drunk by the time he got to Hazel, and somehow had it fixed in his mind he had become a world-famous mountain climber. He drove bravely toward the summit of Mount Hazel, but the altitude got the better of him and he threw up all over Hazel's slopes. Because he was such a good customer, they didn't throw Peter in the Passaic River, but instead locked him in a bathroom to sleep it off. They let him out in the morning, cleaned him up, and fed him breakfast. His head ached, his pockets were nearly empty (something he didn't share with Hazel), and he could hardly hold down half an English muffin.

"What a fucking waste," he said absently. "I don't even remember getting laid."

Conversation turned to the reason Peter was on such a tear, and he quickly got back on stride. "I made some money and decided to celebrate before I move on to my next investment."

"And what will that be?" asked Hazel.

"Dunno. I'm looking around for something good. No quickie, either. Something solid, something with a good rate of return."

"I think I might have an idea for you, Peter," offered Hazel, and within two hours Peter was a five percent partner in the House of Mirrors. By the end of the day the remaining funds (close to 40K) had been transferred, and Peter was meeting with the House's main owner, Paul Protigliano, who promised Peter he would receive 3K a month plus ten percent of income generated from clients he referred. Of course, he had to understand that, like any business, certain "fees" might occasionally be assessed against his take for unforeseen expenses; you know, extra bribes to Newark police, bail in case someone was arrested, abortion costs, that sort of stuff. Peter was also given referral goals every month, and reminded that he had to screen his clients well. Any client-generated mishaps would come out of his check.

For the first several months the deal actually worked. Peter had plenty of contacts through his father-in-law's auto parts business and area car lots, and he worked out an arrangement with a number of car salesmen to send their high roller regular customers for a free romp at the House of Mirrors.

Peter loved his new job, and Sally actually thought he had a steady job—as a "mobile car appraiser." Peter bought himself expensive suits, a new car, and took the family to Disney World for their first-ever real vacation. They stopped by to see Martin, Mary, and Mom, and Peter regaled everyone with stories of his newfound success. During dinner at a fancy Pompano Beach restaurant (for which Peter grandly picked up the tab), Peter handed Martin an envelope containing $1,000 toward his investment.

"Just the start," he said. Originally, he thought he would give Martin and Mary more, but the cash seemed to disappear as they made their way south. Martin and Mary were grateful anyway, Mom glowed, and the kids had their own baked Alaska.

But things didn't go smoothly for long. Peter began to fall behind on referrals, there were more expenses than expected, and pretty soon Peter had to turn in his car for a less expensive model, explaining he just didn't like the new one as much as he thought he would. Within six months, things were desperate. Monthly fees reduced Peter's take to a few hundred dollars and he was having a hard time concealing the looming disaster.

And Peter wasn't the only one in trouble. Because business was way off in several of Paul Protigliano's brothels, he fell behind on his bribe schedule, something for which the Newark police have zero tolerance. The House of Mirrors was raided, its staff arrested, and the once-glamorous interior was trashed. Paul fled back to Brooklyn to lick his wounds. Even Peter knew that chasing after him would be suicide. Kiss Martin and Mary's money goodbye.

The only one who got away scot-free was Hazel. She had advance warning of the raid from a judge she was entertaining and got out of Newark just in time. She moved in with her sister in Scranton, Pennsylvania, converted her carport into a beauty salon, and within several years owned a chain of parlors called Hazel's Hair House, each featuring enormous Victorian mirrors on every wall. They were a huge hit. Hazel married her lawyer, sold the business, and moved to St. Croix.

Peter tried to keep the bad news from Sally but it was impossible, and in one of her rare moments of confrontation with Peter, she told him that if he expected her and the children to stay with him he would simply have to get a job—a real one. She suggested he write to Martin and Mary, too, and let them know the truth about their money.

Peter agreed to all of Sally's conditions, got yet another car sales job, but somehow he couldn't find the right words and the letter to Martin and Mary was never sent. It didn't seem to matter, though, and no mention of the money was made again. Peter, Sally, and the children visited the Florida family at least once a year, and whenever Peter started to bring up the subject of the investment Martin always told him not to worry, they all knew that these things take time, and they had every confidence it would eventually work out.

This was a fairly stable time in Peter's life, and for the next decade he worked more or less steadily in sales, all the while keeping his eye open for a score. But there were no funds available anywhere so Peter had to live on dreams, his modest income, and Sally's paycheck.

In 1988 Delia developed bone cancer. Peter went to see her fairly often, generously financed by Sally who simply couldn't bring herself to say no. She rationalized the expenditures by saying it was for Delia more than Peter.

Delia's illness lasted two excruciatingly painful years, and just before she died, Martin and Mary sold their Florida home, bought an apartment in a retirement community in Elizabeth, and brought Delia back home again so she could be close to her family for her last months.

Peter and Raymond were hopeful that Delia would leave them a nice bundle, but once again it was not to be. What little cash she had she left in a trust for Peter's children (Raymond never married and had no acknowledged children). Clearly, if there was any gold left in the family mine it was held by Martin and Mary, and they had no children. So Peter, usually with Sally and a child or two, started visiting Martin and Mary on a weekly basis. The children were teens at this point and wanted no part of the visit ritual, but Sally insisted that at least one go each time.

The children were right to resist. Everything in the Tall Oaks complex moved in deadly silent slow motion, and there was a slightly nauseating odor about the place, sort of a combination of gardenia and cough syrup. There was literally nothing to do but sit on the couch and make small talk. They couldn't even escape for lunch because Mary prepared the meal, usually chicken chunks boiled in Campbell's celery soup. For variety, she used mushroom soup.

About a year into the routine, Uncle Martin began to show signs of severe decline. He lost weight and his already pasty complexion began to gray. As they were leaving one Sunday afternoon, Peter said something about Martin's bad breath. Sally countered that it was only natural, given his worsening condition. Peter should have left it there, but, of course, he didn't.

"Well, with a little luck, someone will put a pillow over his head and we won't have to smell his rotting tonsils anymore."

Sally exploded. "You hypocritical bastard! How can you say such a thing! He's a sweet old man doing his best to care for his wife. And that's a lot more than you ever do for either one of them. Or for me, as a matter of fact!"

Peter still didn't get it, sputtered defensively about loving his family, but Sally wasn't through.

"You know, Peter, the truth is you're just waiting for them to die so you can get the money."

"What's wrong with that? Who the hell else are they going to leave it to?"

That one sentence, spoken in the Tall Oaks parking lot, completely changed Sally's life. In a split second, all of the denial and rationalizations that had kept her at Peter's side for twenty years vanished, instantly replaced by a sweet sense of absolute calm. It was literally a physical transformation. Her shoulders relaxed, the tension in her neck eased allowing her to raise her head painlessly, her legs and arms felt stronger. At first she said nothing, momentarily lost in the pleasure of feeling the vestiges of doubt disappear. She looked at her hands, clenching and relaxing her fingers, feeling the power in her grip.

Peter didn't seem to notice. He unlocked the car and started to get in on the driver's side.

"I'm going to drive, Peter. Get out."

Peter made an anxious joke, something about "hear me roar," but he got out. Sally slipped into the driver's seat, closed the door, and drove away leaving Peter in the parking lot. When the cab dropped him off at the house, Sally refused to open the door. That meant she also refused to give Peter money for the cab.

"What the hell am I supposed to do?" Peter yelled at the door. There was no answer. The cabbie wasn't about to leave without his money, and in the end Peter gave him his watch.

Peter bunked in the trailer at the used car lot where he was working. Sally had the phone number changed to an unlisted number and refused to answer the door when Peter came around. Their oldest son, Reggie, acted as go-between, explaining that the children were on Sally's side, that "it would be better for everyone" if Peter stayed away. A lawyer had Peter served with papers demanding he either sign a prepared separation agreement accepting half of the furniture, or go to court where there was a strong possibility he would walk out with nothing. He signed.

In spite of Sally's dramatic transformation, Peter believed she would come to her senses and realize that she simply couldn't get along without him. He told his colleagues at the car lot that his wife was having "a hissy fit," and they all had a good laugh about it. He didn't mention the children's attitude.

In spite of his troubles, Peter continued to visit Martin and Mary at least once a week, cheerfully offering a jumble of excuses for Sally's absence. When Mary told him Sally had been visiting separately, Peter simply dropped the subject.

About a month into the separation Peter arrived for a Sunday afternoon visit, took his usual seat by the pretzel bowl, and asked Martin where Aunt Mary was.

"She isn't here, Peter. I asked her to eat in the cafeteria so you and I could spend some time alone, have a nice chat, and talk about the future."

"Great," said Peter, thinking the subject of inheritance might be on the table. He helped himself to a handful of pretzels, and settled back on the couch, a happy anticipatory grin on his face.

"Not so great, Peter. Not so great at all," Martin said in a steely tone, his head trembling slightly.

"What do you mean, Uncle Martin? If this is about your investment I assure you…"

"Shut up, you little shit. I've got a few things to say before Mary gets back, so keep that goddamn mouth of yours shut for once."

Peter started to say something but stopped, frozen in place, a pretzel poised six inches from his face.

"There is no investment, Peter, there never was. Mary and your mother wanted to believe it because for some crazy reason they wanted to believe in you. I knew I'd never see that money again, but it was okay as long as it made Mary and Delia happy. Yes, it was worth every penny to do that."

Peter's arm thawed and the hand holding the pretzel slowly sank into his lap.

"Now listen very carefully, Peter. The only thing that has made life joyous is my dear wife. I have always done everything I could to make her happy, and, frankly, that has often involved protecting her from certain ugly realities. She and your mother are both saints, people with hearts of gold, but neither was ever equipped to deal with disappointment, especially when it involved family. I sheltered Mary—and your mother, too—and in return she gave me a lifetime of love and devotion.

"But I'm old, and now I'm sick and getting weaker by the day. It won't be much longer before I can't protect Mary. Worse, I'll become a burden to her. And I can't let that happen. So I want to make a deal with you, Peter. Now that you and Sally are separated…"

Peter started to protest, but Martin held up his hand.

"I told you to shut up. Now listen, and if you agree to my terms, you may actually get the money you've been sucking up for since your mother died. Are you interested, Peter?"

"I'll do whatever I can, Uncle. I mean, sure I'm on board." Peter quickly ate two pretzels.

"Right now, my will leaves everything I have to Mary. I will be departing well ahead of her, and she'll need the assets for her care, especially if she has—God forbid—a prolonged illness. In her will, all of the remainder will go to you, not a dime to Raymond, that worthless junkie.

"My will is administered by the Bank of Bayonne under the direction of my executor, Mr. Ernst Slaughter, the bank's vice president. He knows all about you, Peter, every stinking, sordid detail. He has the power to cut you off instantly if you fail to live up to my conditions. It's all rather straightforward, simple enough that even you might be able to follow the rules. First, you must visit Mary for at least two hours twice a week as long as she remains in this apartment. Assuming she eventually moves to the medical unit, you will visit every other day for two hours. You won't have to do anything else. The bank will see to her taxes and bills, the nurses have control of her medical needs, and the social worker will order any clothes or personal items she may need. Every month Mr. Slaughter will pay you eight hundred dollars; that is, as long as you live up to the deal.

"This is right up your alley, Peter. You make money sitting on your ass doing nothing but talk. But watch out for Mr. Slaughter. Tall Oaks will provide a visiting log. You will sign in and you will sign out. He will check with the nursing staff to be sure you actually stay on schedule. If you can't be here for some extraordinary reason, you will have to get permission from Mr. Slaughter *before* the visit, not after. You are allowed one unexcused absence every three months, Peter. Anything more and it's over. No eight hundred, no inheritance and no second chance.

"In case you're wondering how much money we're talking about, I'll remove the suspense. Right now our assets total just over one-and-a-half million dollars. This place costs just a few thousand a month. Chicken feed. If Mary has to go to the medical unit the costs will be considerably higher, but even so there will be an enormous amount of money left for you. I dearly wish there was some other way to do this, but, sadly, there is not.

"Now, do you agree to my terms or not?"

Peter agreed. Moments later Mary returned.

"Did you boys have a good chat? No dirty jokes I hope!"

"No jokes, sweetheart, just a little business talk," Martin said struggling to his feet to give Mary a hug.

"He's such a dear, always thinking about us," Mary said after Peter left.

"You're right about that, he never stops thinking about us."

A week later Martin was found slumped over his desk, a plastic shirt bag over his head held in place by a rubber band around his neck. He was wearing his best suit and the tie Mary had given him for his last birthday. An autopsy revealed the actual cause of death was an overdose of pain medication. The plastic bag was Martin's guarantee he wouldn't fail. The post mortem also noted advanced colon cancer with metastases to the liver, lungs, and brain. Death from natural causes would have occurred in a few months at the most, and certainly would have involved unbelievable pain and precipitous loss of control of body functions and cognition.

Mary was, of course, devastated. No suicide note was found and Mary spent two full days searching the apartment over and over for some sort of letter or note. Then she suddenly stopped, sat down on the couch, and smiled.

"Of course there's no note! He knew I would understand. There was no need to say it. He did it to save me from the awful pain of watching him die. That's my Martin!"

Martin was buried in his best suit. Just before the coffin lid was closed, Mary straightened his birthday tie.

Mary went back to her apartment and Peter started his regular visits. Mr. Slaughter opened a saving account at his bank and deposited Peter's eight hundred dollars every month; that is, after carefully checking the logs and talking to the nursing staff at Tall Oaks to be certain Peter was living up to his obligation.

This arrangement went on for three years. Mary played bridge with neighbors, ate in the cafeteria and prayed in the Tall Oaks chapel twice a day. Over time her ability to play cards faded, her once-keen memory no longer up to the task. Gradually, her ability to get around her apartment diminished to the point she needed help preparing even the simplest meals. Then she fell, fractured a hip, and after surgery was sent to the medical unit to recover. She never left the medical unit again.

The pace of Peter's visits increased as did his anticipation of Mary's demise. But Mary was tougher than anyone would have guessed, and another year and $100,000 in medical costs later, Mary was showing no sign of imminent departure. Peter was becoming increasingly impatient, and during his visits sat in the chair next to Mary's bed calculating the amount of money being sucked out of his treasury.

Mary and Peter spoke less and less. Mary seemed to be suffering from the early stages of Alzheimer's, and spent virtually every waking minute "reading" magazines and books. I say "reading" because it really wasn't clear just how much she was actually absorbing. Also, she was sometimes found holding a book upside down, delicately turning the pages in a slow, studious rhythm. The only time she seemed to become animated was when the candy striper (or candy stripper, as Peter fantasized) came around with the library cart. Mary made chirping noises, pointing to her selection. Then with her book propped up on a pillow she again seemed to become happily lost in the pages, upside down or not.

And the visits droned on. By this point the routine was absolutely repetitive. Peter would sign in downstairs, make sure the nurse in charge saw him, kiss Mary on the forehead, take her lemonade, lower her feeding table to chair height, settle into the chair next to her bed, drink the lemonade, daydream about how he planned to spend the money, then fall asleep.

One afternoon he was awakened by Mary's physician who had dropped by for a routine visit. Peter was sent out into the hall and afterward spoke to the doctor, asking in his most solicitous manner how his dear Aunt Mary was doing.

"Her mind is shot, Peter, we'll all have to accept that. But the good news is she's in great physical shape. Her heart is strong, her lungs are clear, and her weight is holding steady."

"That's a comfort, Doctor," Peter said, "But I wonder just how long she can last like this?"

"Oh, my goodness! She could live like this for years or die tomorrow, Peter. But I wouldn't worry, as strong as she is, my guess is you won't be losing your Aunt any time soon."

The good doctor's words reverberated in Peter's brain. "She could live like this for years." With the cost of her care escalating, on top of what had already been spent, Peter knew he could easily end up with only a fraction of what he deserved. At that exact moment Peter decided he had to figure out a foolproof way to speed up the process and help Aunt Mary into the Great Beyond. He would have to murder her, that's all there was to it.

Peter no longer slept through his visits. Instead, he sipped Mary's lemonade and plotted the perfect murder. By this time, Mary seemed to nap more than look at her books. Peter began to keep a log of her naptime, carefully noting the way her breathing changed as she slid into deeper sleep. He reassured the nurses that he would keep a keen eye on Mary and they needn't trouble themselves while Peter was on watch. He tracked the smallest details, noting, for example that after the shift change the new nurse responsible for Mary's wing always got to Mary's room between 3:25 and 3:30 p.m. After that, no one showed up until after 5:00 p.m. when the aide came to wake Mary up and spoon some food into her mouth.

Peter also learned all the nurse lingo and codes, and could follow the medical staff's movements by listening carefully to the loudspeaker system. He was friendly with all of the staff, and frequently brought candy for Mary's overweight diabetic aide. "One bite. What can it hurt?"

He also got the staff used to having the door closed. The glare from the hall light bothered him and made it difficult to read. When staff entered they always knocked first giving Peter time to react even if he was rehearsing the "pillow drop," as he liked to call his plan.

Indeed, a pillow was the perfect murder weapon. It was readily at hand, so much a part of the hospital scenery it was invisible, and once applied was not only certain to work, but would muffle any sounds made by the struggling victim. Peter knew he would have to apply pressure from the sides, not directly over the face, in order to be sure he didn't break Mary's nose—an obvious clue she had been smothered. His planning was so perfect he even considered the potential problem of slobber. If Mary struggled and left spit on the pillowcase, some smart detective might become suspicious. And getting a pillow out from under Mary's head woke her up every time Peter tried it. To solve both pillow problems Peter made a show of asking the nurses for an extra pillow to make his long hours in the chair by Mary's bed more comfortable. After a few weeks, the aides automatically put a pillow in Peter's chair. He stole an extra pillowcase from the laundry cart, hiding it under the chair's cushion. After he smothered Mary, Peter would change pillowcases, and toss the soiled one in the hamper in the bathroom on his way out.

Perfect.

Just to be absolutely sure he hadn't omitted any potentially dangerous detail, Peter staged a series of rehearsals. He planned to strike during the shift change when everyone was in the nurse's station. He unclipped the call button and let it hang by the bed, just in case Mary struggled and somehow managed to grab the device and sound the alarm. Unlikely, but he had to allow for every possible mishap. Then he would loom over Mary, pretending to press the pillow over Mary's face.

Finally, the day came when Peter knew he was ready. All he needed was for Mary to take her nap at shift change. He came on the unit as usual, waved hello to the staff as he always did, pulled the eating tray across his lap, checked his watch, and drank Mary's lemonade.

It was instantly clear that something was very wrong. He could hardly breathe, his skin started to burn, and his vision blurred. He began to choke and couldn't speak. He tried to reach the call button; it wasn't where it should be.

"Looking for this, Nephew?" Mary said, holding up the call button. Peter tried to struggle to his feet, but Mary kicked back the sheet, and with her foot, pushed the eating tray into Peter's gut pinning him into his seat.

"Digitalis, Peter, you just drank a month's worth. I've been saving it for you. Poor boy, you're starting to fade, so I'd better be quick. I want you to know, you little asshole, that I've been on to you for years. I put on a good act for Martin. The woman he loved had to be somewhat helpless and naïve, and the man I loved had to be strong and devoted. It worked perfectly for both of us, and Delia, too. But my blood boiled whenever I saw how you and Raymond treated your family. You thought we were all fools, but it's payback time, Peter."

Peter's mind was swimming, his arms felt like they were tied to the chair, and sweat poured through his skin.

"Don't go quite yet, please. I want you to know that I changed my will just after dear Martin died. I cut you out completely. All of these visits were for naught, Peter. And all that pretending, Peter, it's been a strain, but worth the wait. I left the money to Raymond, in case you still have enough brainpower to wonder who gets it. He gets to keep it unless he dies within one year. In that case, it goes to Sally. And Raymond will certainly die of an overdose when he gets that enormous mountain of cash. So I get to kill him, too."

Peter was slumped in the chair, no longer breathing.

"Oh, dear, looks like you've had a heart attack, Peter. So sad. But all of this work has tired me out. I think I'll take a refreshing nap." Mary replaced the call button, straightened her pillow, smoothed out the sheets, and fell asleep.

HERE AND THERE

The first thing that struck me was the silence. It was frighteningly complete, so much so it smothered the brain-crackling confusion I felt emerging from unconsciousness or coma or whatever it was. Frankly, I couldn't remember what knocked me out, but I wasn't concerned at all about what might have gotten me here. I just wanted to know where the hell I was and why my hearing was so totally shot.

Looking around I began to wonder if my eyes were also gone—or at least the rods and cones color feature—because everything seemed so white. But I quickly realized my eyes were working because I could clearly see the man in the white suit sitting across from me.

"It takes a bit of time to adjust, Talbot," the man said softly. Okay, the ears are working. "And, no, this is not a dream or some earthly illusion. You have passed, Talbot. You had an accident. Do you remember trying to repair the hot water heater?"

It was coming back. "Yes, I remember telling Sally to pull the number six breaker on the electric panel. The rest is fuzzy."

"She pulled number five. They're adjacent. An easy mistake to make, really."

I wanted to say "bitch!" but the word wouldn't form in my mouth.

"That's behind you, Talbot. No need for negative feelings Here."

"This may be a dumb question, but am I in heaven or is this some sort of shock-driven wacky dream and I'm going to wake up on the basement floor?"

"The former, Talbot."

I wanted to say 'Holy Shit!' but again I couldn't manage the words. The man smiled knowingly.

"I realize, Talbot, you never gave the Aftercall much thought. You were too busy with earthly—or should I say 'earthy'—preoccupations." He chuckled. "And under normal circumstances, to be perfectly frank, your life would not even have earned you a position in Precall…"

I obviously looked puzzled by the term.

"Sorry. 'Precall' is a place of neither attainment nor punishment. You simply *are*, but at least you are *not*, if you get my meaning."

I didn't but he continued.

"Anyway, your record is not a particularly resplendent one. However, you did earn a Pass because of one glowing act, a Glorious Achievement so remarkable it erased all of your previous sins. And," he added lowering his already soft voice, "it's probably a good thing the hot water heater got you before you had a chance to wipe out your Glorious Achievement with the sinful nature of your daily existence."

"Good thing," I said thinking it wasn't the water heater that got me, it was Sally.

"Stay with me, will you please, Talbot?"

"Sorry. Could you tell me what the Glorious Achievement was? Was it the garbage truck thing?"

"Indirectly, Talbot. But, yes, it started when you heroically pushed the little girl out of the way of the truck. It was an uncharacteristically selfless act, and quite an acrobatic feat I might add. We were all mightily impressed. But with your record that wouldn't have gotten you a Pass."

"What did it, then?"

"Well, so many people in Pottsville mistook your act for a miracle that overall church attendance jumped thirty-eight percent, including more than two hundred backsliders, *and* fifty-two new souls became not only members of an Approved Church, but *committed* members whose faith has remained unshaken since the incident. That, Talbot, got you the Pass. Fifty is the cut-off, by the way, so you barely made it. But you did."

"Wow! And I didn't even know I had done it."

"True, an irony of the point system. But let's get on to your Orientation, shall we? And, please, hold your questions until the end when I'll tell you that questions are not part of being Here."

He didn't wait for me to respond but went straightaway to an elaboration of Structure and Rules, the first order of business for all new arrivals.

"The robe you are wearing is all you will need in the way of wearing apparel Here. You will never have to remove it, and it—like yourself—will never require cleaning. There is no dust, dirt, or disease Here. Nor is there any discomfort, disability, or distracting desire."

I was catching on. *Probably no doubt, disobedience, or discord, either*, I thought.

"Correct, Talbot."

"You will quickly learn that what you called 'life' below was an empty, unfulfilling experience." My mentor floated to his feet extending his arms, looking up into what appeared to be sky. Actually it was the ceiling, but all the ceilings Here look like blue Jell-o.

"When you thought you were on track you were actually aimless. Here is entirely different. Your earthly body has been replaced with a vessel of absolute purity, your eyes and ears coordinated with your mind to fill you with ceaseless gratitude for the wonders that surround you. You will no longer be distracted by the wish to eat or drink, nor will you be concerned with any of the unpleasant disposal problems associated with those discarded behaviors. You will be completely free to praise your Master, the He in Here who has given you this reward—even though you probably don't deserve it. All the more reason for praise, don't you agree?"

"Sure. Look, the He in Here: is that God? Can I ask that?"

"Everyone does. And no you can't. But I'll let you get by just this once. And I'll be perfectly frank with you, Talbot: He doesn't like the 'G' word at all and the Helpers will report anyone who uses it."

"The Helpers?"

"Yes, there is a lot going on Here and people often need guidance to be sure they stay in perfect harmony. It's the Master's wish."

"While you're being frank, could you tell me why He doesn't like the …you know… word? Or am I stepping over the line. If I am just tell me and…"

"Oh, stop fawning, Talbot. You were too curious on earth and I see the habit didn't die with you. Okay, it's quite simple: He doesn't like the G-word because it's short, doesn't convey any sense of majesty, is often coupled with 'damn' to produce a blasphemous swear word, and spells 'dog' backwards. He hates it and it's forbidden. That's all you need to know."

"I'll get the hang of it, just give me a little time. But before I make another mistake, can I know where Jesus fits into the scheme? Is that a name I can use?"

"That does cause a lot of confusion for newcomers, Talbot. It's a problem that started when one of the Master's cousins showed up in Palestine and started a rumor that he was He in miniature, and He was going to either send him back someday to save the world or else He was going to return and do the job Himself. What nonsense! That would be the end of the world, everyone would either be Here, There, or locked in Prepass. What would He do then? Retire? What a completely silly idea!"

"Jesus was His cousin?"

"Yes, His relatives often go down to travel about, a sort of vacation, you might say. They're supposed to travel incognito, not stir things up." He sat down, seemed to collect himself, and announced he had already said too much. I was told to ask no more questions.

"You'll be in Everlasting Complex MMCC, Level XVIII, room CIX. A Guide will escort you. Just follow the rules—they are printed on your wall—and experience the joy He has given you." I offered my hand in thanks but the fellow had already left, evaporated or whatever—he was gone and I was momentarily alone, sitting on a white bench in a white room with a blue Jell-O ceiling. That was strange beyond words, but stranger still was my lack of anxiety. I can't say I was cheerful or relaxed, but I wasn't frozen with fear, either. I was curious and wondering what was next. There was a sort of opening in the wall, my legs were working, so I walked through onto what looked like a wide street. A short, smiling fellow in white was waiting for me.

"Hello, Mr. Talbot, I'm your Guide, Michael. Mind if I call you by your first name?"

"Sure, it's Robert," I said. I didn't try the handshake thing again.

"Yes, I know. And I also know you're confused and a bit apprehensive. Odd, though."

"*Odd*, are you…" I tried to say "nuts" but the word wouldn't form. I was starting to get the drift of the word thing. I corrected myself.

"Why do you say 'odd'? I mean a few minutes ago I was sitting on the basement floor enjoying a beer waiting for my wife to throw a circuit breaker. Suddenly I'm Here dressed for the shower room wondering what the fu….er…heck all this is about. Isn't everyone the same way, Michael?"

"Not at all, Robert. People are overjoyed to be Here, and they want to start their new life with praise, not questions. By the way, Robert, it wasn't 'a few minutes ago' that you were in your basement. But time as you know it means nothing Here. This is forever, joy without end, so you see it's quite silly to think in terms of earth-time. We do occasionally refer to 'spans' and 'yads.' But that's not important now. Let's get you to your new home, shall we?"

We were standing in what I can only call a vast space on what looked like a wide ribbon of linoleum. There were buildings in the distance and white-robed people moving about in pairs; new arrivals like myself, I assumed, with their Guides heading to one of the housing levels.

"This doesn't look like a street of gold, Michael," I observed, carefully avoiding a question.

"Certainly not, Robert. Gold isn't a suitable building material, and earthly commodities don't have any value Here. Shall we go? It's best to walk, get you used to it; after all, it's an entirely new sensation, isn't it." And, yes, it was. Walking required no effort at all. I could barely feel my feet on the ground or whatever it was. The robe covered my feet so I couldn't even tell if I had shoes on or not. Perspective was completely distorted. Things in the distance approached faster than we were walking. It was almost as if we were hardly moving but everything around us was shifting at lightning speed.

"You'll get used to it, Robert. It's like flying without leaving the runway. I used to be a pilot, that's why I like that image," he added helpfully.

In what seemed like moments—what I would later call a fraction of a yad—we stood in front of an enormous windowless housing complex, white, seemingly hundreds of stories tall, with only one small entrance just wide enough for two people to pass side-by-side. Inside there was a park of sorts with fountains, wide linoleum pathways, and very pale green shrubs made of some sort of rubber-like substance. All of the paths surrounded and ultimately led to an enormous golden-yellow building the size of several football stadiums, a round structure with many doors but no windows. No stained glass Here. On top stood what looked like the Eiffel tower festooned with bells, big ones at the bottom, smaller ones aloft. Clearly this was church central, no need to waste a question on that.

The park—more correctly "Celebration Plaza"—was filled with people, all wearing the same white robes, all moving about slowly, some in small groups talking, laughing, and some solo seemingly lost in happy contemplation. It was impossible to discern gender from more than ten feet away. Either there were no breasts Here or the robes effectively cancelled contour. And it was impossible to tell anything about age. Everyone seemed to be about thirty-five. No one was fat, nor was anyone excessively tall or short.

"I don't see any children, Michael."

"Yes, you do, you just don't recognize them. You see, when a child passes—no matter what age—he or she instantly becomes the adult he or she would have been if he or she had lived. Everyone Here is on an equal footing, Robert. And those who were once called 'retarded' are brought up to the same cognitive level as everyone else."

"And I'll bet the excessively brainy ones are pulled down to that cognitive level."

"You're right, Robert. It's a relatively recent innovation, perhaps in the last two spans. The 'brainy' ones, as you call them, were becoming a difficult bunch and wouldn't stop asking foolish questions. We don't need show-offs, rebels, and intellectualizers Here. It introduces *personal pride* and can distract others from the tranquil joy of our life of appreciation and praise. Besides, now-a-yad the heavy-I.Q. types rarely make it beyond Prepass."

Then there was the music. It played softly but continuously in the background.

"By the way, Michael, the music, it's...ah...unusual. It sounds like a Theremin."

"Well done, Robert! He loves the gentle sound of the Theremin and has made it the official instrument of Here. He is also quite fond of organ music and bells, but the Theremin gets the most play. You'll love the song fests. We have them often and everyone takes part. People who could never carry a tune in church find themselves in wondrous voice Here. I believe you liked to sing, Robert."

"Yes, and I played the guitar. Not well, really, but I enjoyed it. I always thought the official instrument of heaven was the lyre. I figured if I ever made it up here I'd have a head start learning it."

"Please avoid the word 'heaven,' Robert. You are Here, not in heaven. Before the Theremin it was the Aeolian harp. The lyre thing is a myth."

"Fascinating, Michael. I can't wait to hear more."

Looking up at the Jack-in-the-Beanstalk architecture I mumbled, "In my Father's house there are many condos." I couldn't help it. It just popped out.

"Be careful, Robert. That sort of thing won't be ignored for long. I am very tolerant because I deal exclusively with newcomers. But the Helpers have a different attitude. Here is about perpetual joy born on the wings of harmonious praise and complete gratitude. The tiniest hint of discord ruins everyone's state of happiness."

"Sorry. I'll be more joyful."

"Yes, you will, Robert. Now let's breeze up to your room, shall we?" We glided effortlessly up an interior stairway to level XVIII, the numeral clearly carved in the stucco-like wall leading to a long hallway with rooms on each side. We quickly reached CIX. There was no door. The room was small, perhaps six by eight and had little in the way of furniture. There was a bench along one wall covered with taupe pillows, an armless rocking chair, and a table with half-a-dozen books sandwiched between twin bookends of what seemed to be cocker spaniel heads.

"Yes, they are dogs, Robert. We don't have pets Here but people seem to enjoy the dogs. A nice decorating touch don't you think?"

"Definitely," I mumbled scanning some of the titles.

The Readers Digest, *Stories of Inspiration*, Condensed and Abridged
Billy Graham's *Ten Greatest Sermons*
Move That Mountain by Jim Bakker
The Salem Witch Trials: Justice Done!
The Holy Inquisition: Tips for the Practitioner
My Burning Bush by Heidi Fleiss

The last one got my attention.

"Elevate your mind, Robert. It's not what you think. It's about her acceptance of His power to change one's life."

"I didn't know she'd changed. Last I heard she was hawking a line of designer jeans."

"It was ghost written for her, Robert."

Let it go, I thought. "I don't see a Bible, Torah, or Koran, Michael. Can I know why?"

"You should be able to figure that one out for yourself, Robert. All of those other books are loaded with the "G" word. The worst is the New Testament. All that gibberish Cousin Jesus made up to shift the glory onto his puny shoulders annoys the Master. The He in Here is above cheap parlor tricks about loaves and fish or walking around on water. Worst of all, the man married a hooker, Robert! Can you imagine how that went over up Here? Not well, I'll tell you."

"Now let's take a look at the Rules."

There was no missing the Rules. They were printed on the wall where one might expect a window and about the same size. There were only three:

1. Be joyous at all times
2. Let your every thought be on the glory of the Master
3. Live a life of endless praise for the Master

On the table next to the books was the flier, the sort of thing you find under your windshield wiper in the supermarket parking lot—*The Daily Praise*. What else could it be?

"People write stories of praise and joy, Robert. It's always nice to get someone else's perspective, don't you think? Now," Michael said before I got in trouble with what I was thinking, "one more thing—whenever you hear the bells you need to report to the Tabernacle. It could be for a Praise Service, perhaps a class, or a Songs-of-Joy event. You'll come to realize that the call to service replaces what you would call 'time.' There is a reassuring rhythm to the events Here, the measure of life in the infinite. You used to concern yourself with sleep and wakefulness. You will never have a bad night's sleep Here because you never sleep. Another gift from the Master! Now, let's go down for your first class. The bells will sound and you won't want to be late. This is what everybody has been waiting for all their lives, Robert: an explanation of the Cosmos. The true story of how everything came to be! Aren't you excited?"

I have to admit that one did peak my interest. We drifted back to the big park and what I now knew to be the Tabernacle, the epicenter of everything in the Aftercall. Inside, it looked less like a church than a Greek amphitheater, countless simple bench seats arranged in a downward spiral. In the center at the bottom there was a tiny elevated stage. Looking up one could only see more blue Jell-o. In spite of no longer having a functioning gastrointestinal tract (something I confess I secretly missed), I felt slightly nauseous.

"Keep your eyes down there. Robert. Focus on the speaker and you'll feel better."

Michael told me this was where we parted. I was to take a seat and open my mind to the wonders to come.

"And, Robert, I have to warn you—you haven't completely abandoned your earthly tendency to doubt, a dangerous trait you need to jettison immediately. If you persist you could find yourself in trouble with the Helpers. And they won't hesitate to take you to the Committee. From there it's possible you could be expelled to Precall or even…I hate to say it…There. Good luck Robert."

Michael disappeared, and as I sat down, I began to feel the slightest flicker of anxiety. This cannot be good, I thought.

The place quickly filled with cheerful newcomers eager to hear about the Cosmos. All eyes were on the stage, and no one made any effort to speak to a neighbor. Concentrate, I said to myself. Work at it, Here might be strange but I didn't like the sound of the alternatives.

Suddenly a man wearing a blue robe appeared on the stage.

"Welcome, everyone! It is wonderful to see you Here!" A chorus of Thank-Yous, Amens, and Halleluiahs rippled through the crowd. I tried to join in but the image of Sally's hand on the circuit breaker kept intruding.

"My name is Esteban, and I am here to reveal the secrets of the universe and to tell you all about our Master, the one you called—I'll only say this once, He doesn't like the word—'God.' He prefers Master but doesn't mind Lord or Father. Don't—and I won't repeat this—use Yahweh, Allah, or the 'G' word. Now let's get started shall we?"

"Which came first, the chicken or the egg?" There were murmurings in the crowd. Some thought the chicken, others voted for the egg.

"The answer is: Neither one! At first, in the very beginning, there was nothing, at least nothing in the material sense. No rocks, no air, no water, people, or bile salts, no clouds, no plants. Not even poison ivy!" The crowd chuckled. Esteban was clearly quite a wit.

"But!" he said sharply, puncturing the humorous mood, "'nothing' cannot be absolute, can it? Even 'nothing' is something. If there truly was 'nothing' then 'nothing' couldn't exist. So there had to be something even though it was nothing. And what could that be? There is only one possible answer, and it is that which came before either the chicken or the egg, the closest thing to nothing there could conceivably be.

"And that is the Spirit. Spirit doesn't require space, place, or time. In fact, the Spirit existed *before* time, even before there was time extending back into infinity. But even in nothingness, given enough non-time, elements of Spirit had to coalesce—such is the spirit of Spirit. It even disobeys the fundamental earth-bound rule that says nothing can exist in a vacuum. Not so! The Spirit was nothing and it lived and grew in a vacuum. Not only did it exist, but very slowly, in pre-time, the elements of the Spirit mingled, adhered, and shaped themselves into The Creator who, the Master teaches us, dreamed up the idea of time, space, and place, ruptured the vacuum, and started building. He was at that point in non-time floating around the back edge of infinity with no place to call home, no headquarters, so to speak. The Creator was also quite alone so He got busy and used some of his spirit non-matter to create other, separate spirits—lesser spirits you might say. And together they formed a committee, dreamed up the idea of a universe, and tried to decide what sort of thing it would be. That's when they ran into trouble. They couldn't agree on a single concept, so they did the smart thing—each spirit put an idea into a shoebox. Not a real shoebox, of course, but Tradition says it looked like one. Anyway, when all the ideas were in the box, they blew it up."

"The Big Bang," Robert mumbled.

"Exactly. The Big Bang. All the ideas tumbled out in every direction and as they raced along they collided, fractured, and adhered eventually forming suns, planets, comets, meteors—you name it, it was a real hodgepodge. To bring some sense to the whole thing the committee decided to organize it all into galaxies and each spirit took charge of one galaxy. In the case of our galaxy, the spirit in charge was tired of the committee idea, hit upon the notion of a family, and developed a multitude of spirit-offspring, each to have jurisdiction over one solar system. Those offspirits, as we call them, in turn picked individual sons of their own to be responsible for specific planets. Fortunately for us, the Master was put in charge of ours, and He set to work creating what eventually became the world we all knew and loved.

"The Master had help, of course, because he had a family of His own. Thus you see where the family model we have enjoyed actually came from. They all worked together on different plans starting with the difficult matter of how to get everything cranked up on earth. The quaint Genesis story has the basic idea, though it happened over many spans, not a few earth-days. It started with water, sun, and the elements. They were left to cook, and things started to grow, eventually filling the world up with all manner of lizards, broccoli, fish, and eventually dinosaurs.

"Well, that didn't seem to be going anywhere, really, so the Master wiped the slate, took some of the left-over DNA and got a line of monkeys going and over a couple of spans along came humans."

At this point the crowd became restless. Clearly, some consternation was bubbling up, and I was glad I didn't start it this time.

"I know," Esteban said reassuringly, "You're wondering about Adam and Eve, and you're thinking this sounds entirely too close to the dreaded concept of evolution. Let me assure you it is *not* evolution." The crowd seemed to settle, but I couldn't help think it sure enough sounded like Darwin to me.

"Calm yourselves. I feel a few of you are still confused so I'll explain. The DNA thing was, of course, entirely too complex for any spirit to figure out. It had to form over time in the only way it could—by countless trial and error combinations and permutations, with the best amalgams surviving to keep the process going. Once the Master had DNA, then He got the monkey thing on track and guided the process from there. There were, of course, several distractions along the way. He didn't particularly like Neanderthals, for example, so He wiped them out. There were some annoying fish, a lot of unwanted birds, some large moths and the like who were also removed.

"Finally, humans got to the point He could talk to them, and that's when He brought Adam and Eve to Mesopotamia. He gave them their marching orders, but they were headstrong—especially Eve—and, well, you know the rest. Things again got out of hand so he flushed the lot, except for the Noah family, and started all over again. But at that point He and the family got together and in their Vast Collective Wisdom decided to stay out of it from then on. Let it go where it will. If the place blows up, well, then maybe a new start. Or even a new planet. Whatever.

"The family loved the earth idea and started visiting regularly, in disguise, of course. One son, the man you know as Jesus, got a bit big for his loincloth and had to be reined in." The crowd was again restless. "Don't be upset, Jesus was forgiven, eventually, but it did upset the Master that Jesus got in the way of the praise and worship that properly belonged to the Master. But Jesus was a reality, and everyone in the Divine Family agreed that they wouldn't monkey with his reputation." More humor. The crowd settled down again. "So any church that puts the Master first and gives Him the praise is Approved. Those that worship something else, like some fat Chinaman, are not.

"And that is the entire story. It's not exactly what you learned on earth, but now you know the Truth. And you will spend eternity in the joyous presence of the Master, praising Him with your every thought. This is bliss and you are the fortunate few who are privileged to enjoy it." He went on to explain that we were to assemble whenever the bells sounded, and otherwise we were free to wander the plaza or spend time in our rooms in grateful contemplation.

I left the tabernacle and drifted back to my room, trying all the way to get my mind in harmony with the bliss idea. I hadn't been in the room more than a few yads when Esteban showed up at the door. Again, I felt an old familiar jolt of anxiety.

"Are you surprised to see me, Robert?"

"Yes, actually, I am."

"I couldn't help overhearing your questions, Robert, so I thought I'd pay you a visit. By the way, you're not alone. Knowing the Truth is difficult for many, though they usually approach it through a more thoughtful, shall we say, 'ecclesiastic' or 'theological' route than the one you have chosen. You have troubling elements of doubt."

"I can't help but wonder about a few things, it's true."

"Like what? And Robert, I am giving you permission to ask a few questions, an exception that will not be repeated. Make good use of this opportunity."

"Thank you, I'll try. I suppose the thing that is most on my mind is wondering when I will meet the Master, and will I have a chance to talk to Him? I assume you've met Him, what is He like?"

Esteban was clearly perturbed. "No, Robert, you will not meet the Master. No one does. He is far too busy, and why would He honor you—or me, for that matter—by coming to visit any one of us?"

"Well, I sort of thought the idea of it all, you know, church and worship, following the rules, and all of that, was so one day we would meet up with God. Oh! Sorry! I mean, meet the Master."

"The 'all-of-that,' as you call it, was to get in Here, not to be chummy with the Master. You are Here because of His leniency. Be very grateful for that. And the way you show your gratitude is through constant praise, which is very pleasing to the Master, and pleasing the Master brings you joy. In your lowly terms, Robert, it's win-win. He is happy and so are you. End of story. You have one more question, and I have to tell you I'm running out of patience."

"Okay, one more thing—I haven't seen a soul I recognize, Esteban. How do I find my relatives and friends who have passed and gotten Here?"

"You don't, Robert. The Aftercall isn't about you, it's about Him. Feel the joy, Robert."

And with that he was gone. In spite of the muting of any even vaguely negative feelings about Here, I was still left in a slump. My mind went back to the basement and the image of Sally's hand on the breaker switch.

"Bitch." There! I actually said it, and I felt better.

Over time, whatever that is, I fell into the routine of bells, worship, joy, and an occasional careful conversation with some blissed-out neighbor. The only part I really looked forward to was the music service. We sang hymns and songs of praise I had never heard before, but it didn't matter, at least there was some noise. I found myself almost shouting the words. Can you hear me, Master? I'm praising you! Is it loud enough?

Then there was the final visit from the Helpers. They showed up in my room after worship service, three of them, in blue, looking grim. I knew I was in serious trouble.

"We won't mince words, Talbot. You have accumulated eight points and the Rules Committee has voted to eject you from Here."

"Eight points? I don't understand."

"Seven for persistent doubt and one for singing too loudly. Eight points, Talbot, you're out."

"Where do I go from here?" I asked knowing there was no point trying to discuss it further. I was screwed and I knew it.

"We thought about sending you to Precall, Talbot, but that didn't seem like enough. We're sending you There. Good bye."

It happened in an instant. I started to feel dizzy then a falling sensation took over. I drifted in and out of consciousness aware only of flashes of color and sounds like fractured voices and broken trumpets. Then ever so slowly the sensation eased. I felt like someone in an elevator just as it stops before the door opens. My thoughts again became sequential and my anxiety level—absent for so long— suddenly erupted. Oh, shit! I said to myself. You are about to step out in Hell.

But it didn't seem like Hell, at least not the Hell I imagined. I was again in a room, but this one looked like the dean's office back in school. There were books all over the place, windows looking out on a lawn, and flowers in a vase by the desk.

The door opened and a man in a business suit walked in.

"Sorry to keep you, Bob." He extended his hand. "I'm Satan." I started to pull my hand away. "Oh, don't worry. No red suit and pitchfork here. I don't get the chance to meet everybody right when they first arrive, but I did want to greet you personally."

I was reeling at this point, struggling to keep up. "Pardon me if I'm a bit undone…"

"Rough trip down, right?"

"Yeah," I laughed. *Laughed! I actually laughed.* I hadn't had a good laugh since the day I left the basement. "You want to meet *me?* Can I ask why?"

"All questions are welcomed here. And, yes, I do want to meet you because you really upset the apple cart up there in Here, Bob. From what my spies tell me, you were a thorn in their holy side from the instant you got there. Boy, I loved it!"

"You know about Here?"

"Sure, we have a running battle. They hate to lose one to me. But when people don't fit in, they have no choice but bounce them—and they come straight here."

"But what about Precall, can't they just ship them there? Then they're stuck in tar baby forever."

"Precall is a fiction, Bob. There is no Precall. It's just a threat they use to keep souls in line."

"They lie?"

"Like a rug, Bob. Look, the so-called Master is a vain old fool who lost control of his planet centuries ago. Look at the Jesus mishap. He was so distracted he didn't even know what was going on until the end. Then it was too late. He collects souls, yes, he does have that power left, but the rest is all smoke and mirrors. It's really about keeping souls away from me. That's the real competition, Bob. That's what this is all about. You see, many spans ago I had a falling out with the Big Cheese and so I came here to this end of the universe where I set up shop. So make yourself at home, you'll find suitable housing, a lot of old friends, all the books and movies you want. And by the way, all of your body parts work perfectly well here, Bob."

"And the criminals, the terrorists? Are they here?"

"Nope. I simply drop them in a big bug zapper and they're gone."

"No torture, no roasting on a spit forever?"

"Disgusting. Do I look like some sort of sadist? Zap 'em and be done with it. By the way, you can fish here, but it's strictly catch and release. And we don't hunt animals, but you're free to shoot skeet or sporting clays. The food is the same as on earth, the vegetables are all organic, but the meat is artificially made. Looks and tastes the same, of course. I just have a thing about killing living things."

"I don't know what to say, Satan, it all seems too good to be true."

"I know, Bob, but you'll get used to it. I've got to run right now. I'll have someone show you to your house." We left his office and walked out into the sunlight. And there was Sally.

"It took you a while to get here, Sweetheart. Your little run up in Here lasted a lot longer than you realize. And by the way, I'm sorry about the breaker."

She put her arms around me and said, "Want to see our place, lover?"

HIAWATHA

"*Watch it, buddy, don't push!*"

"Hey! It's me, remember?"

"Oh, wow! I'm sorry. I didn't recognize you. How have you been?"

"Good, really good. How about you?"

"Not bad, I guess. Same ol' same ol', you know what I...*hey! Wait your turn!* Rush, rush, everyone's in a rush."

"Yeah, seems like it, but I don't let it bother me."

"That's right, I remember you're always real laid back. I've never mastered that one. I have trouble saying...*Watch where you're going, asshole!*"

"Let it go, it's not worth it. I mean, what's the hurry? The weather's great, plenty of rain for the animals, food's real good, plenty of it. Don't spoil it with a lot of aggravation, know what I mean?"

"You're right, of course, but I hate crowds, especially when I'm trying to...*I've had enough of you! Now back off or I'll bust you in the chops!*"

"Man, you've got a serious aggression problem. Keep this up and you'll put yourself in an early grave."

"I know, I know, but all these jerks just piss me off. And by the way, I think the food is awful."

"Adjective or noun?"

"Very funny. By the way, I don't remember if you have a name?"

"Hiawatha. Do you like it?"

"Hiawatha? How did you pick that name?"

"I like the image. Native American, birch bark canoe, sunset, romance. It's sweet. I like the sound."

"I suppose, but it scares me. I can't swim, and a canoe made out of birch bark doesn't sound too stable…*Goddamn it! Cut that shit out! Back off!*"

"I can't swim, either, but it doesn't make any difference. I trust the canoe, and I have faith it won't tip over. And if I do, so what?"

"*So what?!* Are you nuts? Tip over and you drown, that's what. That's not how I want to go."

"How *do* you want to go? By the way, I don't remember if you have a name."

"Nah. What's the point?"

"The point is you are an individual with a voice, ideas, and a destiny. You should have a name."

"That's all very pretty, but quite frankly, Hiawatha, I see myself as just another face in the crowd. *Yo! Moron! You're in my way.*"

"You'd be amazed how much better your self-image will be if you give yourself a good name. That and a little faith and I think you could turn this hostility thing around."

"I can see the name, but I don't get the faith thing at all."

"It's not complicated. Ask yourself—why am I here? Is it a random act of a quirky universe? Or maybe the purposeful act of a Higher Power? And if it's not chance alone, then it's likely a promise of something far better than this in the future. And to get it, all you need to do is believe, have faith."

"So you think that with a nice name and a little faith you'll fly off into the clouds and live happily ever after? I have a hard time buying into that scheme, Hiawatha."

"It's not hard, and doesn't the chance to shed this earth-bound rat race have any appeal?"

"Sure, but…*You bastard! That's mine! Try that again and you'll be sorry.* Where was I?"

"Faith. All you need to do is accept the promise, believe in it, and you'll be able to ignore all of life's little irritations. Look at me, I'm living proof."

"Okay, I see your point. How about if I start with the name part. If that goes okay, I can work on the…*Kiss my ass, sucker! Get the hell out of my way.*"

"Yeah, maybe we should just start off easy, and…oh my!! Good God!!"

"What's the matter, Hiawatha?"

"I feel really weird! I think I'm dying! It's happening, I know it! The promise is about to be fulfilled! Quick! Promise me you'll have faith! Make the commitment before it's too late!"

"Shit! I think it's happening to me, too! YES! I have faith, Hiawatha. We'll fly off into the heavens, free. I know it, Hiawatha!"

Almost at the same moment, the two maggots shed their skin, flexed their wings, and took flight. Together they soared above the plain, dancing on the warm breeze, sniffing the air for a fresh kill.

LA PONCEDURA

"Lot 49, ladies and gentlemen, the last offering we have from the estate of Jonathan Havemeyer. As described in your catalog, this is a non-indexed package containing approximately eighty maps, letters, and maybe even a bus schedule." The audience didn't rise to the joke. It was getting late and the program's two best maps were still to come. The auctioneer knew the package was a throwaway item and trying to squeeze it too hard could cost the bidding momentum crafted over the last four hours.

Still, it was money—sometimes seemingly dead items fetch good prices. All he needed was an opening bid to bring one of his audience plants into the game, trigger a bidding match and hope his man pulled out at just the right moment.

Larry Kingston had his eye on the package all afternoon. He had already bought two mid-19th-century Texas maps, nothing terribly important but they were colorful and the price was right. Color sells and they were perfect for the display window at his Dallas store. With a little luck, he figured he might be able to double his money and at least recover the expense of driving 600 miles round trip to attend the auction.

But the Havemeyer package fascinated him. During the pre-auction viewing he had been allowed to sift quickly through the collection, though a thick encircling cord prevented him from seeing much more than the map edges. Havemeyer was a famous collector and these were almost certainly culls from his extensive collection. Even so, there was always the chance the old man had missed something important.

Most of the edges had tears, not itself a problem, but several extended into the map borders hurting the value of even the best maps. It looked like a stack of inexpensive 19th- and early 20th-century maps, the sort of stuff he could move for two to four hundred dollars each, more if cleaned up and mounted in a nice frame.

Larry did the math again. If there are 50 good ones fetching an average of $250 each, that's $12,500. Take off framing and overhead and maybe the net would be around 10K. So don't pay more than 5K for the lot.

But there is always the chance there could be a real winner lost in the mix, something no one appreciated in the rush to highlight the big ticket maps. It could be a letter with a good autograph, an octavo [small map] sandwiched invisibly between larger ones, or an offset—a newer map printed on the back side of an older one. Even Texas city and county maps of no historical value sell well to people living on or near some long-forgotten landmark. It was worth some risk.

But just as these exciting tangibles can pay off handsomely, true world reality favors disappointment. There are also an inordinate number of fakes floating around, and without examining a map closely, especially through a strong backlight, a superficial glance tells you almost nothing. The most common tricks are bleaching to remove evidence of mold damage or fading sharp lines to make a map look older. Cleverly done, alterations can be hard to spot. Even an expert like Havemeyer could be fooled.

"Good news, ladies and gentlemen, we are going to remove the two thousand dollar reserve! Who will open at fifteen hundred?"

No one stirred.

"It's a steal at a thousand, ladies and gentlemen. Who will open at one thousand?"

Nothing.

"The old man is spinning in his grave folks. Don't disappoint him. Nine hundred gets us going."

"This could be a treasure chest, ladies and gentlemen. Who will bid eight hundred?"

"Seven hundred to get us started! This is robbery, folks, let's hear it at five hundred."

Finally, a bidding card flicked in the back row. The auctioneer jumped on it with the excitement of a lottery winner, cranking up his tobacco auction chant, arms waving excitedly.

Larry figured the fellow in the back row to be a shill. No matter, I'll just have to be careful not to let him suck me in. Finally, there was a second bid at six hundred followed immediately by several bids from dealers and collectors Larry recognized. The bidding lost steam around $2,500 and that's when Larry pounced.

"Three thousand." He hoped that would be a shutout bid, one that would push the savvy buyers aside and might keep the guy in the back row quiet.

"Three thousand dollars, ladies and gentlemen, do I hear four?" He pointed individually to the previous bidders. One by one they indicated they were out. Larry's heart was pounding. Three K, I can easily swing that.

"Lot 49 going once at three thousand. Don't miss this one, folks." He lifted the package over his head, grimacing dramatically as if it weighed fifty pounds.

"Going twice at three thousand. I can't let this happen, ladies and gentlemen. Last call, all in at three thousand?" He shifted his look from disbelief to grief, like a mother watching her son board a troop ship.

"Four thousand."

Shit, Larry muttered, turning to see who the new bidder was, a bad mistake when trying to maintain the image of indifference. Worse, he missed the move and couldn't tell who made the bid. Clearly, it wasn't Mr. Back Row, but was this his partner or a clever legitimate buyer putting the shutout on Larry?

"Five thousand!" Larry said, immediately recognizing mistake number two—never jump right on top of a large over-bid. Now everyone in the room knows you want the lot and it's just a question of how far you'll go to get it. Everyone else can sit back and watch the fun as the two bidders fight it out. Larry was now the beautiful maiden in the auctioneer's wet dream.

"Six!" shouted the auctioneer. This time Larry caught a glimpse of the man. He was one of the early bidders, someone Larry didn't recognize as either a regional dealer or collector. But he didn't look like a shill. Shills don't want to stand out, and this man was well dressed, wore highly polished Tony Llama snakeskin boots, wide turquoise bracelet, thunderbird string tie and a deadpan face.

"Sixty-five," said Larry trying to apply the brakes. You're over the 5K mark, idiot, he said to himself. Stop. You're getting sucked in. Remember the San Antonio auction. You paid dearly for that blunder.

But Tony Llama didn't hesitate and in a few minutes the bid to Larry was $9,500. He took it and the gavel dropped.

"Sold for ninety-five hundred!! Bidder 249."

Larry felt sick and dizzy. Everyone in the room was looking at him. Mercifully, the auctioneer immediately started hyping one of the auction's two jewels, a 16th century Italian baroque map. Larry waited until the bidding started and made his way to the payment table, wrote a check, picked up his two maps and the mysterious package.

Back at his car, Larry sat staring at the encircling ribbon, his mind tumbling between excited curiosity and deep, deep fear he had just made a colossal mistake. Bad enough to use almost every dollar in his company account, but the worst of it will be Lupita's reaction when she hears the news. He wanted desperately to rip off the ribbon, find a valuable piece and be able to tell his wife that this time his intuition had paid off.

The longer he sat, the more fear pushed curiosity aside. Time to move, hit the road, get some coffee, think about the Astros. Anything but the maps. Of course, it didn't work. It's like telling someone not to think about a dancing penguin.

It was nearly midnight when he finally rolled into the driveway. A light in the bedroom window told him what he already knew—Lupita was up and ready to pounce. And he still hadn't opened the package.

"You paid *how much* for something you don't even fucking know what it is? *Carajo!* You are crazy, Larry! I warned you before you left, my friend, don't spend nothing when you got nothing."

"I have enough to cover the check, Lupita. And I got two really good ones no matter what. It's late and I'm too tired to go through the collection or argue with you. This came from Jonathan Havemeyer. There could be some great stuff in here."

It was weak and he knew it. Even bringing up Havemeyer and gracing the pile with the word "collection" sounded feeble. Lupita wasn't buying any of it and for the next hour she made her feelings known. It only stopped when her six-year-old son, Larry's stepson, Chavito, woke up crying, obviously upset by all the noise. Lupita muttered something in Spanish, turned off the light, and said, "Go take care of Chavito. Tell him you bought some old man's garbage. Maybe *he'll* be impressed."

After Chavito went back to sleep, Larry put the package on the kitchen table, made coffee, sat down, and after his third cup, untied the knot. The excitement factor was gone, replaced by dread and a deep sense of guilt. His only hope was finding something dramatic, just one hot ticket to lead him back from the depths.

The first dozen maps were just what he had expected, Havemeyer rejects with some value but even the good ones needed a lot of restoration. Then there was a series of letters, late 19th-century correspondence about loans, bad crops, and the price of beef. The stamps might be worth something but even the better ones were of poor quality or blurred with cancel marks.

One of the letters, however, did stand out. Written in 1878, it described the shootout in Round Rock between famous Texas outlaw Sam Bass and sheriff's deputies. Bass was killed, and the writer claims to have seen him laid out at the undertaker's office. Excellent! That one will sell. Outlaw memorabilia is hot these days. It ought to bring at least $300. Framed with a picture of Bass, maybe it could fetch $500. It's a start.

He put it in the keeper pile. But it didn't lift his spirits at all. He was half way through the package and his tiny pile of mediocre maps and the Bass letter was dwarfed by the growing stack of rejects. Not much to show for $9,500, but he couldn't stop. He was so tired the maps all began to look the same, but sleep was out of the question. If there was something—anything—he could show Lupita, he might deflect her anger.

Toward the bottom of the pile Larry uncovered a folio map, one printed on a complete sheet of paper (not cut out of a book), measuring roughly 25 by 20 inches. Holding it up to the light, he could see blurring of both color and lines suggesting either a stone printed lithograph or a second or third run copper plate map. Either way, it looked very old. The borders were good and there was hardly any foxing [brown spots caused by mold]. The paper seemed of high quality but unfortunately, there was no visible watermark to help date the paper. If this is a forgery, he thought, someone started with awfully good stock.

The map itself looked Spanish, probably 16th or 17th century, and showed a small city or large town on an island in a bay or lagoon. It was roughly circular, it's edges irregular. Highly stylized human figures were grouped along what appeared to be roads leading to the water and across to the island. In the center of the island a pyramidal structure was circled by a jumble of huts and more figures, these more elaborate and apparently costumed. In the upper right portion there was another pyramid and more costumed figures. Trees and fields with rows of crops filled the rest of the map. Labels and a few lines in Latin were written around the entire circumference, typical of the time maps were turned to be read.

Using a magnifying glass he saw two short lines of script in Latin, possibly a prayer, and under that, an ornate letter, either an "S" or a "P."

From the start, Larry suspected the map was an early Spanish map of Tenextitan [Cortes' spelling of Tenochititlan], a somewhat skimpy version of the famous Poncedura map from the 1530s hanging in the archeology museum in Mexico City. He wasn't particularly excited by it because it was a widely imitated and often faked map, variations of which he had seen many times before. The ornate initial was therefore a "P," but whoever made this one seemed to run out of gas after going to a lot of trouble getting the right kind of paper. The real Poncedura had an enormous amount of detail, especially of the city itself. Virtually every tiny street was in place and there were no costumed natives gamboling around the Zócalo—the central plaza.

Again holding the map up to a strong light Larry noted what seemed to be a partially erased circle on the lower edge about the size of a quarter surrounding a single short word. After working on it for fifteen minutes, Larry finally realized the word was "Fake." A curved line at the top and center of the "F" told Larry it was written by Havemeyer, well known for both ornate writing and the unspeakably bad habit of writing on old maps he either didn't like or rejected as fakes.

That sealed it. Glad I didn't get too excited about it, but it's an interesting piece and there is a market for clever fakes, especially on old paper. On a good day this one could pull $500. Okay, it's a keeper.

It was just after 5:00 a.m. when Larry finished his third run through the pile. He figured the keepers were worth between four and five thousand without too much reworking. And maybe he could repackage the losers with some of his own rejects and get rid of the bunch at another auction. Maybe Tony Llama will show up and give a couple of grand for the bunch.

Lupita found Larry asleep at the table when she got up. The smell of coffee woke him up.

"I'm sorry I was so pissy last night, Larry," she said handing her husband a large cup of coffee. "I just worry all the time we don't ever seem to get anywhere and when you spend money like that it makes me crazy."

"I know, Lupita, and I'm sorry, too. But you know in my business you have to take chances."

"Not ten thousand dollar chances," she said, an edge creeping back into her voice. Larry nodded in agreement and sipped his coffee.

"I am afraid to ask, but did you find anything in your 'chance'?"

"Yes and no, Lupita. There are some good maps, a letter, and one map I have to research. It could be quite a find but I don't want to get my hopes up yet." It was pure bullshit but Larry needed a way out; otherwise, Lupita was liable to reignite and he just didn't have the strength to deal with another explosion.

"Show me," she said defiantly.

He put the map on the table, holding it carefully by the edges as if it truly was a treasure. Lupita glanced at it and asked, "So what is it and what's it worth?"

"It's an early Spanish map from the time of Cortes. If it's real, it's worth a fortune. If it's a fake, it's a beauty and still worth a lot."

"How much is 'a lot'?"

"I don't know, maybe five thousand." Another whopper and Lupita wasn't buying it.

"So when will you know?"

"I'll send a copy off to a few experts and see what they say. It won't take long." Lupita shrugged, took her coffee and headed for the bathroom.

Larry's store was located in the shopping arcade of the fashionable Longhorn Hotel in downtown Dallas. Here, foot traffic was highly selected, generally wealthy people who could afford to indulge their decorating fantasies with colorful maps, autographed letters and documents. Serious collectors also occasionally came by, but most of Larry's income came from impulse buyers.

But location-location comes at a price. The rent was stiff and the cost of paying a skillful clerk and maintaining the image of casual opulence meant he had to move a lot of merchandise. Window beacons included several flashy (and equally pricey) maps plus what he called "bait for rich rednecks," a display of old firearms, wanted posters, and a collection of Texas Rangers' star-shaped badges, all designed to pull customers in from the arcade.

The store was actually Lupita's idea. When they married three years before, Larry's shop was on the fifth floor of an office building just south of Dallas. His business was entirely focused on collectors, mostly through internet trade. She called his office "*Su caverna*," his cave, and convinced him he would never enjoy real prosperity until he took his business to the place where the wealthy like to play. Larry immediately took her advice and made the move.

When it came to making important decisions, even ones involving Larry's business, Lupita usually had her way. He was completely smitten by Lupita, and while others found her abrupt, edgy determination to be intrusive—even domineering—Larry felt those qualities filled gaps in his less bold and indecisive personality.

Lupita was tall, slender, her hair was coal black, and she awakened sexual passion Larry had never before known. Her temper could be fierce, but Larry usually accepted her assertiveness as bold counsel, preferring to avoid open clashes in favor of family comity. He also enjoyed his role as nurturing stepfather. Chivato's own dad had abandoned the family when he was two. He walked out the door and simply disappeared.

Not all of Lupita's ideas worked out, but she was skillful in blaming Larry for poor implementation rather than accepting it as an error in conception. The transition to the Longhorn was costly and when the dream of a dramatic change failed to materialize, Lupita's support quickly wore thin. Larry's income did increase, but his overhead soared, eating up most of the profit. Fat months were few, and Lupita's demands for money were incessant. He briefly considered laying off his clerk, but that would have put him in the store all the time. That would have made him entirely reliant on wholesalers for maps and killed the sense of adventure that fueled his trips to auctions, attics, and antique stores in search of undiscovered jewels.

Being dependent on wholesalers also exposed him to an ethical problem. Wholesalers trafficked in a high percentage of "kites," maps stolen from library books by clever thieves who cut them deep in the binding, frayed the sliced edge and passed them off as single copy impressions. To protect themselves from increasing thievery, libraries searched people after granting access to rare editions, but even combined with camera monitoring, it did little to stop determined thieves.

One virtually undetectable trick was use of a "finger knife," a thin, sharpened sliver of plastic glued under a fingernail. Casual hand movements concealed the cut. As the book was closed, the map was withdrawn, rolled up, and slipped up a sleeve or into a small pocket stitched invisibly under an overcoat cuff. Casual body movement masked the quick moves and blocked the surveillance camera.

As a matter of principle, Larry never knowingly sold a kited map and more than once refunded money when a map was found to have been stolen. Lupita took a dim view of Larry's fastidious business practices. To her, buyer beware was the watchword and Larry's "do-gooder" mentality made him a hopeless sap.

"You think more about customers than your own family" was one of her favorite sayings. To Lupita, it was a pragmatic matter—everyone is a crook at some level. People who don't get it end up living in house trailers.

Larry took his expensive package to the shop, put the good material on display and had his clerk call a few document collectors to see if there were any takers for the Sam Bass letter. He made copies of the Spanish map and sent them off to several collectors who specialized in New World maps.

Within hours he received a reply from a dealer in New York.

Dear Larry,

Ouch! I hope you didn't pay real coin for this dog. I've seen it before—Old Man Havemeyer showed it to me a few years ago. It got him excited, but when we looked it over we both concluded it's a fake, a good one, but still a fake. It lacks the detail of the Poncedura maps, its figures are clotted and the lines are too sharp for its alleged age. The paper is perfect but that also presents problems. How could there be so little foxing, shadowing, and edge wear on a four hundred year old map? Hard to say who did this, and OMH wouldn't say where he got it. The paper is worth at least 1K, and if I were you, I'd try to peddle it as a great fake or else move it for the paper. Of course, if you sell the paper it will end up back on the market again and I know you would never go for that. I offered OMH $500 for it. I'll double the offer for you but I'm not holding my breath.

Hope all is going well for you. Stop by when you get to New York, we'll have lunch.

Parker

"Shit," Larry said. His clerk stuck her head in the door of his tiny office and asked, "Is there a problem, sir?" She wasn't used to Larry using profanity or for that matter, showing anything approaching anger. He assured her there wasn't, put the map in his safe, and tried to turn his mind back to the immediate problem of increasing his cash flow.

Lupita continued to ride Larry, not just about the auction, but in a more general way about her disappointment with their increasingly restricted life style. Larry did his best to mollify her, suggesting they go on a camping trip in the hill country to get away from maps and enjoy the rejuvenating beauty of the Texas countryside.

Lupita wasn't buying it. Worse, she started talking about separation, a horrifying idea to Larry. He countered with his best arguments but Lupita shot them all down. Even the terrible effect splitting would have on Chavito didn't turn her head.

Then Larry received a second response to his Poncedura inquiry, this one from a dealer in London who was also familiar with the map. He had seen a copy before Havemeyer acquired it. He found the map "troubling" for the same reasons Parker gave, but he added a fillip at the end.

"Havemeyer knew I'd seen a copy of it and asked what I thought. I told him it looked like a really good fake, but I couldn't be absolutely sure without a really thorough examination of the map itself. I still feel that way. It is just possible the crude figures and lack of street detail beyond the *Zócalo* indicate this one predates the other Ponceduras. I would love to see it in the flesh, Larry. London is lovely at this time of year.

Regards, F.C. Parkingham, RCMPS, RCHP"

Larry was not the least bit buoyed up by the 'maybe' quality of Parkingham's letter. He didn't have the funds to go to London or even Mexico City, and he knew that Lupita wouldn't be impressed without absolute confirmation and a solid offer to go with it. So he decided to face up to his mistake, call it what it was, and get down to selling maps whose value was certain.

A few days later, however, F.C. Parkingham himself walked into the store. Just happened to be in the states, thought he'd divert, and if Larry hadn't sold it, have a quick look at "a really good fake." The quick look took all afternoon and when it was over, both Parkingham and Larry were convinced they had a very early, primitive version of the Mexico City museum's Poncedura map.

"Congratulations, Larry, you've pulled off every map collector's dream. And right out from under the nose of Havemeyer himself. Nice shot. Any idea what you'll do with it? It's worth at least half a million to someone, don't you think?"

At that point Larry was in a state of bone-rattling ambivalence, still not one hundred percent convinced the map was genuine and if it was, should he think of selling it, using it to draw in customers or take the high road and donate it to a museum?

Lupita, of course, knew immediately what to do with it.

"Sell it, Larry! You just hit gold! This is what we've been waiting for!" Larry mumbled something about getting a second opinion, not rushing, all stall tactics that did nothing but aggravate Lupita. They made love for the first time in weeks but her last words before they fell asleep were, "Sell it, baby. Sell it."

The next several days were hectic. Parkingham had put the word out on the internet, several calls came in from collectors who wanted to see the map and there was a brief piece about the discovery in the *Dallas News*. The prestigious Museum of New World History wanted to send a representative; that is, if Larry was thinking about donating his amazing find.

"Remember, Mr. Kingston, if you sell it, you'll have to give Uncle Sam a big chunk, but if you donate it, your reputation is assured and our accountants can spread the donation value out so you'll never pay taxes again."

Larry also realized he would have to insure the map so he called his agent but the most he could do was insure it for 200K and only if it was housed in a safe deposit vault. The agent joked that any Boy Scout with a penknife and a screwdriver could open Larry's "rinkey-dink" office safe.

By the end of the week it was clear the map was real, and Larry was enjoying some modest notoriety. Foot traffic and sales in the store were up, several collectors stopped by to look at it, but surprisingly, no one was clamoring to buy the map. That didn't bother Larry, though. He was enjoying the income boost and relief from most of the burden of guilt over buying the Havemeyer package in the first place. But he continued to remind himself that his good fortune was blind luck, not genius, so relief never turned into real satisfaction.

He did get a safety deposit box for the map and not a minute too soon. He was awakened at 2:30 a.m. the next morning by the Longhorn Hotel's security chief. "We need you over here right away, Mr. Kingston, looks like someone broke into your store."

When Larry arrived, cops were standing around drinking coffee from paper cups, a detective was looking for fingerprints on the arcade door, the Longhorn's manager was glowering from the lobby, obviously wishing the flashing lights, yellow tapes, and noise would simply disappear.

Inside the store nothing looked out of place, but it was a different story in the office. Larry's desk was pushed against one wall, the safe door was open and its contents scattered around the floor mixed with coins and currency from the change drawer. The police wanted to know what was missing so Larry collected and sorted through his papers and maps.

"Nothing seems to be gone," he said. He was told to double check but still the answer was the same. The detective came to the obvious conclusion the thief was after something specific, something he did not find.

"The Poncedura," Larry said. This was all about the map. If he hadn't moved it to the bank there would have been no insurance and his nightmare would have resumed.

The detective showed Larry how the thief had broken into the electrical panel at the back of the lobby coatroom and cut the juice to the arcade alarm system. A few scratch marks on the door showed how easily the outer lock was penetrated by "a real pro," but how the safe was opened wasn't as obvious.

To the detective, the thief already had either the combination or the skill to work it out quickly. He rolled his eyes when Larry started to recite the number of people who knew the combination, starting with his clerk, his insurance agent, lawyer, and any number of others who knew the safe before Larry bought it—second hand—when he moved into the arcade store.

Lupita and Chavito were up when Larry got back just before dawn. He told them about the break-in and the good news about the Poncedura.

"Thank God, Larry!" Lupita said giving him an uncharacteristically warm hug. "But you know this is a sign. Our Lady gives people signs, Larry. She is telling you this map is unholy and you need to get rid of it."

"Since when is Our Lady in the map business, Lupita?"

"Don't joke about Our Lady, my friend. We need her, and we got to listen to her when she speaks. I'm warning you, Larry, that map came to us like an orphan on the church steps, and we need to find it a home."

It happens every time, Larry said to himself. We start off on one good foot and the other one ends up in a freaking bear trap. But maybe she's right this time, not about the sign crap, but the money might put us back on track. Yeah. Maybe I should sell the damn thing before we have even more bad luck.

And bad luck soon came, in buckets.

It started a few days after the break-in. The Longhorn's manager dropped by to tell Larry the management took a dim view of the recent "incident," and in light of the risk his business was bringing to the hotel, his rental contract would not be renewed when it expired in three months. Nothing personal, of course, but some un-named, "important Longhorn guests" had complained about feeling "vulnerable," a discomfort for which they expected—and would receive—prompt remedial action.

The management was, however, generously willing to allow Larry to move into a location in one of its subsidiary hotels, a recently acquired property convenient to the airport, a large shopping center, and a Super Wal-Mart store.

Even more reason to sell the damn map, Larry concluded. Use some of the money to appease Lupita and the rest to open a low-risk antique store in the old town section of the city. Minimal risk, low heat at home, and for certain, no more map auctions.

Surprisingly, Lupita was only lukewarm to the idea. She embraced the notion of a vacation, a wardrobe update, and a new couch, but seemed indifferent to the part about a new business.

"What do you want me to do, Lupita? Isn't this our chance to literally remake our life together?" Lupita shrugged off the question, said something about having some ideas of her own, turned her back, and walked away. Larry concluded he simply had to move forward with the map sale and hope Lupita got on board when a vacation in Acapulco materialized. She didn't do well with uncertainty.

Unfortunately, Larry's brief notoriety had faded and when he put out the word he might sell the map if the price was right, only a few tepid offers came back. Even the great Parkingham wasn't interested. He tried an ad in the weekly trade rag, *Maps International*, but his $1,500 ad only netted two offers, both in the 300K range.

Lupita was pushing harder than ever, his clerk had found a new job, and he was running out of easy-sale maps. Much as he hated the idea, it was time to hit another auction. Lupita seemed surprisingly indifferent to the idea, told him to take his time and see if he could bring back another Poncedura. He briefly considered selling the map at the auction, but without a lot of hype and advertising ahead of the sale it would look like what it was: the act of a desperate man.

To save money, he drove to the Nashville auction and over two days bought a clutch of reasonably attractive maps. He used his modest notoriety to sniff out a possible sale for the Poncedura but nothing solid materialized. The auction company wanted to offer it at an upcoming sale, but Larry's suggestion of a 400K reserve turned them off.

He drove the long and tedious return trip non-stop. There was no point spending money on a motel when five dollars' worth of coffee would get him home just as well. He was glad to finally turn into the driveway, but jolted into alertness by a police car parked in front of his garage. The deputy county sheriff and Larry stepped out of their cars at the same time.

"What's the problem, officer," Larry asked anxiously glancing back and forth between the house and the policeman.

"No trouble at all, Mr. Kingston, as long as you take these papers, don't make no fuss, get back in your car, and leave the premises peaceably." He handed Larry a clutch of papers, all folded neatly in thirds, the top one proclaiming itself to be a **COURT ORDER**. Larry tried to read the words under the title but he couldn't focus. The cop came to his rescue.

"Let me help you, buddy. Your wife, one 'Lupe Maria Gonzalez Kingston,' has gotten a protective order saying you can't communicate with her except through her lawyer or the court, you can't come within 500 feet of her, and if you do, you'll be arrested."

"Arrested? I'll be arrested? What the hell for?"

"Look, I don't know jack shit about this, but I do know you have pissed her off mightily, and you better get a lawyer, *pronto*. Oh, and that second paper is a summons to appear in court to give your side in the divorce proceedings."

"Divorce? This is crazy…I need to talk to Lupita." He started to move toward the front door but the cop stepped in his way, put his hand on his pistol, and growled, "Look, asshole, I've tried to be nice about this. Get in your fucking car and leave or I'll lock your sorry ass up in County, and you can wait for your court date with a bunch of fucked-up Mexicans. Now leave!"

Larry left, drove to a gas station, and tried to read the papers. The protective order was granted because of "extreme mental cruelty, threats of violence, and failure to provide adequate support and sustenance" to Mrs. Lupe Maria Gonzalez Kingston.

"Support and sustenance? Cruelty? Violence? What the hell is going on?! This is crazy!!"

He sat in the car for over an hour trying to calm down and think what he needed to do next. Several times he started the car intending to go home and confront Lupita, but fortunately for Larry, the image of the deputy and his gun stilled his impulse. Finally, in spite of his agitation, he realized he needed to talk to his lawyer and made the call. His secretary said he had left for the day and suggested he try tomorrow. Larry uncharacteristically exploded, literally screaming that he had to talk to the man NOW!

An hour later he met the lawyer at his office.

Luckily for Larry, his attorney, Bill Lawson, was an old friend and agreed to return to his office; otherwise, Larry almost certainly would have risked arrest trying to confront Lupita. Lawson scanned the papers while Larry paced the office describing the encounter with the cop.

"Okay, Larry, sit down, shut up, and listen to me. This is very serious business, and if you don't follow my directions, you could literally wind up in jail." He waited for Larry to calm down and after brief silence, spelled it out.

"There are two things you have to know up front, Larry. Ignore me at your peril. First—just 'why' this is happening is unimportant. The court doesn't care, her lawyer doesn't care, and to get through this, you can't care either. Secondly, honesty and truth have no part in this. It's all about manipulating the legal system. The bottom line, Larry, is Lupita wants a divorce, she wants it immediately, and she wants just about everything you own in the deal. It's crazy, it's cruel, it's just plain nuts, but it's happening, starting with her allegations of cruelty and her statement that you left her—abandoned her—when you took off last Tuesday…"

"I went on a business trip, Bill, she knew…"

"Shut up, Larry. You aren't listening. It doesn't matter why you went or how many kisses she blew as you left. She says it was abandonment and anything you argue about a business trip will fall on deaf ears, I guarantee it. I know it's a lie, and the court may know it, too. But as long as she's using the system you are screwed. Her lawyer is Ricardo Guzman. He's a real prick, a rattlesnake in a business suit, a guy who does this shit every day and sleeps like a baby at night. She is laying some heavy hay on him to set this up."

"But she can't afford someone like that…"

"Oh, yes she can, my friend, because his last official act in court will be to point to the helpless, demure Lupe Maria who will have been sadly brushing away tears while rubbing a large crucifix, and he'll demand the court order *you* to pay all attorney's fees. I'll protest, the judge will ignore me and ask Guzman how much he expects his fee will be. He'll say he isn't sure but not more than 50K. The judge will order you to pay, set a fifty thousand limit. And that will be the end of it."

Lawson's last piece of advice was to sell everything he could, especially the map, as fast as humanly possible. "The court is going to price your worth way out of proportion to its real value so your best bet is get everything into cash because that's the one thing they can't inflate. Right now, your biggest liability is that map, but don't sell it at an obviously low price or they'll say you deliberately deprived poor Lupe of her support and order you to pay alimony with assets you no longer have. The one bright spot is the court isn't likely to order you to pay alimony when they see she got most of what you have and there's nothing left.

"They've been granted an expedited hearing, so you have exactly nine days to sell what you can and get ready to find out just what a greedy woman and a turbo lawyer can do to a poor *schmuck* with a potentially valuable asset he can't get rid of."

The next week was pure hell for Larry. He sold most of what was in his store to a wholesaler for sixty cents on the dollar, raised a little over $75,000 and bravely turned down an offer of $175,000 for the Poncedura.

He was tempted but Lawson told him he had to get at least close to 300K or the court would punish him with alimony.

Lawson did his best to steel Larry for what he was about to experience in court, but nothing he said remotely prepared him for the emotional tsunami that fell on him that morning. Guzman described Larry as an emotionally abusive husband who was absent from the home for long periods of time, hinting at numerous affairs, and who was unwilling to give his wife enough money to buy even basic necessities. He described Lupita as a faithful, spiritual wife and mother, a once cheerful and outgoing person now crushed under the weight of Larry's sadistic behavior.

As to the settlement, Guzman piously asserted his client only wanted what she deserved, enough to live on and provide for her son. The Poncedura came up again and again, each time its value seemed to climb along with Larry's alleged determination to undervalue "this historical treasure" so he could dupe the court, sell it, and live like a king while poor Lupe would be left with nothing.

Lawson strongly advised Larry not to take the stand. "Guzman will shred you. And he'll make you admit what Lupita already knew—that Parkingham told you the map was worth at least five hundred thousand dollars." That would sink Larry's boat on the spot and anything he said about trying unsuccessfully to get even 300K would be interpreted as proof of his duplicitous nature.

The entire process took less than two hours, including the thirty-minute break the judge took to consider the matter before passing judgment. The house was Lupita's, won in her first divorce; Larry paid the mortgage, and the court granted her all the equity and furnishings plus half of Larry's cash, to be paid through the court within seven days. Larry was allowed to keep his desk, computer, clothing, and the older of their two cars.

Then the kicker. "After considering all the evidence," the judge made what he termed a "fair and a conservative estimate" of $500,000 for the map's value and ordered Larry to pay Lupita $250,000 within ninety days or face "serious consequences," meaning pay up or go to jail until you cough up the money.

Oh, yes, and he also continued the protective order "indefinitely," granted Lupe Maria Gonzalez Kingman her request for the divorce to be final within thirty days and ordered Larry to pay court costs and all attorney's fees. But he did give Larry one break—he turned down Guzman's fifty thousand "estimate" of his fee. He issued a mild rebuke saying the brevity of the entire process did not warrant more than twenty-five thousand. Guzman didn't appear to notice.

"All rise…" The judge disappeared, Guzman hustled Lupita out of court, and Lawson had to literally pull Larry to his feet to get him moving.

Larry spent the first week after the hearing sitting in his crumby motel room drinking coffee, staring into space, and mumbling incoherently to himself. Lawson was alarmed and did his best to motivate Larry, but he wouldn't budge. The suggestion of a psychiatric evaluation angered Larry but seemed to jolt him enough make him start thinking about what he had to do next. He came to the conclusion the only way he could possibly get his life back together would be to sell the Poncedura, pay off Lupita, and try to find a new way to earn a living.

But how in the world could he sell the map when everything he had already done was a complete flop? If he gave it to an auction house and it netted even a relatively robust 300K, he would still have to cough up twenty percent for the sale, Uncle Sam would want another twenty percent, Guzman was in for 25K, and that would leave him with 155K. Even if he threw in all his available cash, he would still be at least over 100K short. No, the absolute minimum he could get by with would be about 475K, clearly an impossible figure.

Larry suggested giving Lupita the damn map and let her sell it and pay off her lawyer. Lawson vetoed the idea knowing Guzman would turn it down flat, and for obvious reasons. He knew perfectly well the map wasn't going to net anything like 500K, selling it would be a huge hassle, and they would be stuck with the brokerage fee, capital gains plus his fee. Better to wait, let the desperate map expert get what he can, take the money, and put his ass in jail if he didn't come up with the whole thing. The judge would eventually spring him, but all his future earnings would be heavily garnished.

"Offering up the map will be our absolute last resort. Guzman will object, but I'll remind the judge that he was the one who put a 500K value on the map, that you would be surrendering your half, in the end an obviously better deal for Lupita. His tit will be in the wringer. If he turns us down it will be an acknowledgement he way overvalued the map and put you in an impossible situation. My guess is he'll tell them to take the map. Case closed.

"But for Christ sake don't stop trying to sell the damn thing. If by some miracle you get a good price you could even have some spare change when this is over without risking jail time."

And Larry did try. He called everyone he knew but couldn't advance the price past 200K. Everyone in the business knew he was desperate. Potential buyers became vultures waiting for his last gasp when the map would fall for a ridiculously low price.

Just under a week before the hearing, Larry got a call that appeared to change everything.

"Mr. Kingston, my name is Ricardo Planchero, and I understand you have a very rare and valuable Poncedura. More to the point, you may be willing to sell it. Is that right?"

"Yes, that is true," said Larry, trying to sound casual. The voice was heavily accented and the name was not one he recognized.

"Well, I am a man with expensive tastes, especially when it comes to art and antiques. I am, I will admit, somewhat vain, and I enjoy the acclaim that accompanies dramatic gifts to museums, and—sometimes— to particularly deserving individuals. That happens to be the case at this time, but I only have what you Americans like to call a 'narrow window of opportunity.' I have talked to people who have seen your map and I am assured it is genuine. Since you are willing to sell, and I am ready to buy, we have only to agree on a price and a few simple conditions.

"So, I will offer you five hundred thousand dollars, a cashier's check to be deposited to your bank account the instant I have examined the map and found it to be genuine. I know this is a handsome price, but again being perfectly frank, I can easily afford it, I hate haggling and I am about to leave the country so the burden of making this sale will fall entirely on you. Do we have a deal, Mr. Kingston?"

"Yes, of course, Mr. Planchero. That is indeed a good price and I would be happy to deliver the map. You mentioned 'conditions'?"

"Yes. First, you bring me the map by Wednesday afternoon at 1:00 p.m. I live in a remote part of eastern Texas and it will require you to drive here from Dallas or fly to El Paso and rent a car that doesn't mind gravel roads. You have two days, which should be more than adequate. It suits my sense of personal security to live as I do. I rarely leave home except to fly out of my ranch, and Dallas is not, you might say, a favored destination.

"The second condition is that I examine the map. That part is easy. You will bring with you the name of your bank, a contact at the bank and the number of the account into which the money is to be deposited. The transfer will take no more than one hour. We will enjoy a brandy while this is taking place and once you hear from your contact that the money has arrived, we will have concluded our deal."

"Is that it, all the conditions?"

"Yes."

"Where do you live, and how do I get there?"

"I live near Juancho about two hours southeast of El Paso. You can find it on a map. It is a small town but has an excellent restaurant, *El Caciche*. Enjoy their *adabo* and my driver will meet you there between twelve and one. He will bring you up to the ranch. It is only an hour's drive and the desert is beautiful at this time of year.

"Do we have a deal, Señor Kingston?"

"Yes. Yes, Mr. Planchero, we have a deal."

"Good. If you will tell me where you are staying and give me about two hours, I will have a colleague drop by and give you some money to show my appreciation and cover your expenses." Larry gave him the name of the motel, immediately embarrassed by the shabby address.

"*Adiós*, my friend, I look forward to meeting you."

And that was it. It was Monday morning and Larry had just agreed to take the map to heaven-knows-where Texas and deliver it on faith to what was almost certainly a drug dealer with money to burn. He had no phone number to call and assumed from the man's tone that if he missed his appointment at the *Caciche* it would be of little concern to Mr. Planchero.

It tortured Larry to think he was probably dealing with a criminal. He began to hope the whole thing was a bad joke and no one would appear with the promised cash. He toyed with the idea of calling his lawyer but decided against it. Lawson would almost certainly say it sounded fishy and advise against it. But how could he pass this up? It could hardly be a robbery, why go to all that fuss to do what could be done more easily right in Dallas? And if it were a hoax, well, it would be good just to get the hell out of town for a couple of days on someone else's dime.

Two hours later there was a knock on his door, and a man in a white double-breasted suit, impenetrably dark sunglasses, and a wide grin handed him an envelope, touched the brim of his Panama hat, and left without saying a word. The envelope contained $5,000 in crisp one hundred dollar bills.

Larry fanned the money out on a table, his emotions bouncing from excitement to relief, then on to worry and back to excitement. "Fuck it!" he finally said out loud. "The world is full of crooks, so if I can use one to my advantage to get out of this mess, so be it. I'll get back to being honest later on."

The trip to Juancho was just over 650 miles. To be sure, there was the possibility of a breakdown in his aging Honda, so Larry rented a brand new Jeep Cherokee with leather seats and a killer sound system. He retrieved the map Tuesday morning, got the deposit information, and told the bank manager to expect a call from him around two o'clock Wednesday afternoon. Then he hit the road with a stack of new CDs and a thermos of coffee.

The trip across west Texas was a breeze and he was in San Martin in time for dinner. Juancho was only two hours away so, with travel pressure off, Larry allowed himself an enormous steak then retreated to his motel room with a bottle of tequila and four lemons. He woke up with a fearsome headache, chased it away with breakfast, coffee, and several aspirin. He was on the road by ten and in the parking lot of the *Caciche* at noon.

He took a seat at a table overlooking the parking lot, the briefcase holding the map between his leg and the wall. His stomach wasn't up for a plate of fiery hot *adabo,* so he settled for a bowl of tortilla soup and a glass of milk.

Just before one o'clock, a man wearing a white linen suit and bright red leather cowboy boots stepped out of a dust-covered Land Rover. He had on the same Panama hat he wore when he delivered the cash to Larry two days before.

"We meet again, Señor," he said extending his hand. "I trust you had a nice ride." He glanced briefly toward Larry's car.

"Yes, Mr...ah..."

"Alvarez, but please called me Paco."

"Yes, Paco, a very nice ride. Can I get you some lunch?"

"No, Señor, perhaps later, but we have to get going. Señor Planchero does not like to be kept waiting." He tossed a twenty dollar bill on the table, waved to the owner, and walked back to the parking lot. Larry followed, trying to appear nonchalant.

"You can leave your car here, Señor Kingston. Alberto will watch it for you." Five minutes later they turned onto a wide gravel road headed into the vast desert to the south of the little town. Paco, while friendly and proper, was no conversationalist, especially when Larry tried to probe about his employer. His only comment was, "Mr. Planchero is a man of business. You will like him."

An hour later, the car slowed and turned onto a minuscule dirt road marked by a small, crooked, weather-beaten sign that read, AZTEC MINE—KEEP OUT.

"Not much of an entrance," Larry joked nervously.

"Señor Planchero likes his privacy. You'll see."

The road wound around a hill abruptly ending at an abandoned shack. A rusted ore cart lay on its side next to a twisted pair of steel rails leading up the hill to a wide slit in the face of the hill.

"We are here, Mr. Kingston," Paco said. "Come with me and meet Señor Planchero." Larry cautiously stepped out of the car, his anxiety boiling into fear as the desolation of the scene enveloped him. He held the briefcase against his chest, his arms folded around it as if both protecting the map and hanging onto some sense of control in a situation that was becoming more ominous by the second.

"Around this way, Mr. Kingston," Paco said, his voice cheerful and non-threatening. They walked around the shack, Paco in the lead, Larry several steps behind. More mining equipment was scattered about the landscape along with an old pickup truck melting into the sand.

Paco stopped in front of a small mound of sand next to an open hole. "We are here, Mr. Kingston."

"And there is no Mr. Planchero, is there, Paco? You plan to steal the map."

"Well, there is no Planchero, but we do have Sancho," he said, pointing into the hole. Larry could hardly speak. His heart was pounding; he felt dizzy, nauseous, and disoriented. In spite of his terror he looked into the hole. It was about five feet deep and at the bottom lay a body, face down; an enormous black stain covered most of his back.

"A gentleman doesn't dig out here in the desert, Mr. Kingman. It isn't dignified. There are always people willing do that sort of work."

"You killed him? You killed that guy? Why? What sort of monster are you?"

A voice came from the back of the shack. "He's my monster, Larry, and he's really very sweet when you get to know him."

Larry slowly turned around. "Lupita!!"

"Yes, my dear husband, it's me. And Paco is my partner, Larry. We have been very close for a long time."

"Dear God, Lupita! You did all this to steal the map? You killed someone to steal the map? It's crazy! You could have had the map in another week or you could have stolen it in Dallas. And you plan to kill me, Lupita?! This is crazy. Why? Why?" He sank to his knees, unable to stand. Tears filled his eyes blurring the image of Lupita sitting on the steps of the crumpled cabin.

"We already tried to steal it, Larry. *Maricón!* You got it out of the store just in time. Now we got a new situation. If you give me the map, I get stuck with the taxes, paying the stupid lawyer, you walk away free as a bird, and all I get is pocket change. If I get Paco to steal the map, you are off the hook 'cause it's not your fault, and I end up with a big lawyer bill, no money, and a map I can't sell.

"But if *you* steal the map and disappear, the lawyer gets nothing from poor little me, you are a wanted man, and when we sell the map in Mexico to a very real buyer who wants it and has money to burn, we got no taxes, no nothing but cash. So the only way it works is for you to disappear. It's very simple Larry." She nodded to Paco.

"No!! Lupita!!"

Explosion. Pressure. Falling.

ADDENDUM:

Bill Lawson started to worry about Larry the day after he left the motel. Two days later, he called a friend in the Dallas police department to see if anyone had information about Larry. The cop called back five minutes later with the news that a rental company had also called about Mr. Kingston, fearing he may have made off with a new Grand Cherokee. When the car was found a day later, Larry went from "reported missing" to "wanted on suspicion of theft and unlawful flight."

The judge refused to postpone the hearing in spite of Lawson's vigorous protest. He granted Lupe Maria an immediate divorce and gave her all of Larry's property, "Every last paperclip." She was also given sole ownership of the map, should it be recovered.

Mr. Guzman asked for a new ruling on the issue of fees, given the change in circumstances. Lupe started to cry, lest the judge temporarily forget her delicate nature and impoverished circumstances. After a brief recess to ponder the matter, he ruled that the former Mrs. Kingston would only have to pay her attorney $2,500. He softened the blow for both by adding, "When Mr. Kingston is apprehended you can each sue him to recover your money."

After selling her house at a bargain basement price, Lupita and her son went to Mexico for a visit and did not return. About six months later, Paco Alvarez's bullet-riddled body was found in a drainage ditch outside Nuevo Laredo. Chavito attends a very private boarding school in Morales, Mexico, has his own bodyguard, and travels to and from school in a bulletproof SUV.

No one knows what has happened to Lupe Maria Gonzalez Kingston.

REMEMBERING THE HOLY WORD TRAILER PARK

Don't bother looking through the county records for any evidence that the Holy Word trailer park ever existed. You won't find permits, right of ways, or that sort of stuff, and being so far off the main road, not too many folks from around here ever saw it. Most of the ones who did have died off, and those few who do remember it would probably prefer not to. Besides, it only lasted a year or so, but it was one hell of a year, I'll say that.

The big fuss nowadays about the Hatfields and McCoys has created excitement about "hillbilly lore" here in east Kentucky, dredged up a lot of old memories, and twisted some stories around so you wouldn't know the truth unless you were actually there. It's the same sort of thing that turned Butch and Sundance into a couple of wisecracking romantics and Jesse James into a stay-at-home dad with an unfortunate night job.

And now someone has gotten a whiff of the goings on at the Holy Word trailer park, and unless the story gets set straight, there will soon be a Holy Word weekend festival, a country band singing the *Ballad of Skunk Hollow,* and coffee cups and tote bags for sale covered with naked pictures of the Darling sisters.

So I will tell the story, exactly as it happened forty-two years ago.

Near as I can tell, it all started because Kid Toliver was squatting on Clint Boggert's land, living right there inside Boggert's mine, and when Clint got wind of it, he went up Skunk Hollow with two of his sons to put Kid Toliver off his land. He wasn't real mad at Toliver at that point because there wasn't anything in that old mine except spiders and maybe a bear or some diamondbacks. But he sure didn't like anyone being there without his say-so, especially after the fact that Toliver's old man put a load of buckshot clean through Clint's Aunt Clara when both of them were drunk and got in one of their hellacious fights.

Anyway, when Clint and the boys got to the mine, Toliver beat feet into the mine to consider his options. Clint decided to ask for Divine Guidance, and all three of them got behind the truck to pray. Toliver, being the hothead he was, took advantage of the moment and let go a few rounds from his .22 rifle. One of the bullets bounced off the side mirror and hit Clint in the elbow. That ended the prayer session, and in between cussing and yelling, Clint said the Lord told him Toliver was Satan in disguise, and He wanted the mine closed so this sort of thing didn't happen again. One of the boys went and got a dozen sticks of dynamite, wrapped them in a bundle, snuck up beside the mine, and chucked it down the shaft. It went off with a hell of a bang, collapsed most of the main tunnel, and that was the last anyone heard of Kid Toliver. To tell the truth, I really don't think anybody missed him.

Clint said he had another message from God saying he needed to protect the mine from Satan returning in the form of someone else, so he hauled a house trailer up and parked it right in front of the mine entrance. There was a big flat area there where the ore trucks used to park, so it was perfect for a trailer. In fact, it was big enough for a dozen trailers. Skunk Creek ran down the mountain year 'round with the best water you could find, and while it was true the old mine's electric was down, the power company main line was only a mile away on the state road. Clint already had a well dug for the mine so it was easy to run a pipe to the trailer. All he needed was power.

Clint had a cousin, Jeeter, who worked for the power company so when Clint told the company he was reopening the mine and needed juice, Jeeter arranged to have a new line run up the hollow to replace the old one. He had Clint apply for the account as "The Reverend Clinton Boggert" so he would get church rates on his power. Of course, Clint didn't have any real church credentials, but that didn't matter since it was well known he was a prayerful, born-again Man of God and that was all he needed.

That was the start of the Holy Word trailer park.

When the power company ran the line up the hollow, Jeeter was there to install the meter, an old one he found in the warehouse, discarded because it didn't seem to be able to keep up with the incoming electricity. And it was Jeeter who saw the potential for a money-making trailer court in the clearing in front of the mine. After all, Clint could run water and power himself to at least six more trailers, and as long as he showed up at the power company office every month to pay his bill with the number off the meter, there was no danger anyone from the company would go all the way up the hollow to check.

Clint let out the word that he was accepting applications, and over the next month or so five more trailers were hauled in and connected up. The park itself was about half the size of a football field. The road in came through the goalposts at one end, ran straight up the middle, trailers on each side facing the road, ending dead center in front of the mine opening at the other end . The park was a little higher at the mine end, but given it was half way up a long hollow, it was surprisingly flat.

Clint's fee structure was highly attractive. Monthly rent was $50.00, including $35.00 for the lot, $10.00 for electricity and $5.00 for road maintenance. Water from the well was free. The septic system, however, was a bit of a problem. Putting in a large septic tank and drainage field big enough for six trailers was way beyond Clint's budget, though he promised to dig a field sometime soon.

In the meantime, he planned to tap into the slurry pipe that used to carry water pumped out of the mine down the hill about a half mile where it dumped out into a ravine. The pipe ran pretty much dead center through the park under the road and it wasn't a big trick to attach a drain pipe from each trailer lot. The pipe itself was old and had a lot of roots growing through it. Clint knew that too much solid waste would likely stuff it up in a hurry so renters were invited to dig their own latrines on the edge of the lot over the creek for what Clint delicately called "the big stuff."

In those days, lots of folks lacked indoor plumbing, so no one complained, especially with rent such a bargain. The same was true of telephones. This was way before cell phones, and only a fraction of the folks in that area had phones, mostly party lines so jammed up with static you could hardly listen in on what your neighbors were saying.

With six trailers, Clint was bringing in $300.00 a month with virtually no overhead. He plowed the road once in a while and paid about $40.00 for electricity, but otherwise he didn't have to lift a finger and money rolled in.

As soon as the last trailer was installed, Clint held a consecration ceremony, formally dedicating the Holy Word trailer park. He urged his flock to count their many blessings, gird their loins against the works of Satan, and be sure to pay their rent by the first of the month. No exceptions.

The first renter was June Heffner, some distant relative to Clint, just out of the county lockup. He did one day shy of a year (a full year got you sent off to the penitentiary) for transporting moonshine in a county vehicle he "borrowed" from the school board parking lot.

He was desperate for a place to stay, had no money for rent, and heard Clint might have something he could use in exchange for work. He promised Clint he had seen the light while in the slammer, had forsaken his wicked ways, and wanted to tread the righteous path. Clint loved a repentant backslider, absolved him of sin, and installed him in the trailer in front of the mine. He kindly forgave the first month's rent, but made it clear that after one free month he expected June to turn his newfound virtue into regular rent, same as anyone else.

This solved June's immediate housing problem but left him with the question of where he was going to get the rent money. As other trailers started to arrive, June bargained another month's rent in exchange for helping set the trailers up on blocks, hook up the water, and dig latrines.

June was a resourceful man with an extensive knowledge of the distillery business. He immediately saw the opportunity God had thrust upon him by positioning him a mere thirty feet from the entrance to the collapsed mine. The first hundred feet or so of the main shaft was easily cleared of debris creating the perfect place for a still. Providence had put everything at his fingertips. While the well water was full of iron, stained everything orange, and smelled like rotten eggs, the water in the creek (above the latrines) was pure and sweet. There was plenty of dried oak from fallen trees all over the woods, the kind of wood that burns slow, even, and with almost no smoke. By putting a large funnel-shaped piece of tin connected to a stovepipe above the fire, June was able to run most of the smoke up the pipe, out the mouth of the cave into the back of his trailer where he married it to the vent coming out of his stove. By running the trailer stove whenever he was running the still, he created suction and all the cave smoke came out of his chimney. It wasn't even odd to see stove smoke in the summer. The hollow was cold all the time, and folks liked their trailers hot.

Of course, there was the problem of the pipe between the cave and the trailer, but you couldn't see it unless you went behind the trailer and June piled a bunch of junk around to make that hard to do. Within a month, June was back in the whiskey business, slick as can be, with plenty of customers waiting for his high quality product. Anticipating a brisk business, June saw the need for an assistant, someone to soak his mash and help mind the fire when it was running twenty-four hours a day. Also, he needed someone who could not only drive but actually had a driver's permit.

That someone was Wanda Tuttle, an edentulous recovering crack addict who had sworn a Solemn Oath to live a sinless life and never touch drugs again. She was going to stick strictly with alcohol and never stray back to her old ways. June and Wanda had tried to live together once before though it didn't work out. June accused her of being unfaithful (repeatedly), and she retaliated by moving out and having one of her boyfriends threaten June with bodily harm if he messed with her again. Bad mistake. Don't think for a second that June would ignore a threat, especially when his woman is involved. The boyfriend's car went up in smoke along with his favorite .22 pistol. He got the message, moved out of the county, and eventually Wanda moved back in with June.

The next problem was getting it by Clint. After all, he didn't condone people living in sin, and June didn't want to threaten either his cushy living circumstances or his new business. He introduced Wanda as his sister, and sensing Clint might not buy it, he pointed out the additional advantage of having two people in the manager's trailer. It increased security, and having a woman's touch in the park was good for attracting the right kind of renters.

Clint seemed to accept it but shook his finger and said if he found out June was lying he would remove his protection against demons and throw his sorry ass out of the park.

Even with Wanda on board to drive, June still had a transportation problem, and he sure enough wasn't going to repeat his recent mistake with the school board car. He went back to Clint, asked if he could use his truck once in a while and said he'd be glad to pay for gas and maybe a little extra for wear and tear. Clint knew exactly what June was up to and berated him for retreating from his promise to live a sinless life. June assured him he was only making the stuff, not using it, and upped the ante a little by offering Clint a cut for the regular use of his truck.

Clint reasoned it wouldn't be a violation of his Sacred Oath of Purity to let June use the truck. After all, Clint wasn't going to drink the stuff (he preferred beer) and transporting isn't the same as making it. He reasoned that it would be wise to have one of the boys go with June and Wanda to keep an eye on the cash and make sure he got his cut—forty percent to start. June fumed and stomped around a while over the price, said it would kill his business, no one ever treated him so low, and on and on. Clint chewed tobacco, spat, and rubbed his sore elbow waiting for June to come to his senses, settle down, and realize he didn't really have a choice. And so the bargain was struck.

Within two months June was generating about ten gallons a week, retailing at $20 a gallon. June was happy, making good money, and Clint and the boys were pulling in over $300 a month for a few hours' work. Life was getting better at the Holy Word.

The next folks to arrive were the Angel sisters, Carla and Connie, both in their eighties and most recently thrown out of the Moose Hall retirement park for starting a fire in their trailer. Something went wrong with the space heater they were using to melt wax to make angel candles for the Senior Center craft sale. While the fire didn't get past the living room, it wasn't their first so they were promptly evicted. Happily, their guardian angel led them straight to Clint and the evolving Holy Word trailer park.

Given their surname, it isn't hard to understand the sister's fascination with angels, all sorts of angels. Their collection included stuffed angels, cutout angels with paper wings, blow-up angel balloons, angel toilet paper covers, and lots of homemade halos festooned about over lamps, on pictures, and around every doorknob. Over the couch in front of the TV hung a large fuzzy rug showing several angels hovering over what, at first glance, looked like a huge pair of hairy balls. Get closer, however, and you would have seen two bears huddled together in peaceful, protected hibernation. There were angel lamps (with and without lava), angel potholders, an angel doormat, and at Christmas, a huge angel mobile spun in drunken circles in front of the door. When the door was opened, the wind caused the angels to spring into action frantically tapping silver icicles with tiny candy canes.

The outside of their trailer was covered with pictures of angels commissioned by the sisters while they lived at the Moose Park. Neighbor kids were given paint and brushes and told to paint angels all over the trailer. It caused quite a sensation. Initially, the sisters assumed it was all about art and angels, but when they looked a little closer they found some fairly graphic examples of what the kids thought angel sex might look like. Now it was all cleaned up and the little lighted wooden angels by the door welcomed visitors to what the Angel sisters called "Almost Heaven." Wrong state, but still too fitting to pass up.

Clara and Connie were practiced snoops, scavenging gossip from naïve neighbors who had no idea they were being worked over by a pair of pros. To the Angel sisters, it was entirely proper to know everything going on, starting with sorting the righteous neighbors from the sinners.

That way you can protect yourself and keep that clever bastard, Satan, from sneaking up behind you to take advantage of a lapse in vigilance. No telling what kind of wickedness he might deploy in an unprotected moment.

At night, they drank coffee laced with a little tonic to steady the nerves and studied their "intel" to see what evidence there was that angels—both good and bad—were at work in the park. Everyone was studied for evidence of a subtle halo or slight glow. They were also on guard for false angels. More than once they had been fooled by intoxicated people at first thought to be talking in tongues.

They had a younger sister who lived in another park, larger by far and closer to town. She had a car and faithfully took her sisters shopping, to the Senior Center at least twice a week, and the Mountaintop Holiness Church every Wednesday and Sunday. They lived on social security surrounded by every form of angel prop imaginable, protected from the wickedness of the world by invisible guardian angels whose wings gently soothed their anxieties. The tonic helped, too.

The next to move in was the Mavouleen family, Merle, Martha, and their ten-year-old son, Miles. Merle was a coal miner retired prematurely by a back injury none of the doctors seemed able to treat. The coal company refused compensation, accused him of coming to work drunk and in no shape to calculate the right amount of dynamite to use to keep the roof from collapsing.

With Merle sidelined, they had to move to more affordable housing, and Martha was forced to work two jobs just to keep up. She drove a school bus and worked in the elementary school cafeteria.

While Martha was working, Merle stayed in the trailer practicing guitar, hoping to spark a career as a country music singer in the mold of his hero, Hank Williams. First thing every morning, he dressed in cowboy clothing, though he usually skipped the boots and stayed in his battered slippers. Then a few pain pills to relax his back (and encourage creativity), and he was ready for a prolonged rehearsal. He played the same three songs (*Cheatin' Heart, You Win Again,* and *Lonesome Blues*) over and over and over, day after day, knowing that one day it would all come together, the perfect blend of voice and instrument. Close your eyes and you'd swear Hank was back from his heroin overdose, in perfect form, and again ready for the Big Time.

Miles was an elusive youngster, always in the woods around the park, often with his .22 looking for a squirrel or a nice young deer. He was intensely curious, and like the Angel sisters, he wanted to know what was going on in the various trailers. He found he could easily slither past the lattice skirt surrounding the trailer undercarriage. Once under the trailer, he could move about unseen to get directly under the action. The floors were paper-thin and anything said above was easily heard.

By walking along the steep creek bank he could approach all of the outhouses unheard and unseen. He liked to peek between the cracks and quickly became expert in human anatomy, waste control, and a few autoerotic behaviors which, while initially puzzling, worked themselves out through imitation and practice.

Next to arrive was Grampaw Clancy, another of Clint's distant relatives and like Merle, a retired coal miner. He owned his trailer outright and, unlike Merle, his problem—black lung disease—was acknowledged by the coal company. He received both social security and a disability check making him one of the better-off members of the Holy Word community.

Grampaw Clancy wasn't particularly social and was rarely seen outside his trailer. He weighed over three hundred pounds, and getting out of his lounge chair was quite a task, so much so the chair was also his bed. He saw no particular reason to go outside, and if folks wanted to visit, they could talk to him through the open door. His only real outside contact was his nephew Dewayne Gabbler, a gay Bible salesman whose territory included Skunk Hollow. He lived somewhere in town— Grampaw Clancy wasn't interested in the where and with-whom details— and visited faithfully twice a week to bring groceries and cigarettes. He had his own room in the back of the trailer where he kept an extensive collection of women's clothes. He was especially fond of corsets, garter belts, and cast off prom dresses.

Grampaw Clancy didn't seem to give a hoot what Dewayne did as long as he brought the groceries and cigarettes. Black lung made him terribly short of breath, so much so he had to stay tethered to a huge green oxygen bottle next to his living room chair. He was warned not to allow an open flame anywhere near the bottle, and when he first got the bottle, he struggled outside to smoke. That got old in a hurry, so he experimented with smoking closer and closer to Big Green, as he called it.

When that didn't blow him up, he realized the warnings were just some kind of government bullshit and within a month he was again smoking in his favorite chair, happily puffing away without the slightest worry. He didn't even bother to take out the little nose tube or shut off the oxygen flow. You can't believe anything the dang government says anymore.

The next trailer belonged to the Darling sisters, April and May. They were "professional entertainers" who worked the bars near the big mine on the other side of Hutton. They commuted in a converted bread delivery truck, which doubled as an office, conveniently outfitted with a cot and portable toilet. Typically, one of the girls would entertain a customer in the back while the other sister drove slowly around town, careful to avoid sudden stops or sharp turns. A thump on the partition behind the driver meant it was time to return to the bar.

The sisters also made and sold "crank," what today is called "meth." At that time, crank was mainly a trucker's drug, something that could be swallowed or snorted, gave the user a tremendous jolt of energy, and made drunks both horny and impotent—a perfect combination as far as the Darlings were concerned.

Making crank was relatively easy in those days because the key ingredients were common and not yet restricted. Even so, it was a dangerous process requiring cooking potent chemicals over an open flame. The biggest danger, beyond explosion and fire, was inhaling the stuff while it was cooking. The Darlings ruined quite a few batches because they were too stoned to manage the end of the process. But as long as what they ended up with could be dried out and crushed, they sold it. Truckers and drunks weren't too fussy about quality.

Ever safety conscious, the sisters cooked their brew over a camp stove in the bathtub and never used their product when they were working. They also observed a strict code of distribution ethics that prohibited sales to neighbors.

"You don't shit next to the well," April used to say.

You might be surprised to know that the Darlings didn't seem to touch off any alarms in the Angel's house of angels. Because they worked at night, the sisters were a presence in the park during the day, always cheerful and ready to help their neighbors. Miles found them particularly helpful, especially May who liked to visit and always requested her favorite song, *Your Cheatin' Heart*.

Beyond being friendly, Clara had proof positive the Darlings were benign. She just happened to be walking by their trailer one afternoon and couldn't help but peek through the living room window. The bathroom door was open, and she saw both sisters down on their knees next to the bathtub praying by what seemed to be candle light coming from the tub. An odd place to pray, maybe, but it doesn't matter where you pray as long as you mean it.

The Darlings also bought a lot of homemade angel cookies and angel cake from their kindly neighbors. Like their principle of clean water management, shopping locally does wonders for community relationships.

The last trailer belonged to a snake-handling preacher named Mr. Higgs. He was a giant of a man, about six feet five inches tall, heavyset but not obese, and like his Biblical idol, John the Baptist, he dressed entirely in leather clothing he made from deer and bear skins. Adding to his wild look was the fact he was unusually hairy. Black, oily, untended hair hung below his shoulders, his eyebrows looked like Brillo pads, and his gray beard was stained red around his mouth and chin from years of non-stop tobacco chewing and spitting.

But it didn't stop with whiskers and long hair. The back of his hands were black with matted hair, and tufts of it poked out of his shirt around his neck. His voice was deep, booming, and menacing.

Of course, the voice was nothing compared to the fearsome diamondback rattlesnakes he kept somewhere in his trailer. No one ever went in to find out if they were caged up or just free to roam around. The first day he came to the park he stood at his door with a four-footer held high over his head, preached a rip-roaring five-minute sermon on the fate of evil doers ending with something that sounded like "The doors of hell will open with serpents to those who ignore the signs!!" He retreated inside, slammed the door, and wasn't seen for days.

No one who saw the performance will likely forget it or fail to appreciate its corporal meaning—stay the hell away from my trailer or you're going to get snake bit—or worse. In case they missed the message, there was a reminder painted in six-inch block letters across the side of the trailer:

IN MY NAME THEY WILL PICK UP SERPENTS
IN THEIR HANDS
MARK 16:18

For slow learners, another sign over the door said:

KEEP OUT OR ELSE

It was never clear where Mr. Higgs' house of worship was, or even *if* it was. He rarely went out unless it was dark and always left his lights on. The only people he talked to at all were the Angels, probably a kind of professional courtesy. They were brave enough to approach the trailer, usually with a batch of freshly baked angel cookies. But they were never able to peek inside because the windows were covered and he always spoke through the closed door.

"Just leave them on the step. Thank you and God bless you, sister."

Miles Mavouleen came closest to figuring the whole thing out. He had two shots at it but he was too young to really grasp what he was seeing. For obvious reasons, he didn't dare crawl under Mr. Higgs' trailer, but he did do some aerial reconnaissance from his favorite climbing tree, a big white oak that loomed partly over the trailer. Like most trailers, it had a vent hatch on the roof, and sometimes Mr. Higgs opened it, especially in the daytime when the interior lights wouldn't be noticeable.

What he did see through the thick screen in the portal one afternoon was foliage, green plants packed together like Miles imagined a jungle would look like. Of course, he didn't associate the bright green marijuana plants with the greenish tobacco his daddy liked to smoke. In the end, he decided the inside forest was there for the snakes and that meant they were clearly on the loose, not penned up in a cage. It made Mr. Higgs seem a few inches taller and a lot scarier.

His second clue was the way Mr. Higgs handled the serpents. Miles had been catching snakes for years and like Mr. Higgs, one hand always held the creature just behind the head making a bite all but impossible. To Miles, it just made good sense. If he had known more about snake handlers, he would have wondered why Mr. Higgs would need anything beyond divine protection to keep from getting nailed.

The trailers were arranged with June and Wanda in the top center, right in front of the mine, Clancy and the Darlings on the creek side and the Angels, Mr. Higgs, and the Mavouleens on the other side. Because space was tight, the trailers were close to each other, almost touching, but they all opened onto the center road creating a sense of space and community.

For a few months, everything seemed to go smoothly at the Holy Word trailer park. Clint was happy with the sharp increase in tax-free income, and all of the residents went about their lives in seeming harmony. Even Mr. Higgs appeared to soften a bit. When June's bluetick coonhound ran off, he joined in the search and was the one who found the dog up an adjacent hollow. He also found a fat rattler to add to his collection.

Meanwhile, over near Taylor Mine Eight, a jailbreak of sorts took place. A group of fifteen prisoners from the county lockup, the same pokey from which June had recently graduated, were out on the road sweeping off coal clumps and gravel. Deputy Farley Owens was watching the group, 12-gauge shotgun loaded with buckshot at the ready, when his ex-wife, Florence, drove up screaming he hadn't sent her any child support in two months. They got into a terrific fight and Owens momentarily took his eyes off the group.

Buck Terrell and his cousin George Webb took advantage of the moment to slip away down an embankment to the railroad tracks, well out of sight of Deputy Owens. The other inmates bunched up so Owens wouldn't immediately see if anyone was missing. By the time Florence peeled out and Owens was back on task, Buck and George were around the first bend running like hell to grab onto the last car of a slow moving coal train.

When Owens realized what was going on, he herded the remaining inmates into the cage on the back of the county truck and radioed for help. Meanwhile the escapees were tucked up behind the coupler on the back of the train.

I need to tell you something about jumping a coal train for you to understand why they couldn't stay with their ride for too long. The wind and motion of the train produces invisible clouds of coal dust, so much that anyone riding unprotected on a coal car will choke to death within thirty minutes. The boys knew the danger and covered their mouths and eyes with their shirt, but they were too out of breath from running to control their breathing and had to jump off the car after it had only gone a few miles.

They were riding along the banks of Eutaw River, so when they jumped off they got in the water to wash off the coal dust that had already gotten in their hair, ears, and turned their clothes black. Once they could breathe again, they turned their clothes inside out to hide the COUNTY INMATE on their shirt and orange stripe on their pants. Then they took to the woods, climbed out of the river gorge to the top of the hill; from there, they followed the ridgeline back toward the nearest town, Hutton. They got there as it was getting dark, stole some overalls from a clothesline, and made their way to the home of the only person they knew in Hutton, a former county inmate they met when he was doing three months for indecent exposure, Dewayne Gabbler.

Just before the boys arrived, Dewayne was trying on his newest acquisition, a bright green prom dress picked up at a yard sale for a mere four dollars. It was an excellent fit, maybe a bit tight around the middle, but the bust was just right for his see-through bra stuffed with gym socks. As he cracked the door to see who was knocking, the boys burst through, knocking Dewayne over throwing the billowing dress over his head.

The boys were terrified they had the wrong house and had just assaulted a woman who was sure to start screaming. They both pounced on Dewayne trying to hold him down and get a hand over his mouth. Dewayne fought back, and indeed he did scream, but the masculine voice yelling "Get the fuck off me!!" made them realize they had the right address. It took a few minutes for everyone to calm down and for George and Buck to explain their situation.

The last thing in this world Dewayne wanted in his house was two wild-eyed, escaped convicts, especially since he knew the sheriff's bloodhound was dead certain to track them right to his door at first light. He had to get them out of there, but where could he take them? They all had a few drinks and some high-powered grass to steady their nerves and help them come up with a plan. At first, Dewayne just wanted to take them out of the county, let them out, and wish them well, but the boys were having none of it. They told Dewayne that if he didn't come up with a better plan they were going to stay right there and all three of them could go back to jail.

That's when Dewayne came up with the bright idea of hiding them in Grampaw Clancy's trailer. Hell, no one would think of looking for them at the Holy Word. They bought it, so he had the boys duck through the backside of town and meet him on the highway. That way the bloodhound would track right past Dewayne's and it would look like someone picked them up off the road. They got to the trailer park about an hour later, pulled up to Grampaw Clancy's trailer, and slipped inside.

The old man was passed out in his lounging chair and didn't even stir with all the commotion. The boys made a bed of sorts in the back room and Dewayne got ready to leave. They were all pretty loaded at that point, but George was still sharp enough to raise an important point.

"You can't leave, Dewayne. The old man is going to shit green when he wakes up and finds us here. We'll get busted for sure. You've got to be here to keep him calmed down." They had another strategy session, supplemented by the rest of their booze and some of the old man's pain medicine, and in the end, Dewayne consented to stay to make proper introductions in the morning. A good decision because loaded as he was, it is highly doubtful he could have made it safely down the mountain on Clint's slippery gravel road.

When they got up in the morning, the old man was still sound asleep, Dewayne was itching to leave, so they decided to wake him up and explain the situation. Problem was, the old man wouldn't wake up. That's because he was dead.

It took a while (and the rest of the old man's pain pills) to formulate Plan One—back the car up to the door, dump his body in the trunk, and take him up to the landfill. Doing all of this in broad daylight seemed a bit shaky, but the landfill wasn't open at night, and he would be found if they tossed him out anywhere else. And that would inevitably bring the police straightaway to Dewayne.

Plan One fell apart when they tried to move the body. It weighed several hundred pounds to start with, and was starting to bloat, making it impossible to get a good grip on his already meaty arms and legs. It took the better part of an hour to wrap him up in a blanket, tie the bundle, and roll it from the chair to the front door. The neighbors were moving about and even if they hadn't been, it would take a lot of time and energy they didn't have to get him out the door and into the trunk. And what about getting him inconspicuously out of the trunk into the landfill? Clearly, Butch and George couldn't go along to help, and Dewayne would never be able to do the job alone.

Okay, time for Plan Two—chop him up into convenient chunks, toss them into the trunk, and let Dewayne make a solo trip to the landfill. George didn't like it at all.

"Did you ever try to gut and butcher a deer in your living room? This bastard weighs twice what a deer does, and he's already starting to rot. It'll make a stinking mess, and we'd never get the place cleaned up and aired out. I don't want to be here when you stick a knife in his guts, I'll tell you that."

"So what the fuck are we going to do with him?" demanded Dewayne.

"Bury him, that's what," said George.

"And just where the hell are you going to bury him?" Dewayne's anger and frustration were growing as the drugs wore off and the body continued to swell in the hot, airless trailer.

"Right here," said George pointing at the floor. "We're going to cut a hole in the floor, dig a damn hole, dump his smelly ass in, and cover him up. Nobody can see under the trailer and we can take turns digging."

And that was it, the best—indeed, the only—solution to the problem. Dewayne was sent off to get a shovel, buy beer, and see if he could score some more grass while the boys went to work on the floor. They pulled back the linoleum, pried up the plywood flooring, and punched through the thin aluminum skin. They hadn't figured on the location of the steel support beams under the trailer and had to widen the hole to center it over an open area. By the time they finished, both were exhausted, fell asleep and didn't wake up until Dewayne arrived with a shovel and the beer, but no dope.

Dewayne reported that the jailbreak was big news and everyone had a theory about where they were hiding. After a few beers, the digging began, but it was slow going, and by the end of the day, they only managed to dig a shallow hole.

"You couldn't bury a groundhog in that hole," observed George. "And that tub of lard is really starting to stink." By noon the next day the hole was deep enough and they tried to push the body through the floor head first. They got the head and chest through the hole but couldn't get the gas-filled abdomen to fit between the supports. They couldn't pull the body back, either, so there was Grampaw Clancy, head down in the hole and his feet, stiff as a board, sticking straight up in the air.

Getting the old man past the support beams wasn't going to work unless they deflated the corpse. No one wanted to do the job so they drew straws and Dewayne "won." They all knew there was going to be one hell of an explosion, so Dewayne tied a knife on the shovel handle and threw it at the body from a safe distance. The first two shots went wide but the third hit dead center and, as predicted, putrid air blasted through the narrow cut. It sounded like a whoopee cushion attached to a weather balloon. The skin around the cut began to tear open followed by a lava flow of green slime that oozed out and spread around the body.

Just then there was a loud knock on the door. The three froze in place, trying not to breathe.

"Who is it?" yelled Dewayne.

"It's me, Clara Angel. Is everything all right? Smells like the toilet is backed up again."

"Yeah, Miss Angel. That's it. Me and the old man are working on it but thanks for asking."

"Well, I'll just leave some cookies out here for you, but you better get 'em before June's dog does."

It took a while and a lot of gagging, but they finally managed to stuff the corpse into the hole, sweep most of the green mess in, and cover it with a thin layer of dirt.

RIP, Mr. Clancy.

That ended the immediate problem, but the brain trust had to come up with a plan for what was next. It was clear that Grampaw Clancy had to stay alive for Dewayne to continue to collect the monthly disability checks. Of course, the boys had to stay out of sight until things quieted down and there was some new catastrophe to take people's minds off the great escape. Even then, without some clever cover, it wouldn't take long for everyone to realize there were two new men staying in the trailer, and that would be the end of their freedom. They had to be especially careful with June since he knew them well from their time together in the county lockup.

The answer to everyone's problem was obvious. George, being the bigger of the two, would become Grampaw Clancy, and Butch, dressed in some of Dewayne's attire, would metamorphose into Clancy's kindly but extremely shy niece, Mildred, who had come to look after the old man when Dewayne was away. If anyone happened to get a peek inside, they would see Butch in the old man's lounger watching TV, his head partially hidden by the big oxygen bottle. They might also catch a glimpse of sweet Mildred attending to her duties, though she had to be careful not to let anyone see her hands. The prison tattoos on her knuckles (LOVE on the left, HAIT on the right) might raise gender questions.

And it worked quite well. The boys hated it, but the thought of going back to jail was worse. Besides, Dewayne had plenty of money to keep them in beer and sometimes a bag of grass. They got through the winter without a hitch and as the snow melted away and the trees started to bud, they began to make plans to leave. Dewayne decided to move his wardrobe back to Hutton, install someone else in the trailer, and tell the neighbors that the old man had taken poorly and had to be moved to a nursing home.

Unfortunately for Dewayne and the boys, they didn't make their move fast enough, and they were all swept up in that final, catastrophic convulsion that brought down the entire Holy Word trailer court.

It started in the cave. June was just finishing a superb batch of whiskey. The fire was burning, the duct was removing most of the smoke and the product dripping out of the condenser was pure and sweet, almost 200 proof. June had been testing it all day, each sip reaffirming the quality of the batch. Eight gallons were already bottled and a ninth was slowly filling.

That's when June felt the sudden urge to relieve himself in a big way. Not wanting to leave the process for too long at that crucial stage, he decided that just this once he would do his business right there in the cave, back in the tumbled down part he had never explored. With his alcohol lantern (why use kerosene when pure whiskey works just as well and is free?) he climbed back among the rocks and fallen timbers until he found the perfect perch, a support timber lying knee high across a gap wide enough to sit comfortably and think about the twin pleasures of bowel relief and impending sales.

He put the lantern on the beam, dropped his overalls, sat down on the timber and wiggled his rear end into the firing position. But something on the floor under the beam caught his eye so he stood up, turned and peered over the beam. In the rubble he saw a man's face staring straight up at him, eyes wide open and mouth stretched into a hideous grin. He froze in place for a millisecond, but in spite of the combination of alcohol and shock, he instantly recognized Satan, screamed, turned, and tried to run.

His first steps tangled his boots and overalls causing him to fall face down in the rubble. He yelled, twisted, cursed, and crawled away the best he could, dead certain the Devil's steely claws were about to rake him to shreds. Of course, he didn't have time or the presence of mind to grab his lantern, so his only light was from the still, a beacon only faintly seen through the tangle of rocks and timbers.

No one in June's position could be expected to calmly analyze the situation and realize that this was not Satan, but the face of a corpse in rigor, skin taught, face frozen in a sardonic grin, preserved by the cool, arid conditions of the cave. The rest of Kid Toliver's body was scattered invisibly under the rubble.

June frantically clawed his way toward the fire, stood up and got enough of a grip on his overalls to hobble faster. Unfortunately, he chose that instant to look back and ran straight into the tin smoke cover over the fire. The sharp edge sliced across his forehead right to the bone. Blood gushed down his face swamping his vision. He spun back but crashed into the still, knocking it and himself over. His knees and overalls were in the fire; worse, the alcohol from the still was instantly ablaze.

"Hell!! I'm in hell!!" he screamed, running, tripping, falling, bouncing off rock, and rolling in the direction of the mouth of the cave. Blood was everywhere, the fire behind him was now roaring, its flames licking the roof of the cave in a race with June to escape into fresh air.

June fell out of the cave, but even in the bright light, he couldn't tell which way he was going. He reached up for some kind of support but unfortunately grabbed the duct pipe, which instantly ripped out of the back of his trailer. Inside, Wanda was stirring mash in preparation for the next batch of whiskey when she heard June screaming for help. She ran into the living room just as the smoke duct pulled away from the wood stove vent leaving a round hole in the wall. Through it she briefly caught a glimpse of June covered with blood, tangled in his smoking pants, rolling on the ground yelling and cursing Satan, and the fires of hell.

Flames from the stove danced out of the torn chimney up the wall as well as out the hole, sandwiching the flimsy wall in its fiery grip, instantly igniting the wall and roof.

Wanda grabbed her shotgun, ran out the door screaming for help, and headed for the back of the trailer. Right at the front corner, she and June collided. He bounced off his hefty partner, spun away, and still bleeding heavily from the forehead cut, headed straight toward the Angels' trailer. Wanda was only slightly dazed, recovered, and chased after him. June hobbled along, overalls at his ankles, trying to kick the damn pants past his boots. But he couldn't escape the overalls trailing him like a headless, mocking shadow.

The Angels opened their door to see what the ruckus was about just as June crashed in knocking Clara flat on the floor. Galvanized by the sight of a half naked, bloody satanic creature attacking her sister, Connie grabbed her walking stick and hit June on the head as hard as she could. Just then Wanda loomed in the door, grabbed the trailing overalls, and pulled June down the steps. Somehow June regained his footing and lurched blindly away toward Grampaw Clancy's trailer.

Clara, too, was on her feet, covered with blood but thinking clearly enough to go for her father's double-barreled shotgun, an ancient weapon no one had fired in fifty years. Unfortunately, the sisters had loaded it with modern ammunition, power the old twist steel barrels could not tolerate. Smoke from the cave and June's burning trailer swirled around the open area between the trailers making it hard to get a clear shot but she got a glimpse of the bloody figure and fired.

There was a thunderous blast, which split the first barrel wide open and knocked Clara backward causing her finger to pull the second trigger. That blast opened the other barrel and threw Clara against the wall. She was unconscious when she slumped to the floor.

Clara's first shot sprayed the area with buckshot, missing Wanda but catching June square in the back. The barrel failure took a lot of the power out of the shot, but it still had enough shot to put June down for the count, though it didn't kill him.

The second blast sailed over his head into the side of Clancy's trailer, blew out the living room window filling the room with buckshot, glass shards, and smoke. Luckily for Butch and George, they were standing by the door when the window erupted next to them. They were cut by dozens of pieces of flying glass but not by buckshot.

Wanda, seeing June fall, went into a rage, crawled around in the smoke screaming obscenities trying to find her shotgun. When she finally found it, she unleashed a shot in what she thought was the direction of the Angel's trailer. Luckily for the Angels, the shot went in the opposite direction and tore an enormous hole in the bathroom wall of the Darling's trailer. While it missed the Darlings, it went straight through the bathroom crushing the light fixture over the bathtub. Sparks from the ruptured light fell into the tub right on top of a fresh batch of crank. The fumes ignited and within seconds the room was a raging inferno.

The Darlings were a lot more level-headed in a crisis than their neighbors. They were always prepared for a fast exit and kept their money and drugs in a large purse at the ready behind the door in case of an emergency. They made a dash for their van and were gone in less than a minute.

Merle Mavouleen rushed out of his trailer in full Hank Williams attire, guitar in hand, his son, Miles right behind him. Even though the eruption was only moments old, two trailers were ablaze, fire and choking thick smoke were billowing from the mine entrance, June looked like he was dead, and Wanda was howling like a banshee. At that exact moment, Mr. Higgs leaped out of his trailer holding an enormous rattlesnake over his head. He was screaming something but the roar of the fire and Wanda's cries drowned him out.

Just as Mr. Higgs made his appearance, George and Butch made a run for it, knowing that the flames from the two adjacent trailers would soon engulf theirs, too. They couldn't really see where they were going in the thick smoke, but they were aiming for the woods, trying to shoot the narrow gap between the Angels' and Mr. Higgs' trailers. They miscalculated—who could blame them?—and emerged from the smoke running full tilt, George with his oxygen mask prop still around his neck and "Mildred" holding her long dress waist high. They barely missed Mr. Higgs who was so startled he momentarily lost his grip on the rattler's head. The snake took advantage of his lapse and nailed him twice in the neck. The pain was instantaneous, and Mr. Higgs dropped like a rock, losing control of the snake as he fell. They hit the ground together. The snake took advantage of the moment to lash out one more time before darting for the woods.

In what turned out to be Mr. Higgs' only good luck of the day, his jacket absorbed the bite.

That was all quite enough for Merle Mavouleen. He yelled for Miles to follow him and without checking to see if the boy heard him, took off down the gravel road, his terrible back injury in sudden remission. Miles had his own idea about what to do and that was scramble up his favorite oak tree to watch the scene play out from the safety of his high perch.

When the fire first broke out, a forest ranger in a fire tower twenty miles away spotted the smoke and immediately called the forest service emergency center. Within seconds, flames were visible. State and local police were notified and calls for help went out to volunteer fire departments within a fifty-mile range.

The first to arrive was a forest service fire truck. It did its best to rush up the narrow road, dodging ruts, potholes, and nearly running over what looked like the ghost of Hank Williams. Hank didn't stop, just ducked around the truck and kept going toward the highway.

No one in that truck will ever forget the scene they blundered into. Flames were still coming out of the mine entrance, three trailers were alight, and there were three people on the ground. The one covered with blood appeared to be dead, the woman next to him was completely unhinged, and a hairy giant was writhing in agony from what turned out to be two severe rattlesnake bites.

The reason I can tell this story in such detail is quite simple—I was there, sitting in that oak tree. You see, my name isn't really Miles Mavouleen, I made that up. Like I said at the beginning, it would have been better if this story was never told, but it got started so I feel I owe it to folks to tell it like it was and not let it get distorted. Just remember, this happened a long time ago, and you can't judge people by today's standards.

I don't know what happened to everyone, but I do know some of it. Clara survived her brush with Satan, and she and Connie moved in with their other sister. June also survived, though it was close, and he lost a lung to buckshot. When he recovered, he was arrested for making moonshine whiskey, but because of his poor health and the lack of usable evidence—just about everything was destroyed in the fires—the charges were dropped. He and Wanda moved into town, but June only lived another year. I'm not sure what became of Wanda.

Mr. Higgs barely survived the rattlesnake bites. He was arrested for growing marijuana, jailed to await trial, but he was so loud and disruptive, a judge ordered an evaluation in a state psychiatric hospital. He stayed about two months, then simply walked out and disappeared. No one had any interest in trying to find him.

George and Butch lasted less than a week in the woods, turned themselves in, and finished their sentences plus another ten months for escape. They, too, long ago split up and left the area.

Dewayne very cleverly told police about his poor grandfather, blaming George and Butch for the entire thing. He also sent off a letter to the Disability and Social Security folks telling them of Mr. Clancy's sudden passing. The checks stopped and not another word was said about it. I saw Dewayne a few years ago in another town. He owns two women's wear shops and serves on the city council.

My family moved to Kansas where Dad got a job in a music store, Mom continued to drive a school bus, and I finished school, went to Kansas State, and now I'm married, have a family, and a career as a newspaper reporter.

And finally, Clint Boggert. No one quite knew what to charge him with, but given the mayhem at the Holy Word trailer park, something had to be done. In the end, he was charged with operating a trailer park without a license and fined $25.00. Clint was furious, but there was nothing he could do but pay up. After all, when you break the law, you have to pay the price.

THE EXECUTIONER'S
VINE

Lauren Blackbridge's first pregnancy did not go well. Even before she realized she had missed a period, she was overcome with nausea and vertigo. Her doctor presumed it was nothing more than a debilitating virus, but her condition accelerated, forcing hospitalization to treat severe dehydration. Blood work was ordered, including a pregnancy test. Everyone was shocked when the result came back positive.

Lauren's obstetrician was dismissive of the idea this was a simple pregnancy gone wrong. "Too much puking too fast," he observed. "It has to be an ectopic pregnancy." More tests were ordered. But those results were negative. Extraordinary or not, this was indeed a straightforward pregnancy.

After a week of intravenous nourishment, Lauren was sent home on a Saltine and water diet.

Money was not an issue for the Blackbridges, and a group of nurses was quickly fielded, a major blessing considering the emergence of other complications, including painfully swollen breasts requiring around-the-clock ice packs. Other than Saltines, the only food Lauren could hold down at all was stale bran muffins. Regrettably, her diet caused severe constipation and the development of enormous bleeding hemorrhoids.

The nausea cleared at a glacial pace, and by the fourth month, Lauren was able to eat small amounts of regular food and take brief walks around the grounds of their Greenwich, Connecticut, home. By the fifth month she was strong enough to tolerate surgery to deal with the hemorrhoids. She spent most of the next several weeks soaking her backside in a warm bath.

The last three months went fairly well, discounting the emergence of mild diabetes, and when Lauren finally heaved across the nine-month line she begged her doctor to induce labor, "To end this goddamn nightmare" as she delicately put it. Her doctor felt the same way, admitted her to the hospital and started the induction. Mrs. Blackbridge labored mightily, but in vain, for twenty-six hours.

Finally, a C-section was performed and Lawrence Hanover Blackbridge was extracted from his mother's womb.

Larry weighed in at a startling 10 pounds 3 ounces, and except for some transient jaundice, he seemed quite healthy. But he was colicky from the start and had a nasty habit of gumming his mother's nipples with such ferocity she was forced to give up breast feeding. "It was like nursing a Vise-Grip," she said. It took almost six months before Lauren would allow her husband any sexual gratification, and then only after getting fitted with a diaphragm *and* starting birth control pills.

From the start, Baby Larry showed little interest in sleep, and that, of course, meant the Blackbridges and their servants were severely sleep deprived. By his first birthday, Larry had calmed down, was eating well, taking some initial steps, and already had a six-word vocabulary. The Blackbridges celebrated by leaving Larry in the care of servants while they took a three-week cruise on their 85-foot yawl, *The King's Ransom*.

In spite of her precautions, Lauren again became pregnant and immediately considered having an abortion. Her husband was appalled at the idea, but when none of the horrors of her first pregnancy reemerged, she cautiously settled into the idea of seeing it through. In fact, it was as non-eventful as a pregnancy can be, and in spite of her previous C-section, Lauren delivered her second son, William Culbertson, naturally after a brief and relatively painless labor.

When mother and Baby William returned from the hospital, Larry displayed none of the aggressive behavior Lauren had feared, briefly thought to be a positive sign. Instead of antipathy, he appeared totally indifferent to William. He didn't seem to mind his mother's obvious delight in nursing William, nor was he outwardly perturbed if he had to wait for a servant's attention while William's needs were met. True, there were little things, like tossing a block in William's general direction, or spilling his milk on the baby, but nothing that couldn't have been a simple accident.

All of that changed one night when Lauren responded to a shrill cry from William's room. To her horror, she found Larry in William's crib seemingly trying to push the infant over the railing. A child psychiatrist was consulted, and after hearing the story from the distraught parents, she advised Lauren to spend more time with Larry, and—just to be safe—suggested a latch on William's door well out of Larry's reach.

Larry, of course, used a chair and a silver asparagus server to defeat the lock, though he didn't actually enter William's room. He seemed content to let it be known that locks were not a barrier.

With everyone on alert, Larry seemed to retreat from any overt action against William. The psychiatrist said he was "frightening smart," and simply content to set everyone's nerves on edge. Servants began to refer to their shift as "guard duty" or "on patrol." Microphones were set up in the children's rooms and play areas, monitored at all times for any sounds of distress. By the time Larry was ready for kindergarten, the household was more relaxed, but even so, everyone celebrated his absence from the house—even if it was just for a few hours.

Larry and William were both handsome, bright children, and to the outside world appeared relaxed and congenial. Larry loved school and quickly distinguished himself as an instant learner with a voracious appetite for anything related to nature. He began to bring bugs, snakes, and other crawling creatures into the house. At first it was just an annoyance, but as his fascination—especially with snakes—increased, so did the unexpected living room encounters with toads, skinks, snakes, and turtles.

Again, the psychiatrist was consulted. Reasoning that Larry would not likely respond to prohibitions and threats, she advised "substitution therapy," a scheme designed to deflect Larry's interest away from serpents toward something more manageable like plants. Since expense was not an issue, carpenters grafted a large window greenhouse onto one wall of Larry's room. Then they invited him to find plants on the estate and transplant them into his indoor garden.

It worked. Larry instantly took to the new system and began to move all manner of plants and vines into his room. The only problem was containing his horticultural exuberance. But Larry responded to the logic of growing fewer plants well, and quietly settled into his new hobby. Servants called him "The Plant Man of Alcatraz" because of his reclusive preoccupation and the fact they all hoped he would someday end up behind bars.

At the age of ten Larry bought his first carnivorous plant, an event that pushed him in an entirely new botanical direction, one that many years later resulted in his discovery of the Executioner's Vine.

His first plant was the *Dionaea muscipula*, the Venus Flytrap. Larry delighted in pulling the wings off flies before dropping them into the sticky open jaws of the hungry plant. It takes about a week for the plant to close, digest its meal, and open anew for business, and Larry had more than a dozen plants chewing away at the same time. Every school science project involved plants, usually carnivorous, and most of his ample allowance was spent on plants and growing equipment.

Learning was an effortless matter for Larry—as long as he was interested in the subject. Otherwise, he put little to no effort into his studies, passing history and English by a thin margin, while rarely missing perfection in science, geography, and math. He mastered Latin names with ease and wanted to study the language in the sixth grade. But French was offered in the sixth, Latin in the eighth. Larry refused to attend French class. Threats of detention, angry tirades from both the principal and Mr. Blackbridge, even threats of expulsion from the posh private school all failed to move Larry. Finally, the school caved in, and Larry was allowed to take Latin.

By contrast, William was a quiet, non-discriminating learner who easily but unobtrusively absorbed whatever came his way. He was also a natural athlete and—as you would expect—always elected to the Student Council. Larry was well-coordinated, played soccer with modest enthusiasm, but otherwise he had no interest in sports or student activities, nor did he appear to care what anyone else thought of his aloofness.

But Larry had his threshold for taunting, even if it wasn't obvious on the surface. For example, the stealth hit on William when he was finishing the ninth grade and Larry the eleventh grade. William was slated to receive six awards for various academic and athletic achievements at the end-of-the-year awards ceremony. Larry was—as usual—going to get two, the science and Latin prize. William's growing fame and Larry's resentment collided in a quickly hatched plan to keep William out of the limelight.

Using a thick pair of rubber gloves, Larry soaked a rag in a solution of water, ground poison ivy leaves, and sumac pods, then fermented the brew in a plastic bag. In the afternoon of the day before the awards ceremony, he feigned a twisted ankle at baseball practice and hobbled back to the locker room before any of the others returned to dress for class. He took William's underpants out of his locker, and wearing the gloves, carefully dabbed the toxic rag in the undergarment and returned it to the locker.

William began to itch at dinner, but a hot bath seemed to quell the discomfort, and he went to bed hoping whatever it was would pass by morning. But he woke up at 3:00 a.m. in agony. His entire midsection was flame red, and his penis and scrotum were swollen to three times their normal size. His parents rushed him to the emergency room, a severe allergy to laundry soap was diagnosed, and William was admitted for around-the-clock soaks, IV fluids, and steroid injections.

Sadly, he missed the awards dinner.

William wasn't Larry's only victim. He particularly hated his English teacher, Miss Proctor, a Calvinist spinster who made it her life mission to expose her students to "the grand symphony of perfect syntax." For fun reading she preferred Hawthorne, Mather, and Wigglesworth (particularly *Day of Doom*). Larry ground his teeth and tried to maintain invisibility in her class, and in fairness to Miss Proctor, she did not call on him any more than the rest, but Larry didn't see it that way. Over time he came to think she had it in for him, a suspicion confirmed one awful day when she penned the words "The pen is mightier than the Sword especially when wielded by Righteous Men" at the end of a term paper on Pope's *Rape of the Lock*. Just what the sword had to do with snipping off Arabella Fermor's hair was obscure, but the C+ at the bottom of the page was crystal clear.

"Oh, really?" thought Larry slathering his growing fury with the soothing balm of revenge. "We'll just see which is more powerful—the pen, the sword, or *Pueraria thunbergiana*." (Kudzu to the rest of us.)

Miss Proctor lived on the outskirts of Port Chester in a house on the edge of what used to be her family's truck farm, lately a newly-minted track of split level homes grandly called Sunshine Acres. Miss Proctor was insulated from her *déclassé* neighbors by a thick band of woods surrounding her home. There she enjoyed modest isolation and the joy of her considerable flower garden, laid out in neat rows nourished by an ancient but functional overhead watering system.

Feigning illness, Larry skipped school one muggy spring day. With Miss Proctor safely trapped in school, Larry went to her house— more correctly her woods—with a large bag of kudzu seeds, and methodically planted them in an huge circle around her house. And for good measure he tossed a handful in her compost bin and on the ground behind her garage. It was an exhausting day, and at dinner that night, his father noticed how "drawn" his son looked and asked if he felt up to returning to school. Larry bravely told his dad he would try.

It took about a month before the alarm sounded. Miss Proctor hadn't noticed the vines growing up the back of her garage, but when they crept around the corner headed for her cold frame, she chopped it back. Her local nurseryman identified a leaf as kudzu and recommended contacting the county agriculture agent. The agent apparently had more important vegetation on his plate and failed to return her calls.

By this time the vines were slithering in sinuous synchrony out of the woods toward the houses in Sunshine Acres. The Property Management Committee held an emergency meeting, attended, by the way, by the county agent whose daughter lived in the pathway of the menacing green tendrils. Spraying was suggested since it was obvious chopping the vines was a losing deal. One resident objected to the use of chemicals so close to the little stream that ran through the woods.

"Fuck the stream!" someone yelled, and the spraying proposal was passed with only one nay vote. Six county employees dressed in space suits with tanks of poison on their backs attacked the woods but couldn't penetrate the dense tangle of interlacing vines. A helicopter was brought in to bomb the woods from above. It was perhaps a bit too effective, destroying not only the vines, but most of the trees as well. Some of the spray drifted into Miss Proctor's yard and finished off her garden.

It was big news in the local paper and a topic of discussion at the Blackbridge's dinner table, especially the part about Miss Proctor's nervous breakdown and sudden retirement from school.

Larry's collection of plants and books was so extensive the family had to convert the attic space over their five-car garage into his combination laboratory, study, and living space. He read everything he could find on plants and was at sixteen the youngest member of ICPS—the International Carnivorous Plant Society. He wasn't the least bit interested in football, dating, or watching television, though he did like movies, particularly detective films, Hitchcock thrillers, and his absolute favorite, *Little Shop of Horrors*.

Larry wanted to attend the University of California at Riverside because of its renowned botany program. He had already read most of the papers published by its professors and doctoral students and was particularly drawn to the work of Professor Norman Ellslant, an expert in plant propagation and a major force in ICPS.

Larry wasn't immediately accepted by UC; they were impressed with his science and math scores, but his middling English SAT performance gave them pause. Also, an unsettling number of letters of recommendation came from partners in Mr. Blackbridge's law firm, but only one letter from his school. Larry's science teacher described Larry as an obsessive learner with a great future in academic botany. In the end, they took him, but not until he spent an uncomfortable six weeks on the "second list."

Once at UC, Larry selected as many "interesting" courses as possible, lived comfortably for a year with three roommates in university housing and, of course, joined the Botany Club. There was a good deal of breath-holding at home, but as the year went by with no sound of crisis or dismissal from the west coast, they—parents and staff alike—relaxed, hoping they would only have to deal with Larry at holiday time.

Larry was, like most of his classmates, a bit overwhelmed by college life, especially the pressure he felt from roommates and his few other friends to enjoy his new-found freedom from prep school rigidity and watchful parents. The main solvent in their emancipation was alcohol, and to a lesser extent, marijuana. Not surprising, given Larry's concern for control, he didn't like intoxication. He saw it as an enormous waste of time and, worse, the thief of his sense of personal vigilance. He saw this play out in the way his friends used alcohol, either to act like bigger fools than they already were or to aid in the seduction of naïve coeds.

He was annoyed by drunken behavior but indifferent to the exploitation part. In fact, it made sense. He had no special fondness or feeling of attraction toward women, and he considered using a chemical, like cannabis or alcohol, a logical short cut to the tiresome and expensive process of seduction.

To the few who knew him at all, Larry was a smart but harmless square. His feelings of contempt and hostility for those around him were well masked. Larry kept score, to be sure, but he did it quietly and with a smile on his face. In spite of his oddities, you couldn't really ignore or dismiss Larry, and his verbal alacrity, confidence, and sense of direction kept him at least marginally in the social swim. Women found him attractively mysterious, and his lack of sexual assertiveness made him a safe and entertaining male companion. The fact he was obviously wealthy didn't hurt either.

By the end of his freshman year Larry was ready to shed any pretense of social interest and told his roommates his plan to move off campus and live alone. They asked if he wasn't concerned that living so far from the school wouldn't be lonesome or limit his chance to make new friends.

No, Larry wasn't worried on either count. "Besides, all the friends are used up."

They parted on good terms and Larry turned his attention to finding the right kind of house, one that made him comfortable, was private, secure, and had plenty of room for his research. For the last ten months, Larry's parents and their staff had been watering and feeding his collection of plants, snakes, lizards, and turtles, and they were sick to the gills with it. When he found a suitable place, they rejoiced at the news and happily packed his books, plants, and various reptile cages into a moving van. The moving company charged an exorbitant fee to make the trip, but Mr. Blackbridge was more than happy to pay. "Money well spent," he said as the van lumbered away. "The only thing that would make it any better would be if the whole lot burned up in the middle of Arizona."

No one disagreed.

Larry found the right home in an isolated area near the San Bernardino National Forest. Tyler Castle had been on the market for over five years, but even though it was priced to sell, no one showed any interest in the old stone house with its twin turrets, rusting iron perimeter fence, and caved-in swimming pool. Getting the place up and running would cost a fortune and the taxes, already crushing, would escalate with every improvement.

None of that made any difference to Larry, and he immediately set about rebuilding the main floor, some of the second floor living quarters, and the basement. What had once been an enormous wine cellar was the perfect place for snakes—cool, dry, windowless, and only one door—escape-proof, just in case a venomous serpent managed to slip its cage. It also had a large closet with a thick oak door, the perfect place to store the few bottles of wine Larry did occasionally enjoy.

He built three separate greenhouses where the collapsed garage had been. The swimming pool was filled in and topped with several native oaks. In the end, he had to go to the well several times for money, but his parents didn't seem to mind. "Whatever you need, son, just so you're happy." And stay in California.

And indeed he was happy. Academically, Larry was having an easy time with his course work, acceptance into graduate school was certain, and his home had become a successful, though extravagant, extension of the world he began in Connecticut. Everything was perfect.

Then Eric Sepp showed up.

Eric transferred from an obscure school in central Ohio at the start of his junior year. Son of an unemployed steel worker, widower, and dedicated alcoholic, Eric had effortlessly consumed all that Trailer College had to offer. His grades, athletic ability, affable personality, and backing by the Trailer Moose Lodge made him an attractive transfer applicant. He easily qualified for a full scholarship, was given a room on campus, and all of his books were paid for by the Trailer Moose Lodge. About the only expense left was for food and clothing, but Eric was used to working and gladly accepted a night job stacking books at the Orbach Science Library.

By Eric's standards, the pay was ample and when work was slow it gave him a chance to study books in his area of interest—botany.

Larry took little note of the newcomer, though he was annoyed by Eric's sunny disposition and what he felt to be an excessive enthusiasm by the Botany Department for their newest student. It amused Larry to call him Trailer Trash—not out loud, of course.

Annoyance turned to smoldering resentment as it became clear that Eric was going to become a formidable adversary, an evolving scholar with a zeal for learning every bit the equal of Larry. Add to that his unsolicited popularity with fellow students and, even more troubling, with faculty. If that wasn't bad enough, within a few months of his arrival, Eric was being actively courted by the graduate school faculty.

Though Eric didn't realize it, he and Larry were on a collision course, one that could become ugly if, no matter how unintended, the oblivious interloper crossed an invisible line. Fortunately, there were over 400 zoology/botany majors to dilute their interaction and it wasn't until the end of their senior year that Eric committed the unforgivable sin of besting Larry by winning the Cheeseman Award for academic excellence.

As runner-up to the Cheeseman, Larry was given a generic Promising Undergraduate award, hardly a strong enough balm to soothe his raw wounds. Thomas Cheeseman (1845–1923) was a renowned New Zealand botanist and Larry's long-time hero. Capturing the award would have given Larry's own work the confirming recognition and peaceful symmetry he always coveted.

Larry was not unaware of his interpersonal shortcomings, and while he generally didn't give an aphid about what others felt about him, he didn't want to be rejected or ridiculed by his colleagues. He actively suppressed his hostility in the presence of others and always wore the face of a cheerful if preoccupied researcher. He wanted his avoidant behavior to be seen as a reasonable and benign extension of his voracious appetite for knowledge, not the expression of a cold and troubled mind.

Eric Sepp would pay for stealing the Cheeseman, make no mistake about that.

Graduate school was more challenging for Larry than he had imagined it would be, especially on a social level. Gone were the mega-classes and comfortable anonymity of his undergraduate years. Now classes were small and comity replaced competitiveness and grade anxiety. Even more challenging, the barriers between student and professor were gone. People called each other by their first name and intimate dinners were frequent and unavoidable.

The only way out for Larry was to accept the situation, immerse himself in work, move as much of his research as possible to the greenhouses at Tyler Castle, and socialize as little as he could get away with and still not attract negative attention. This is just practice, Larry told himself. When you're a professor of botany or a leader of industry, you'll have to host these goddamn parties. Get used to it.

And there was the unresolved problem of ruining Eric Sepp. That would happen, in good time, at just the right moment. Opportunity's call can be heard by those who maintain constant vigil.

Larry's work focused on the biochemistry of plant interaction, the way plants seem to know how to express or suppress themselves in unison, depending on soil, air, and climatic conditions. Unlocking those secrets would allow agricultural businesses to manipulate plants into greater exuberance and productivity than conditions would normally allow. Patents on this technology would have untold value. Agribusiness executives would crawl to his door just to have the chance to bid on contracts.

Eric Sepp was also focused on crop yields, but he was interested in the role amino acids play in soil health. He was trying to unlock the mystery of how to develop crops that secrete soil-enhancing, large-molecule amino acids that, like nitrogen-fixing bacteria, actually leave the soil stronger, not weaker, after harvest. Also, the large molecules would create a natural osmotic effect pulling water from the air thus reducing pressure on meager irrigation resources. Farmers in underdeveloped countries could use their land constantly without the need for fallow years. The potential impact on the world's food supply would be incalculable.

As Sepp's work began to show some initial promise, he was given a small greenhouse complex adjacent to the university's experimental citrus groves. Larry took the risky step of writing a letter to his chairman questioning the wisdom of putting evolving, unpredictable work so close to the vulnerable citrus fields. His concerns were quickly dismissed.

Perfect, thought Larry. The oracle has spoken and the trap is set. Ignore the oracle at your peril. "Now," he mused, taking a drag on his favorite meerschaum pipe, "all I have to do is sit back and wait for the fates to let me know the next step."

And Larry would have time to consider that step because he was about to spend two long and unwanted weeks in China, guest of the government of the People's Republic of China, Division of Workers Agriculture, Department of Research, Division of Plant Biology, all located on the sprawling Struggle for Freedom and Justice campus of Foo Uaji University in Beijing. To Larry it was a colossal pain in the ass, part of a useless annual exchange between a clutch of graduate programs and F.U. It was simply his bad luck to be chosen for this dubious honor, though he knew better than raise a ruckus about it and risk appearing like a spoiled, ungrateful child.

At least he liked Chinese food.

The trip across the Pacific was endless, and to make matters worse, there was a cranky infant just two seats behind Larry. The kid alternately cried and screamed for the first two hours of the flight. Larry finally broke, summoned the flight attendant, and in a loud voice demanded to know if it would be possible to give the child a tranquilizing suppository to shut him up. Passengers who heard the outburst were horrified, but Larry instantly felt better and fell asleep, soothed by the knowledge that those around him now had two reasons for sleepless irritation.

Larry and the other ten graduate scholars were taken immediately to F.U.—no sightseeing on the agenda—and assigned bunks in the austere Future Labor Leaders dormitory. They ate noodles and lifeless vegetables brewed in thin chicken stock three times a day. The rest of their time was spent either touring monotonously similar growing sheds or listening to speeches about the glorious work being done by their inspired students.

It was pure hell, and Larry detested every moment, a powerful challenge to his capacity for contrived forbearance. The days ground by without a single scrap of new or even vaguely interesting information. Finally the last day arrived and the group was told they would have one more tour before heading to the airport. This time, they were taken to an entirely different structure whose name was uncharacteristically devoid of chauvinistic embellishment. The small sign over the steel entrance door simply said "Vines."

Immediately inside, the group was jammed in a small windowless chamber where two attendants dressed in white jump suits busily vacuumed everyone from head to shoes. Then they were admitted to the laboratory through another heavy steel door. Everyone wanted to know the reason for the precautions and once inside, their guide answered somewhat cryptically that it had to do with "contamination" and let it go at that.

The tour was pretty routine, only today's blather was about vine biology; again, no useful details provided. As the group approached each workstation the students, or workers, or whatever they were, would come to attention, bow collectively then stand in smiling silence as the guide babbled something incoherent about more glorious achievements. At the end of the last lab was one more door, steel like the others but with a large reinforced glass portal.

"What's in there?" asked Larry expecting to be rebuffed. Questions, they had all learned, were generally unwelcome.

Surprisingly, their guide answered that it housed one particularly interesting vine, one prone to sudden bursts of growth that if not immediately contained could threaten the entire laboratory. Larry was instantly on alert and asked if it would please be possible to see the vine up close. Please.

The guide conferred with his assistants for several minutes, then talked to the two workers inside the unit through a speakerphone next to the door. Yes, the group could enter, but they were to stand together in the center of the room and not touch anything. The door was opened and they crowded into a room the size of a Levittown bedroom. The walls and ceiling were clad in stainless steel and the floor was concrete. A single, narrow U-shaped growing bench was attached to the walls. There were no shelves under the benches and no suspended growth lights above. All light came through ceiling lights, protected by heavily reinforced glass. Hand tools were hung in neat rows from the front of the benches, and a single watering hose was coiled by the door. A small pan full of clippings hung from the lip of the center bench. The only other objects in the room were three large fire extinguishers.

The plants themselves were surprisingly few and entirely unremarkable. In all, there were perhaps forty stainless steel containers, each about ten inches high containing a single vine neatly trimmed to about six inches. The leaves were on the small size but the stems were more like trunks, probably, Larry reasoned, the bonsai effect caused by obsessive trimming.

An awkward silence followed a brief whispered exchange between the room's attendants and the guide. Keep your mouth shut, don't blow this one, Larry told himself.

Finally, the guide began, starting with the name of this peculiar plant—the Executioner's Vine. His English was choppy but the story was clear. These are last survivors of a vine whose history dates to the Eastern Han Dynasty (25–220 CE). What makes the vine so curious and menacing is its unpredictable growth spurts, sudden hyper-proliferate bursts in which a single plant can grow as much as five feet in an hour. Unattended, one plant could fill the entire chamber in a day.

Larry's heart was pounding, his mind on fast forward. Their guide, seeing the collective look of disbelief, chuckled slightly (humor was not on the agenda at F.U.), said something to the attendants who also allowed themselves a brief smile, then continued his speech. The vine got its name from its earliest use by the Han courts. A criminal convicted of murder was instantly beheaded unless there was some remaining element of doubt about his guilt. In that case, the prisoner was tied to a chair in a small, heavily built wooden hut. A vessel holding a single vine was put behind the chair and the door was sealed. Twenty-four hours later the door was opened and if the man was crushed to death by the vine, he was obviously guilty, the door was shut and the hut burned to the ground.

If the plant did not grow, the man was released and the plant set aside to wait its next assignment. According to tradition, the plant only accelerates in the presence of evil and that is why even today, care is taken to select morally pure attendants and limit visits by outsiders. Another round of chuckles.

Folklore aside, he said, the unsolved research question is what triggers the plant and could that gene or chemical be used to increase growth in other plant species. "And now we go," he concluded, turning toward the door.

"*No!*" Larry screamed in his head. "Sir, could I ask why there are fire extinguishers?"

The guide looked irritated but answered that once a vine is triggered, the only sure way to stop it is to deprive it of water, too slow for an emergency. Fire would work but obviously can't be used in this chamber. That leaves freezing and so there are fire extinguishers. "But we have never used them. Now it is time to go."

"One more thing," Larry said moving toward the clipping tray. "What do you do with the clippings?"

"Stop!" yelled the guide, but in that moment, Larry tripped, falling against the bench then onto the floor. As he hit the bench, he scooped several leaves out of the trimmings tray, and as others lifted him to his feet, he slipped the leaves into his inside coat pocket.

"So sorry, terribly embarrassed," he muttered as he was helped out of the room. The guide was obviously furious but contained himself. "To answer your question, the clippings are burned," he said with cold correctness. End of tour.

Back in his room, Larry examined his treasure. He managed to snag three leaves but only one had much of a stem. He rolled all three together in a thin coat of wet toilet paper, then folded his handkerchief around the small bundle and put it in his breast coat pocket, displayed in proper innocence. He had no difficulty with Chinese customs, and on the flight home, he made hourly trips to the toilet to inspect and moisten his booty.

He allowed himself several congratulatory glasses of wine, and was high as a kite on merlot and endorphins when he hit American customs. When the customs officer asked him if he had any agricultural products in his possession, Larry laughed and said he did not. "I'm a botanist, sir. Bringing in such products would be like carrying coals to Newcastle, don't you think?"

The customs officer wasn't amused but, fortunately for Larry, dismissed him without comment.

Larry got back to Tyler Castle as fast as he could. Two of the leaves, the ones without an attached stem, were clearly dead and already starting to discolor. Sure enough, over the next day they shriveled to a crisp and he tossed them into his compost pile. The third leaf seemed to be hanging on. Larry made up a nutrient solution in a beaker with a rubber diaphragm stretched over the top. The stem was poked through a small hole in the middle supporting the leaf, allowing the stem full immersion and easy observation through the glass.

In the beginning, he inspected his prize hourly, even through the night. Normally, if a cutting was going to make it, tiny growth hairs would become visible at the cutting site within two days. Otherwise, it was likely a goner.

Larry's leaf did nothing. It seemed to be stuck in neutral, not showing any sign of growth nor the slightest loss of color. But one week into his vigil he noticed the leaf was starting to wrinkle and the bright green color faded noticeably—both grave signs absent any growth hairs. Larry's grand plan for the Executioner's Vine was sagging fast.

And Larry had another evolving problem. Because of the China trip and his preoccupation with the vine slip, his regular work was being neglected. Undergraduates complained about cancelled classes and unread papers, and he had missed an important deadline to report on research for his thesis. Larry was summoned to the chairman's office and questioned about the strange turn in his behavior. Initially, the meeting was collegial but Larry's inability—or unwillingness—to account for himself frustrated the chairman. Tapping his finger on Larry's last quarterly research report, he described it as "thin soup."

"Get it together, Larry, that's all I can say. We've cut you a lot of slack but you've got to produce." End of meeting.

Larry was boiling mad, went home, and got drunk. He barely made it to his morning undergraduate class but did his best to appear engaged and even stayed after class to answer questions, something he rarely did before. He put in an appearance at the central lab, made a show of gathering some glassware, and attended a late afternoon lecture by a visiting biologist. He was exhausted by the time he got home, and didn't even bother to check the precious vine.

Instead, he went straight for the wine and sat crumpled at his desk trying to deal with unfamiliar feelings of self-doubt. "What the fuck is going on?" he muttered to himself over and over. By the time he was halfway through his first bottle of wine things were starting to clear up. Yes, of course, it's all about unfinished business. It's all about Sepp, the golden boy, that piece of Midwest shit masquerading as a scholar. I can't get back on track until I deal with him. The vine idea is dead, get that out of your head.

"Maybe," he thought, "I'm being too indirect about this. Instead of discrediting him to eliminate the problem, I should simply get rid of him. Straight to the point, no Sepp, no problem." That felt really good and Larry sensed his confidence starting to grow.

"I need a hit man, that's it. Or maybe a hit snake. Even better."

Larry went to his cellar to talk it over with his serpent friends. Every lizard, turtle, and snake had an affectionate nickname. How about Bonnie, the green mamba? She's fast and deadly. Or perhaps Clyde, his king cobra, might be right for the job. Deadly, to be sure, but too inclined to put on a good show rather than strike. Or how about Fang, the Russell's viper—really cranky, aggressive, toxic as any snake in the world, and quick as lightening. They can hide in any crevice, invisible until it's too late.

But even through his boozy exhilaration it was obvious he couldn't simply turn an exotic snake loose in a greenhouse and expect it to do his bidding. No, it wasn't the snake he needed, it was the venom. And if he used venom from something local like a Pacific rattler, the absence of the snake would be consistent and wouldn't raise an eyebrow.

Larry returned to his den to have another drink and ponder the delivery question. Then he remembered the vine and decided to check it one last time.

Hairs. There were hairs on the end of the stem. Holy shit! Hairs! In spite of its appearance, it was alive and growing! By morning the hairs were almost an inch long. Again, Larry had to show up for classes, but this time his enthusiasm was real. By the time he returned in late afternoon, the hairs filled the entire beaker. Larry gently transplanted the proliferating leaf into moist soil in a large clay pot. By the next morning, the vine was almost three feet long and beginning to grab and stifle adjacent plants. Larry trimmed the plant back to a foot in length and burned the trimmings.

The vine continued to grow a little faster each day forcing Larry to trim it twice a day. Clearly, he had to make his move quickly before he lost control altogether. The best time to strike would be on a weekend to give the plant unattended time to do its work.

Early Saturday night Larry finished his third trimming in eight hours, then transferred the plant to the trunk of his car in a large, tightly closed industrial trash bag. He drove as fast as he dared to the orange groves and parked well away from Sepp's greenhouse. The bag had swollen up like a weather balloon and Larry had some difficulty extracting it from the trunk. Hidden by darkness, he carried the awkward package to the greenhouse. He could feel the vine expanding as he went. He was barely able to get it through the door into the growing area. He slit open the bag and dumped the writhing vine onto a table of plants. The clay pot had already broken into several chunks and Larry had trouble in the dim light finding the pieces. Each time he grabbed a piece the vine would start to wrap around his arm. He finally managed to disentangle himself and wrestle the clay pieces and plastic away from the clinging tendrils. Looking back from the door, he could see the boiling mass of vines growing and pressing against the plastic outer wall.

He circled around the greenhouse and had no trouble seeing the bulge in the wall. He punctured the plastic skin and jumped back as the vine ripped through the wall spilling a mass of vines only thirty feet from the chain link fence surrounding the citrus grove.

"So long Sepp," Larry muttered as he drove away.

Larry kept his radio tuned to the local station Sunday morning waiting for the news to break. But there was no news. How could they miss it? Somebody had to see what's going on. Around three in the afternoon, Larry broke down and drove to a picnic area near the citrus grove. Standing on a picnic table, he had a pretty good view of the groves and the top of Sepp's greenhouse.

Nothing. He saw nothing. No vines smothering the orange trees, no green monster crushing the greenhouse. Nothing. He drove right up to the greenhouse and looked at the spot he had released the deadly vine. That's when he saw it—a huge pile of dead, already rotting vegetation oozing out of the wall like a lanced carbuncle.

Eric Sepp stepped out of the greenhouse. "Some mess, eh, Larry?"

"Yeah," Larry sputtered, "What the hell happened?"

"I have no idea. By the way, what are you doing here?"

"Oh, I hoped I'd run into you to see if maybe you could take my 101 on Thursday at eleven. I've got to be away." Sounded weak, Larry thought. "I wanted to ask in person, not on the phone. I mean, it's asking a lot."

"No problem, Larry, I'll do it. But while you're here, come look at this."

The vines lay in a brown tangle on the bench and through a gaping hole in the wall. "Any ideas, Larry?" he asked picking up a handful of crumbling leaves.

"Christ, what a mess. But, no, Eric, no idea at all. Looks like some sort of hybrid vine went nuts. Maybe it's a prank, someone's idea of a joke. Vines aren't my thing. That's your bailiwick, Eric."

"A prank, yeah, maybe, but who would go to all this trouble for a prank? And what vine grows that fast? At first I thought it was *Persicaria* (*Persicaria perfoliata*, the Asian tearthumb or mile-a-minute plant, fastest growing of all vines), maybe a contaminant from a recent shipment, but the leaves are wrong and there are no barbs. Who knows?" he said with a shrug. "Well, I'll clean it up and fix the wall. And don't worry about the class, Larry, always glad to help."

Larry muttered his thanks and drove back to the castle, his mind swimming in confused circles. He went straight to the cellar and grabbed a bottle of wine without even looking at the label. He stopped in front of Fang's cage. Flashing its tongue, the snake raised its head and pulled into a tighter coil.

"I should have let you do the job, old boy. You would have settled his hash in a fucking instant."

Back in the kitchen, Larry opened the bottle, filled a glass unwashed from the night before and drained it in one long gulp. As he was refilling the glass, he heard a crash coming from the greenhouse. "What the fuck is that?" he grumbled yanking open the back door. A metal garbage can lay on its side next to the compost pile. "Freaking raccoons," he said slamming the door.

If Larry had looked a little closer, he would have seen the problem wasn't a garbage hound but two large vine clusters surging out of the compost pile. The garbage can was in the way, between the pile of rotting vegetation and the back of the house. While Larry sat hunched over the kitchen counter drinking his wine, the twin columns coiled together, gathering both speed and bulk. Within thirty minutes they were crawling along the outside wall of the house, one branch moving up the back steps toward the kitchen, the other wrapping around the side of the house, up the front door, and through the open transom. Once inside, the roiling mass moved down the hallway between the dining room and the kitchen.

Larry was jolted out of his stupor by the crash of broken glass as the window over the sink literally exploded under the pressure of the massive weight of the vine.

"Holy shit!" he yelled, momentarily staggered by the sight of the vine tumbling through the shattered window. He knocked over the stool he was sitting on, tripped, and half crawled, half ran to the hallway door, hitting it with his shoulder as he twisted the knob. The door barely opened, just enough to allow vine tendrils to circle the opening. As he reeled back, the lights began to flicker.

"Think, man, think!" he shouted out loud trying to calculate his next move. It only took an instant to see his one line of defense—the cellar.

"Light, I'll need light." There were battery powered emergency lights in the cellar, but he knew he would need more. He risked stepping on the vine to open a counter drawer, find a flashlight and a package of extra batteries. He shoved the batteries into his shirt and grabbed a large knife from the counter. The vine was already wrapping itself around his ankles. He slashed himself free, lunged through the cellar door, and slammed it shut behind him.

He stood on the top step panting, fighting panic, trying to figure out his next move. The lights flickered and went out. Moments later, the emergency lights came on. This is crazy, it can't be happening. "STOP IT!!" he screamed. The only answer was the sound of glass breaking, wooden chair spokes snapping, and something scraping against the cellar door. He waited on the top step scanning the edges of the door for intruding tendrils. The door was practically airtight, a precaution he had taken before setting up his cellar herpetarium.

No tendrils. The door made aching sounds but it was holding. Larry leaned against the stone wall trying to slow his breathing and marshal his thoughts. Seeing the door hold was a huge relief but he knew he would need a backup plan in case it failed. Unfortunately, the door opened inward, and if it bulged at all, the vine would certainly surge through.

The only place left was the storage closet. That door was made of oak, two inches thick and heavily reinforced with large cast iron hinges. It opened out so any pressure on it would only seal it tighter. Air might be a problem and so would light. Larry disconnected the two battery powered wall lights, put them on a shelf with the extra batteries for his flashlight, and quickly filled a dirty bucket with water. The only other tool he could find in the semidarkness was a hacksaw.

The upper door cracked loudly then burst open. Larry dove into the closet slamming the door shut as hard as he could. He sat on the floor, panting, fighting the urge to puke.

Breathe slowly, Larry. Slow it down. Don't waste air. Get control, he told himself over and over. He looked around, quickly assessing his situation. "I'm in my fucking tomb," he muttered. "But I'm not dead yet. FUCK YOU, VINE," he screamed at the door.

The closet was about eight feet wide and five feet deep. The door was centered and the back lined with empty shelves and wine racks. Larry's wine supply had dwindled to a dozen bottles of assorted French Bordeaux. He sat on the floor staring at the door, his breathing now regular and slowing down. He could hear the muffled sounds of havoc outside the door. Loud cracking noises could only mean the cages were being crushed. His friends would have no place to hide.

Larry knew he couldn't survive too long in the closet, but if death was inevitable, he wanted to be in control of it, not in the grip of that goddamn vine. It gave him a brief feeling of satisfaction to think all he had to do was get stupefying drunk, pass out, and suffocate. Let the vine choke on his corpse.

Yeah, that's my escape hatch. But, I'm not there yet. Looking at the door, he reasoned the most vulnerable part would be the minute space between the door and the floor. The lip of the threshold was simply too thin to hold back the green monster.

Caulk it like the boards on a boat, that's it! he thought. Jam it tight and maybe that will block the bastard. He pulled off his pants and cut the fabric into long strips, then, using the knife, he tried to press the material into the crack. But the fabric was too thick and he immediately snapped off the tip of his knife. He sat back again to rethink the situation. It was growing quiet in the cellar but he could hear the vine scraping across the door.

His shoulder hit a wine bottle and he briefly thought of just saying the hell with it right now. He took out a bottle, held it up, and laughed out loud. "You never have a corkscrew when you need it." Then an idea hit him. Wet the fabric with wine. That will make it easier to jam in the crack and maybe the alcohol will act as a repellant to the vine. He scored a circle around the neck of the bottle with the hacksaw, then broke the neck off with one sharp smack with the back of the hacksaw. The break wasn't clean but it didn't shatter the bottle. He took a long draught, spit out a few glass splinters, and poured the wine on the trouser strips. This time he was able to get the fabric into the crack and after a half an hour and two more bottles of wine, the job was done. He took another congratulatory pull and sat back to consider the situation.

So far the door was holding. He turned off the flashlight and one of the two emergency lights. He didn't want to find himself in the dark. The room was cold and Larry knew he would run out of air, the only question was when. It might be worth feeling around the top of the wall in case there was some chance air could seep in through a crack in the stone wall. Just hope the vine doesn't figure that out, too.

Larry used the shelves to climb to the ceiling then wet his hand to make it more sensitive to any minute breeze. Finally, in the center of the back wall he felt a very slight sensation on the back of his hand. Using the knife, he pried away some loose concrete and was able to increase the flow slightly. It wasn't much, but holding his face against the wall he could suck in some stale but reassuring air. Another victory, another drink.

He was exhausted and had to pee. The bucket held his water supply so there was no choice but piss on the floor.

Larry fell asleep on the floor somewhere around three o'clock in the morning. Three hours later, he awoke with a jolt because of pain in his left foot. It took a moment to turn on the light but even before he saw it he knew the vine had penetrated the vault. Green fingers had pushed under the door wrapping themselves around his foot and lower leg. He grabbed the knife and slashed furiously at the vine. The stems were tough and hard to cut through; worse, in flailing at the vine, the knife broke off at the handle.

Larry pulled off the severed tendrils, wrapped the blade in a strip of fabric and cut the vine off at the crack where it had penetrated. He poured wine into the crack to prepare for more caulking and noticed that the vine retracted.

Alcohol! I was right, it doesn't like alcohol. By the time he finished re-soaking and caulking the door, Larry was dizzy and nauseous. *Air, I need air,* he thought. He climbed up the shelving, put his mouth over the crack and drank until his head cleared and he could return to inspect the door.

The bottom was holding but the center showed a slight inward bulge. If it wasn't stopped the seal would break and no amount of wine would stop the inevitable. Larry pulled two shelves loose and tried to wedge them between the door and the back wall but they were too long and he couldn't force them in place. Again, he was dizzy and had to go for more air. Then he set about cutting the shelves to size with the hacksaw, an exhausting task. It took over an hour to cut each piece. Not only was the blade not meant for wood, but he had to cut back vine and climb the shelf for air in a constant, numbing cycle.

He finally managed to wedge the two boards between the back wall and the door forming a rigid platform wide and strong enough to support his weight. It meant he no longer had to sit in the growing puddle of urine, but more importantly, he could stand on it and just reach the air hole.

The door held and for a while Larry was able to stay awake, but the dizziness became overwhelming and twice he fell off the boards trying to stand up to get some air. He was soaked in urine, shivering, and down to his last bottle of wine. One emergency light was out and the other was getting weak.

It's over. Time to check out. Fuck it, being dead has to be a lot better than this, he thought. After one more painful trip to the air hole, he managed to break the neck off the last bottle, poured half of it in the direction of the bottom of the door, and set about drinking the rest. He passed out after just two gulps.

Larry woke up puking, trying to remember why he was lying in the dark, dizzy and breathless on a cold, wet stinking floor. *I must be dead. Dead is just like the closet. Yeah, the closet. Shit! I'm still in the closet.* He felt the bottom of the door but there were no vines poking through.

Air! I need air. He couldn't find the flashlight so he groped his way onto the boards, pushed himself up to his knees, then very slowly inched his way up the wall to the air hole. He sucked on the hole until exhaustion forced him to lie down. But his head was clearing and he found the flashlight. It was dead, but after a struggle with the package of batteries and two more trips for air, he reloaded the flashlight, cringing at what he would see when he turned it on.

But, other than hacked up tendrils on the floor, there was no sign of the vine anywhere. He pulled up one end of the caulking expecting to see the vine surge through. Nothing happened. He pulled up the rest of the cloth strips. Again, nothing. He put his ear to the door. No sound. He remembered the sudden death of the vine at Sepp's greenhouse, and the way it seemed to rot as quickly as it grew.

Holy shit, he thought. It's dead. Dead! He thought of the Chinese guide saying the only way to stop it is to freeze it, burn it...or stop its water supply. Of course! The bastard ran out of water. The vine's turbo metabolism requires an enormous amount of water. It sucked every molecule out of the ground and when it was dry the vine collapsed. And with no water it would literally desiccate and quickly crumble under its own weight. It all made crazy sense.

Larry struggled to keep his footing and breathe slowly as he pried the platform boards away from the door. Then one more exhausting trip to the air hole and he was ready to open the door. But the door wouldn't budge.

"No!!" he screamed, slamming himself against the door. His feet slipped out from under him and he fell onto slimy floor. He knew he wouldn't make it back to the air hole again, and he was too feeble to try to shoulder the door open. His mind was closing down. His hand was on one of the boards...the board...the wedge. That's it! He pulled himself onto his knees, twisted and locked the doorknob in the open position. Without trying to stand, he wedged the board between the wall and the door. Using the board for support, he managed to stand then fell chest down onto the board.

The door moved an inch but not enough to clear the jam. Again, he struggled just to sit up, and again, he fell onto the board. The door moved another half-inch and Larry felt a gush of warm, sweet smelling air. Air!! He lay on the board for about ten minutes breathing, gradually feeling his mind start to clear.

He was finally able to stand, and shining the light through the half-inch slit, he saw brown-green leaves, tendrils, and stems in a lifeless mass piled almost to the top of the door. He kicked over the water bucket, stood on it, and peered through the crack at the top of the sea of vines. In the five minutes it had taken to do that one task, the mass had settled several inches.

I'll just wait a little longer, warm up, get my strength back, and by then I'll be able to get the door open. Thirty minutes later the mass had settled almost half way down the door, and Larry decided to try again. This time he managed to widen the crack to about an inch giving him a wider view of the cellar. He saw broken parts of cages and what looked like several pieces of turtle shell, one attached to a small piece of skin.

Everything is gone, but I beat the fucking vine! "Do you hear me? I beat you!! I beat you!!"

He didn't notice Fang slither through the gap.

How Dorothy Carrington Withers
Married the Notoriously Intemperate
Industrialist Morton Cuttman
and Lived a Long and Happy Life

C.W., as Dorothy was known, met Mr. Cuttman at a charity ball and within weeks they became engaged. C.W.'s mother warned her daughter about Mr. Cuttman's well-known problems with both temper and alcohol. C.W. ignored her.

Within three months of their wedding Mr. Cuttman was unfaithful, often leaving his wife alone for weeks at a time in their Long Island mansion. C.W. ignored it.

One night at dinner, Mr. Cuttman choked on a piece of steak. He staggered to his feet, hands gripping his throat in the universal Heimlich recognition signal. C.W. ignored it.

C.W. inherited an enormous fortune, married an artist, and moved to Paris. They had three children and lived a long and happy life.

POLLY

Dick Tardigrade was a man who valued routine. His mantra, one he repeated to himself several times a day, was "Proper prior planning prevents piss poor production." True, his turgid lifestyle didn't invite close friendships, but to his boss at the accounting firm of Crisp, Sharp, Keen and Reckoner, he was the perfect employee.

While not especially religious, Dick had a verse from Matthew framed over his desk—"Every Hair Shall Be Counted." Indeed, he approached every task—no matter how trivial—with the same enthusiasm for perfection, though it would be unfair to say he was without humor and at least a modicum of social grace. He readily participated in the office sports pool, always brought a gift for the Christmas party, and would on occasion join his fellow employees after work for a drink at a local bar.

Dick was accepted by his colleagues as nerdy but loyal, reliable, and utterly harmless. While others pushed to show off their skills and move up the corporate ladder, Dick appeared content with his station, comfortably aloof from office politics.

Underneath his well-regulated surface there was at least a fragment of resentment over the fact that other, less competent but socially slick, associates advanced while he remained stationery, appreciated but not rewarded. Anger was not an allowed impulse, however, and when he felt its icy fingers wrapping themselves around his brain he would counter with the warming realization that he is the tortoise, the others are foolish hares, and one fine day it will be Crisp, Sharp, Keen, Reckoner and Tardigrade.

"All things come 'round to him who will but wait." Wasn't that what Longfellow said? More words to live by. And in the meantime, his life was entirely adequate.

Dick lived in a small house on a quiet street, virtually invisible to his neighbors, though they did appreciate his tidy yard, modest holiday decorations, and generosity to kids at Halloween. In many ways he was the perfect neighbor, friendly to a point, not eccentric or someone to warn the children about.

Dick maintained an orderly home, exercised regularly on his stationary bike, liked to read about science, and was always up to speed on politics and the economy. He subscribed to both the *New York Times* and *Wall Street Journal*, consuming the *Times* with his morning coffee and the *Journal* after returning from work.

Dick was, as he liked to say, in his groove. Everything was going along at a predictable and satisfying pace. Then Polly came along.

It was a Tuesday, Dick remembers that quite well, and as usual he was up ahead of the 5:30 alarm, showered and dressed by 6:00, ready for his coffee and the *Times*. He turned on the porch light, opened the door, bent over to pick up the papers, and came eyeball to eyeball with a tall, green and red parrot.

"Aaawk! Hello, Joe. Aaawk!"

Dick leaped back, tripped over the threshold, fell, and ended up sprawled in the doorway facing the parrot who stood his ground on the *Wall Street Journal*, seemingly unperturbed by Dick's crash landing.

"Aaawk! Hello, Joe!" said the parrot cocking his head slightly.

"What the hell kind of joke is this, anyway? There's a goddamn parrot on my porch at six o'clock in the goddamn morning and…HEY! You're standing on my paper! Don't you dare shit on my paper!" Dick quickly regained his feet but didn't make a grab for the paper lest the parrot rake him with its large curved beak.

The two stared at each other for a full thirty seconds, each unsure of the other's next move. Dick had never been that close to a parrot, and in spite of the shock of their encounter, he was intrigued by the bird's size and the dazzling color of its feathers. Then he noticed what seemed to be an envelope under the creature's right wing.

"Aaawk!" said the parrot, breaking the spell. He hopped off the papers, over the threshold, marched into the front hall, looked around quickly, and flew into the living room up onto the back of Dick's favorite recliner. The envelope fluttered to the floor.

"Aaawk! Hello, Joe!"

"Jesus Christ! This is insane. Get the hell off my chair! If you shit on my chair, I'll knock you into next week!"

"Aaawk! Hello, Joe!"

"And my name isn't Joe, you freaking feather duster, it's Dick. Try that one, smart ass."

"Aaawk! Hello, Dick!"

"Holy shit! Did I hear you say 'Dick'?"

"Holy shit, Dick! Aaawk!"

"My God, I can't believe this." Then he noticed the envelope on the floor, picked it up, carefully looked inside then removed a folded note. The writing was childlike, big block letters, slightly tilted, but each line was straight, orderly, and readable.

> Hello, my name is Polly, a bit cliché, I know, but I'm stuck with it. I hope you will consider having me as a housemate. I am good company, I eat just about anything you do, and if you leave the toilet seat up, I will never make a mess. A little water in the sink in the morning is appreciated. I am told you are a man of honor, highly dependable, and honest, exactly the sort of human I have been searching for.
> Sincerely,
> Polly

"Leave the toilet seat up? Wow, this is one sensational joke. I wonder who would go to all this trouble just to pull my chain?"

"It's no joke, Dick. I'm Polly, and I hope you'll consider my proposal."

Dick stared at the bird, his mouth sagged open but no sound emerged.

"As to the toilet seat, think about it. Look at these claws. They're big, I'll grant you, but not big enough to get a grip on a toilet seat. I've slipped into too many bowls, Dick. I like my bath water to be clean and pure, same as you."

Dick stood frozen in place, still unable to speak.

"You don't look good, Dick. Maybe another cup of coffee, then we'll talk." The parrot flew off the chair, down the hall into the kitchen. Dick followed, his gait zombie-like. "You'll have to pour your own coffee. I'm good, but I have my limitations. By the way, do you have any fruit? I'm starving. I was out on that damn porch for three hours. And please, no crackers. I hate crackers."

Dick managed to pour the coffee, got an apple out of the refrigerator, put it in the middle of the table, and slumped into a chair.

"I don't mean to be a *nudge*, Dick, but how about a plate? You don't eat off the table, right?"

"Of course, sure, a plate. A plate for my talking, thinking, and if I may say so, somewhat bossy parrot."

"Hey, man, I don't want this to get off on the wrong claw…little parrot joke, Dick…really, I don't mean to be difficult. I want this to work. I'm sorry if I have offended you."

"Sure, no problem. Listen, Polly, um, this is really a bit overwhelming. How about if you eat your apple, I'll go talk to myself in the mirror, and if you're still here when I get back, I'm either going to the nut house or to work."

"They may be interchangeable, for all I know. Sorry, just trying to bring a little levity to the situation. Sure, go have a soul talk while I take this McIntosh apart."

Dick stared at himself in the bathroom mirror for a solid ten minutes, his mind spinning, trying to figure out how the joke was being played. But no matter how carefully his analytic mind looked at the situation, he kept coming back to both the improbability and impossibility of it being a joke. Polly was not a flying stuffed bird, no ventriloquist was hiding in the broom closet, it wasn't a hologram, and that only left two options. Either Dick was hallucinating or there was a talking parrot with a genius IQ eating an apple on his kitchen table.

There was only one way to handle this—go back to the kitchen, and if Polly was still there, hallucinations were eliminated. Before leaving the bathroom, Dick raised the toilet seat.

"You're still here, aren't you?"

"Yep, sure am. And that means you're not nuts. Great apple, by the way. Really hit the spot."

"Look, Polly, I think maybe I am crazy, but on the off chance you're for real, it would be helpful if you explained a few things…"

"Sure, Dick," Polly said hopping onto the back of a chair across the table. "Fire away."

"Well, for starters, help me get my mind around the fact you can talk. Then maybe something about how you know so damn much."

"Reasonable questions. That's where everyone starts. It's actually rather simple, when you think about it. Parrots have been around forever, long a companion to man. We live as long or longer than you humans, so we have had eons of exposure to language and information.

Fly on the wall, bird on the perch, always listening, taking it all in. We're actually pretty snobby about whom we hang around with, so over time we mated only with the best and the brightest. Think of it as fast track natural selection. What you see before you, Dick, is a highly evolved *Psittacitformes*, species *timneh*." Polly paused to let it sink in.

"We are a small but tight club, Dick, and to anticipate your next question, we don't reveal ourselves because we hate becoming somebody's entertainment. It's bad enough being labeled a pet but far worse to show up on the *Tonight Show* or the featured act in the Parrot Jungle."

"So why reveal yourself to me? Aren't you afraid I'll call Jay Leno when I leave the house?"

"Nope. You won't because you have integrity, Dick. If you give your word, you keep it. That means I can live here in safety and considerable comfort. The alternatives are a pet shop, being tied to a perch in a smelly nursing home, or stuck in a cage at an ersatz jungle theme park. You get a cheerful housemate, and I can keep up with my favorite soaps."

"Soaps?"

"Yeah, soaps. I love the soaps. Seeing humans make tearful idiots out of themselves knocks me out. Anyway, it's getting late, and you either have to call in sick or get going. We can continue later, okay?"

"Sure, later. But I've never called in sick. That would be dishonest."

"That's what I like about you, Dick. It's why I'm here."

Dick had to run to catch the bus, barely acknowledged the regulars, and was so distracted he missed his stop and had to walk four blocks back to the office. When he failed to attend the morning team meeting, his boss called to see if he was sick or needed help. Dick mumbled something about feeling badly and was told to go home and take all the time he needed to get well.

All the way home on the bus he rehearsed what he was going to say, that is if Polly was still there, and he hadn't imagined the whole thing.

"Welcome home, Dick! I thought you'd be back early. It's a lot to take in all at once." Polly was perched on the back of Dick's chair watching *Yesterday's Bride*.

"Look, Polly, we've got to talk. Can we shut that thing off and have a chat?"

Their "talk" went on for four hours and by the time it was over, Dick was convinced Polly was the highly evolved feathered anomaly he said he was. At 47, Polly considered himself to be in his prime, though a recent three-year incarceration chained to a post in a Florida petting zoo had taken its toll. He escaped by feigning illness, then biting a handler while being carried to the vet.

"Normally, I hate violence, Dick. And I know the guy is going to have a hell of a scar to remind him how much he hates parrots. You see, desperate situations call for extreme measures. But now I'm free, and it looks like this may work out for both of us, right?"

Dick was far from convinced, though he did find himself increasingly fascinated by the bird, and by the end of their conversation he agreed to a two-week trial run. If either was dissatisfied, they would part, no questions asked. And if it didn't work out, Dick agreed to rent a car and take Polly to the destination of his choice.

For the first several evenings Dick approached the house with enormous anxiety. What if Polly wasn't there? What did that say about his mental health? Who would believe him? And if he went to a psychiatrist to talk about his lost talking parrot roommate, he would be committed to a Thorazine asylum for the rest of his days.

But Polly was always there, ever cheerful and glad to see him, ready to relinquish the recliner to the weary accountant and hear about his miserable day. The two-week deadline passed without mention, their arrangement by then entirely clear. The rules were simple. Polly would be a tidy and upbeat companion, always neat and clean. No feathers in the butter dish, no poop anywhere except the toilet, and he would remain ever vigilant in case of fire or prowlers.

Dick's obligations were simple: provide a comfortable home, access to TV, good food, and never refer to Polly as a pet or try to exploit him. On those rare occasions when Dick entertained, Polly would stand statue-like on a perch and stick to his "Hello Joe" line. Once a week Polly asked Dick to leave an upstairs window open at night so he could rendezvous with friends and catch up on goings on in the parrot world.

The arrangement seemed to be working perfectly. Dick's work was better than ever, a promotion was imminent, and Polly was spending less time with soaps and more time with educational TV, including an on-line course in avian medicine—in Dick's name, of course.

Then one day while having coffee in the break room, a passing remark by a coworker caught Dick's attention. The man's daughter had won a regional spelling bee and was featured on a network talk show.

"And get this, they paid her five hundred bucks for her ten minutes on the show. Christ! What'll it be if she wins the nationals?"

They all laughed, and Dick didn't think much more about it, at least not until his boss told him he was being promoted to assistant senior division accountant. He was pleased with the recognition and happy to move from a carrel to an office, but when he heard his raise would only amount to $300 a month, his heart sank.

His first thought was about Steve Cohen's frigging daughter and how she made more in ten seconds spelling "logomacher" than his raise would give him in a month.

Polly was entirely sympathetic. "That's not a raise, Dick, it's a tip. You have every right to be cranky. Maybe you should get your resume together and take your considerable talent somewhere you'll be appreciated."

"No, Polly, I've thought about it, but old man Crisp has been really nice to me in other ways. They need me and when they realize it, they'll make it up to me."

"Sure, if you live as long as a parrot, maybe." But the discussion was over and Dick refused to discuss it further, though he continued to stew about it. The image of little Shelley Cohen and her $500 check haunted him. He lectured himself about the corrosive effect of negative emotion, tried concentrating on positive memories, but the harder he tried the more he thought about how badly he was getting screwed.

He imagined being in a spelling bee for accountants. Mr. Crisp was the emcee. "The word, Dick, is 'arbitrage.' You have ten seconds to spell it."

"That's easy, Mr. Crisp! F-U-C-K-Y-O-U!"

They both agreed that in business, principles and morality mean nothing. It all comes down to money. The higher-ups use the lower-downs to peddle their goods and services to a naïve public, pocket the money, and soothe the working stiffs with platitudes and promises of a better payday just ahead. If the workers get restless or question the scam, they get a pink slip and new recruits are rushed in to fill the void.

The unthinkable was starting to push its way into Dick's awareness. Suddenly it wasn't freckle-faced Shelly on the fantasy TV screen, it was Dick, and he was making tons of money. Can you spell "talking parrot"? But how in the world could he ever get Polly to go along with the scheme? He couldn't exploit Polly, that was against the rules, right?

The idea went from recurrent to obsessive. Over and over, Dick asked himself how he could pull it off without Polly's help and still make a bundle in the bargain. The answer hit him while he and Polly were watching a wildly popular reality show about a burned-out rock star and his lunatic family. Cameras caught their every move. Even the bathrooms weren't off limits.

Of course! A reality show about Dick and Polly. All he needed to do was film their time together, Polly at home during the day and some extra footage of Dick at his office. With commercials, each show would only need about forty minutes of action. Over an eight- or nine-month season it should be a snap.

Of course, there would have to be some plot thread, problems and crises strung together to create tension. It can't all be based on the novelty of the anthropomorphic bird. But that can be worked out later. Step one will be getting footage to present to a studio. Then a contract and some up-front money.

Dick used his computer at work to research spy equipment, tiny cameras he could conceal so Polly would have no idea what was happening. He's smart all right, but let's remember, he's still a parrot. Clever, to be sure, but not clairvoyant. Besides, whose frigging house is this, anyway? He chose me, not the other way around. And for all his bluster about exploitation, just what the hell do you call what he's up to?

"I've become the goddamn pet! That's the truth of the matter," Dick muttered to himself as he ordered the latest miniaturized spy camera and recorder both neatly concealed in a leather attaché case, its tiny lens peeking invisibly through the keyhole lock.

"Nice case, Dick." Polly said when Dick arrived home with his new purchase. But Dick was ready, having anticipated Polly's observation.

"Thank you, Polly," he said brightly. "I figured if I am going to be an assistant senior division accountant I can damn well look the part. Like you say, Polly, it's all about the costume." (Polly often said that if parrots had been born looking like grackles, no one would have paid any attention to them.)

"Now you're getting it, Dick. Watch out Reckoner, here comes Tardigrade!"

Perfect! The moment passed and nothing more was said about the matter. Dick cleverly carried the case to and from work for two weeks, leaving it in various places around the house, even "forgetting" it on occasion. Still, nothing was said about it.

Finally, the big moment arrived, time to put the plan into action. It was a Friday and Dick turned the device on at work to test it one last time before a weekend of filming. It worked perfectly and would run for a full two days on one battery charge. When he arrived home he casually put the case on a living room table, one whose location gave him the maximum coverage of the living room and most of the kitchen. He prepared Polly's favorite dinner—shrimp cocktail, carrots almandine, French fries, and apple pie.

"What's the occasion, Dick? Mind you, I'm not complaining, just curious." Again, Dick was ready.

"I'm surprised you don't know, Polly. This is our six-month anniversary. Let's make it a special weekend, okay?"

"Fantastic, Dick, here's to you." Polly took a big drink of water and gargled loudly—a parrot's way of expressing great satisfaction. Dick hoped the tape picked that one up loud and clear.

Saturdays were Dick's day to go shopping, stock up, and rent a good movie. As usual, they made their shopping list together at the kitchen table then Dick caught a bus for the short ride down to the mall. Today he planned to splurge and take a cab home. On the way back he thought it was time to buy a car, maybe a BMW. The hell with taxicabs.

The first sign of trouble was the crunch of broken glass on the front steps. Looking up, Dick saw that the window over the front door was shattered, the glass scattered over the porch and steps.

"Shit!" he yelped, leaping up the steps. A large bottle of ginger ale tumbled out of his grocery bag and exploded on the threshold as he burst into the front hall. The living room was a mess. The smashed television, stereo equipment, cables and wires, books, magazines, and broken lamps lay in a hopeless tangle on the floor. It was the same in the kitchen. Cabinets open, food everywhere, sugar and flour canisters broken on the counter. Dick's attaché case was in the middle of the kitchen floor, its back ripped open, the camera and recorder torn to pieces, its parts mixed into the mess on the floor. Upstairs, the only damage was to the light fixtures in Polly's bedroom and the smashed out bedroom windows.

There was a note in the seat of his recliner written on the back of the invoice from the EZ Surveillance Company. It had been in the spy case.

Dear Dick,

    Sorry about the mess but I couldn't leave without being absolutely sure there were no other hidden eavesdropping devices. I am sad it has come to this but quite honestly I sensed it coming over the last month. You just haven't been yourself, Dick, not since that kid won all the money in the spelling contest. I've seen this before. Something always triggers it and before long, what used to be just right is suddenly not nearly enough. Then the scheming starts and I have to be on my way. You got out of your groove, Dick, and I don't think you'll be able to get it back. But look at good side, you're now primed and ready for the corporate life. While you get comfortable in your new persona, I'll continue my search for a human who knows how to keep his word.

Sincerely,
Polly

BAD NIGHT
IN THE BRONX

Hoover Kowalski, the only son of Maria and Lech Kowalski, was born about 3:20 a.m. on August 14, 1934, in the back seat of a Checker Cab on Webster Avenue in front of Carmen's Italian restaurant. Just as Maria gave one final involuntary push she looked up and saw the illuminated picture of a bowl of spaghetti in Carmen's window. In that instant Hoover shot across the seat into his father's lap. The placenta was delivered in the driveway of Bronx General Hospital.

"Who's going clean up this mess?" demanded driver Oja Majoris. Lech Kowalski paid the fare—plus a generous twenty-five cent tip—said he was sorry about the placenta and disappeared into the emergency room with Maria and squalling baby Hoover.

The *New York Post* reported the story **BABY BORN IN CAB!** Noting that Hoover weighed in at a robust 9 pounds 2 ounces and that both he and his mother were doing fine and expected to leave the hospital in three days.

Asked by the reporter how the name "Hoover" was chosen, Mr. Kowalski said proudly, "He is named after President Hoover in honor of his many achievements. I'm a Republican, and I don't care what people say, he is a great American and a great president. History will show I'm right, and hopefully our son will grow up to be just like him. I know he'll be a great Kowalski!"

The paper also took note of Mr. Kowalski's employment as "keeper of the apes" at the Bronx Zoo, and quoted a fellow worker who said, "Lech has a way with the apes. It's as if he can somehow communicate with them. Everyone else is afraid of the animals, but not Lech. I'll tell you, we'd be lost without him."

The media glow didn't last too long, but it was good for a lot of flowers, some baby clothes, diapers, and several baskets of fruit. The Kowalskis returned to their third floor walk-up on East 180th Street across from the Asia Gate entrance to the zoo. Before Maria's pregnancy, the Kowalskis lived on the sixth floor in a cramped studio apartment in the back of the building facing a windowless shirt factory. The refrigerator didn't work very well and heat—seemingly in defiance of the laws of physics—didn't rise above the fourth floor. In spite of the difficulties, the Kowalskis never complained, and when Maria became pregnant, the superintendent arranged for them to take over a choice third-floor corner apartment overlooking 180th Street.

Baby Hoover was an angel from the start. He rarely cried, and when he did, a change of diaper or snack at his mother's breast quickly soothed him. Maria had quit her job at the laundry hoping she could be a full-time mother, but after six months, the Kowalskis had to face the fact they couldn't survive on one salary, and Maria reluctantly went back to work. It was a painful decision compounded by the necessity of working at night to spare the expense of a daytime babysitter.

Still, baby Hoover didn't seem to mind, and he quickly (and quietly) grew from an infant to a toddler, though he seemed to be less inclined to walk than climb. He scaled the chairs, bookshelf, and bathroom vanity, and by the age of one was able to climb onto the table next to the 180th Street window. It quickly became his favorite place to sit and even nap. The Kowalski's worried he would topple off, and they put cushions around the table, but Hoover never lost his balance.

His vocabulary was slower in coming, but by the time he had mastered the table climb he could say a few words. Along with "Mamma" and "DaDa," he had several that always seemed to delight him even though no one else could understand them. His father joked that they actually sounded like ape words, the kind they utter while being groomed by a fellow ape or sitting contentedly on a high perch out of sight of the public.

The Kowalski's hardly saw each other during the week. Their day began and ended with a hand-off of baby Hoover along with a quick summary of any new words or behaviors over the past twelve hours. But Sundays made all the toil and deprivation worthwhile. They were together as a family and not a treasured moment was wasted.

The day always began with a moment of hushed intimacy before Hoover stirred, unless—of course—Maria was physiologically inconvenienced. After a hearty breakfast of sausage and eggs, the family attended Mass at the Holy Shrine of Mary Mother of Our Savior. After the service Maria packed a picnic lunch and the family headed for the zoo where they spent the rest of the day. Even in the dead of winter, the Kowalskis took advantage of Lech's unlimited free access.

These outings always delighted Hoover who squealed with joy as the family made its way through the zoo's myriad pathways, but especially so as they neared the ape house. They entered through a back door into a large hallway that circled behind the various enclosures. Invisible to the public, the area gave the keepers access to the cages for routine cleaning and feeding. There were also smaller cages where individual primates could be sequestered for veterinary services. Here there was no thick glass or protective moat to keep the public safely out of reach of the wild jungle creatures.

The apes were separated by group: chimps, orangutans, monkeys, baboons, and gorillas. The Kowalskis made the rounds, and Lech greeted each group with sounds and hand gestures. The monkeys seemed least inclined to react, unless offered some sort of fruit treat, but all the rest crowded about the feeding port excitedly waiting to greet their keeper.

The most animated of all, however, were the gorillas. Clearly, they enjoyed a special bond with their keeper.

In everyday persona the gorillas appeared apathetic, lounging about in bored indifference not only to the gawking, peanut-throwing public, but—curiously—to each other. When they spoke at all it was usually in low, clipped growls or grunts, and when they moved, it was in extreme slow motion. There was none of the howling, chest-pounding, vine-swinging behavior the public had come to expect from the wildly popular *Tarzan* movies.

The public reaction to the gorillas was generally one of disappointment—"Smaller than I thought. Lazy bastards, don't they ever move? I'll bet they don't have tires to play with in the jungle. How come they don't have more hair? See if you can hit one with a peanut, maybe that'll wake him up."

And when one of the apes—male or female—decided it was time to put on a genital display, the entire ape house could be cleared in a matter of minutes.

"Disgusting! Did you see that? Hide your eyes, Bunny. Don't tell me we're descended from those vile, flea-ridden creatures. Anyone who believes that nonsense should be tied up in front of those smelly things for an hour. Just one hour! That will cure anyone!"

Crowded around the feeding port, one by one the inmates reached through the bars and touched hands with Lech, a ritual that took several minutes to complete. Lech greeted each ape with grunts and chirps, occasionally laughing at what seemed an inside joke. Maria was never comfortable touching the gorillas herself and worried when Lech held baby Hoover too close to the bars. Hoover loved that part.

World War II was hard on the zoo, but people still came, finding relief from the constant drumbeat of scary news and a source of cheap entertainment in a time of food and energy rationing. Lech was too old for the draft, but many of the other employees were not, leaving Lech with a greatly expanded set of responsibilities. Maria worked the night shift in a factory sewing uniforms. Happily, the Kowalskis' Sunday ritual was uninterrupted.

Hoover started public school just before the war, and while he had no specific problems with either the work or his classmates, it was clear to his teachers and parents that he was basically uninterested in the entire process. Thinking Catholic school might provide a better stimulus, Hoover was transferred in the middle of second grade. It was an instant disaster. His teachers complained he paid no attention to his catechism lessons, and the only time he seemed the slightest bit interested in academics was when something about animal or bird life was discussed.

His teachers tried punishing him with threats of eternal damnation, trips to the Monsignor's office for stern reprimands, and swats with a ruler on his palms and forearms. None of it seemed to make the slightest difference to Hoover. Finally, in total exasperation Sister Angelica Mercy locked him in a windowless storeroom for the day. When she opened the door expecting to find a beaten and contrite boy, she found nothing. Hoover had escaped.

It seemed impossible, and Sister suspected the janitor had sprung her prisoner. But he swore on his mother's rosary that he didn't do it. When they looked carefully at the room they saw a grate had been removed from the heat duct in the ceiling and realized that Hoover had somehow managed to climb up the wall, loosen the grate, slip into the narrow opening, and crawl down to the furnace room; there, daylight showed through the open hatch at the top of the coal shoot.

Hoover's mother was told that her son had left school "without permission." No mention was made of his incarceration or escape. Maria was frantic, and ran across the street to the zoo to find Lech.

When she entered the ape house, Hoover and his father were busy making banana mash for the baboons.

Hoover was expelled and returned to public school the next day. After that there were no more fights over catechism, and both Hoover and the school settled into a long-term arrangement of mutual tolerance. Hoover moved invisibly from class to class, grade to grade, and graduated from high school just before his eighteenth birthday.

For the previous three summers he had worked for the zoo in Grounds Maintenance, and on the day he graduated he applied for full-time employment, hoping to be assigned to the ape house with his father. It was already clear to the management that Hoover would someday replace his father as Senior Keeper of the apes, and his request was granted. For Hoover this was a dream come true, and Lech was proud his son was following in his footsteps. Maria, however, was apprehensive. She had hoped her son would want to go to college (she had long ago abandoned the idea he would enter the priesthood) and make his mark somewhere other than the Bronx.

Every morning Lech and Hoover packed their lunch buckets and walked together to the zoo. They worked in total harmony caring for their "family," as they collectively termed all of the apes. All but the monkeys, that is. They remained simply "monkeys."

It was clear to Lech and his son that the apes, especially the gorillas, were a civilized crowd, wrongly imprisoned, and in need of constant nurturing and encouragement to deal with their constricted life across the moat. The Kowalskis were also tuned in to the gorilla language, and to a lesser extent that of the chimpanzees. The rest were irrevocably primitive and said the same six or seven angry things over and over. Except for the monkeys, of course. They were a hopelessly juvenile group of jabber heads, beyond understanding, and uninterested in bettering themselves.

Lech had mastered most of the basic gorilla sounds and their accompanying gestures. He could carry on a fairly clear conversation, though his limited lung capacity made some exhaled words impossible to pronounce. Hoover was a tireless student of gorilla epistemology, spending hundreds of hours with two of the older females who patiently went over words until their student mastered both meaning and pronunciation.

Hoover was increasingly inclined to linger after his father went home. The two oldest females, named Alice and Jenny by Hoover, and the three most dominant males, Josh, Leonard, and Epstein, gathered at the food gate at the back of their enclosure to share some fruit or sugar cane and talk with their keeper. They loved to hear what was going on around the zoo, especially hot gossip about other animals—as long as it wasn't about snakes or monkeys.

In spite of Hoover's fluency in the gorilla tongue, the conversations were, in the first few years, a bit jerky, and unless an unfamiliar word was particularly important, translation discussions were kept to a minimum. Hoover had always taken for granted the idea that gorillas are highly organized and fully capable of basic logic. What surprised and delighted him was the realization that they are also in touch with their feelings. Moreover, the raging-beast image the outside world associated with gorillas was largely a put-on designed to keep other animals (especially humans) at bay.

It all seemed totally natural and exciting to the Kowalski men. For Maria, however, it was more complex and conflicted. While she genuinely enjoyed their enthusiasm and the harmony that existed between her husband and son, there was a price to pay. Over time she became increasingly peripheral at home. Dinner conversation was usually about apes, and the Sunday ritual did not permit variation. Even a trip to a near-by beach on a sweltering summer day was not on the menu.

And holidays—the traditional week or two of the Yellowstone variety—simply didn't happen. Part of the reason was devotion to work, but there was also a practical issue—both Kowalskis couldn't be gone at the same time. Who would care for the apes in their absence? And it didn't occur to Lech to take his wife off for some time alone.

But even the time off and endless ape-focused conversations were tolerable compared to Maria's *real* issue. Having rejected the priesthood, her back-up dream was that Hoover would find a suitable young lady—Catholic, of course—marry, and make Maria's life complete with grandchildren. There was, however, no sign that Hoover would fulfill his mother's fondest wish, and slowly Maria became depressed and withdrawn. She tried to talk to her husband about it but he was dismissive. Don't push. Give the boy time. Maybe you need a hobby to take your mind off grandchildren.

Maria tried giving extra volunteer time to the church, but Father Fitzpatrick put her in charge of childcare in the Unwed Mothers Home, which only made matters worse. When Maria asked for a transfer to the alter guild she was refused.

"It's a Holy Mission, Maria," the kindly Fathers said. "It's ordained by God, you can't refuse His wish." A few months later God solved the problem: He gave Maria a bleeding ulcer, and she was allowed to quit.

Lech was slowly changing, too. As it became clear that Hoover had more of a connection with the apes (even the damn monkeys) than his father, Lech gradually became less involved. The gorillas noticed it and tried to cheer Lech up. They encouraged Hoover to be more inclusive, and to his credit, Hoover tried. Plainly, Hoover was not intentionally displacing his father; it was Lech himself who was retreating from the field. The fact he had always imagined turning the banana bin over to his son made it easier to conceal the serious and growing problem behind the mask of his long-standing assumption. But over time the mask fell away, and Lech began to see the toll their entrenched life was having on Maria.

Hoover, on the other hand, was entirely satisfied with his life, consumed with his gorilla family, and oblivious to his parent's deepening despair. All of that changed, however, when Maria attempted suicide. It seemed to come out of nowhere—an overdose of sleeping pills, five days in the hospital near death, and gradual physical recovery. But the experience left her more depressed than ever, and Lech was forced to spend a significant amount of time with his wife. He had months of unused sick and vacation leave, but when it was nearly exhausted and Maria's black mood had not lifted, Lech realized he had to do something radical.

At that point he was in his early fifties, too young to retire with a pension. But no matter the cost, it became obvious they had to leave the Bronx. They moved to Cape May, New Jersey, and Hoover took over the apartment. The change was good for Maria. She loved the ocean, took endless walks on the beach, and quickly improved. Lech took a job managing a large kennel and he, too, soon brightened. The pay and benefits were better than at the zoo, and while he missed his beloved ape house, he quickly accommodated to the new milieu and concentrated on learning to speak dog—an easy job compared to the complexity of the gorilla tongue.

At first they visited Hoover every month, but over time their trips became less frequent and within a few years they only journeyed to the city for Christmas and Easter. When they first left, Hoover felt quite alone and was himself a bit depressed. Suddenly he had to shop for essentials, cook his own meals, do his own laundry, and pay bills—all new experiences for him. But unlike his mother, Hoover had a large and vocal support group, and they rallied around their leader.

Epstein was the comedian and always had a new joke ready for his keeper:

What do you call a human whose nephew scratches his ass in public?
A monkey's uncle!

Why do humans throw peanuts to gorillas?
They want the gorillas to show them how to open the shell!

What's dumber than a monkey?
Nothing!

Alice was the philosopher. She counseled Hoover to meditate and seek enlightenment by focusing on the richness of emptiness. Jenny thought Hoover should find a lady friend, maybe ask the popcorn girl out on a date. Leonard thought vet school made sense (not grasping the idea that college was a prerequisite).

But over time Hoover adjusted to the separation from his parents; after all, it was his life work to nurture and protect his primate family, not be distracted by light bills and the need to shop for coffee and toilet paper. Those simple irritations were best dealt with quickly—a few notes on the refrigerator helped—that way he could remain focused on his work.

And at work virtually all of his problems came from one place— the zoo's administration, the source of an endless flood of schemes all fixed on improving the bottom line—no matter what the effect on the animals. Usually the plans were harmless or fizzled out before stumbling though the bureaucracy. Still, some made it through, and Hoover was always on alert, poised to throw his *sabot* into the gears of any truly menacing idea.

Sometimes the plans were downright amusing. Take, for example, the idea about mating. Just about every animal, reptile, amphibian, bird, and fish had been coaxed into reproducing in captivity. Rabbits, cats, mice and rats, guppies, and sand fleas will gladly spew offspring about the house and yard. Even lowly fruit flies, given a rotting fig, will reproduce by the billions.

But not gorillas. Sure, they will engage in sexual behavior, especially when the crowds have left and the lights are turned down. But there is a world of difference between sex play, which more often than not has to do with territory and dominance, and sex designed to produce viable offspring not to be eaten or used as a tennis ball.

Successful gorilla coitus in captivity had taken place only once before—on January 9, 1956 (Richard Nixon's birthday, curiously enough) but did not result in a live birth. Time was running out.

The environmental movement and anti-animals-in-bondage groups were already making it clear that captures in the wild would soon be forbidden, and without a reproduction program, zoos would have to downsize or even fold their ape houses. Think of the damage to the revenue stream!

Zoologists were hard at work studying the problem, sometimes in the Kowalski's ape house, though in the past they had not consulted the lowly keepers. What could they know? Lech and Hoover understood the problem, but since they weren't asked they simply went about their chores amused by the silly ideas the ape mavens advanced.

One plan, for example, was based on the supposition that unlike the human reproduction model, one based on the lofty ideal of monogamous attraction and a conscious wish to achieve parenthood, gorillas lacked the ability to bond with each other for more than a few convenient minutes. Reproduction, therefore, was a random event, which could only be successful if closeness was encouraged by putting plenty of attractive females in every enclosure with a dominant male. If a pregnancy did result, the birth was to be observed and the newborn immediately separated from its mother.

When the Ape Density Plan (or "ADP," as it was known) failed, the Augmented Ape Density Plan (AADP) was implemented. The goal was to agitate the males into defensive intercourse by bringing in a large, unknown male gorilla borrowed from another zoo. That animal was placed in a small cage next to the larger enclosure. Quite deliberately no toys or perches were allowed in the stranger's cage so he would focus all of his irritation on the animals in the enclosure. Fearing they were about to be replaced by another dominant male, the resident males were supposed to demonstrate ownership of their group by wholesale rape. Surely someone would get pregnant, she could then be sequestered, and when she delivered, the baby could quickly be snagged.

It didn't work, of course.

Another idea was to put pairs of gorillas in small barren cages with the idea boredom would drive them into each other's hairy arms and pregnancy would surely follow. Start printing extra admission tickets.

But it, too, was a flop.

The problem, of course, was that the apes knew exactly what was going on, and they weren't about to fall for the scientist's deceptions. The reason was obvious to Hoover long before he discussed it with the family. Simply put, gorillas resent their captivity and while they pragmatically accept the idea they can't escape back to the jungle, at least they won't pass on the burden of life behind bars to offspring. Children are far too precious to do that.

But the threat of forced procreation was real. The zoo was not to be denied its wish for a crowd-gathering, money-making baby gorilla simply because the damned apes wouldn't cooperate. Hoover, of course, was privy to every scheme, immediately reported it to the family, and together they hatched a plan to thwart whatever was afoot.

Most of the plots were easily defeated though there were some close calls. The worst—really the scariest—involved famed zoologist Dr. Franz Cumka, a celebrity in the field of Captive Population Reproductive Behavior. Dr. Cumka bragged there wasn't a caged creature in the world he couldn't, by one method or another, induce to reproduce. He made the circuit with his administrative assistant and doctoral candidate, Lois Leachman. They had been collaborating for over a decade and while their methods were a closely-held secret, it was widely known they credited gorillas with certain human instinctual drives, innate behaviors that could be manipulated into expression under the right conditions.

Dr. Cumka and the almost-Dr. Leachman arrived with considerable fanfare. They announced that they would be camping in the service area of the ape house as their work was carried out at night. All employees were instructed to stay away after closing time, including night watchmen. After three weeks of non-stop work, they gave up and skulked away. In a brief letter to the board, included with a substantial bill for their services, their lack of success was blamed on the gorillas, not their method. It seems the group had been together so long it had stifled their need to impress each other with sexual behavior.

The truth was far different, as Hoover already knew.

Hoover followed the Cumka/Leachman shenanigans from the sidelines, enjoying every morning report from the family. It seems that as soon as all of the employees were safely out of the building, the scientists shed their clothes and started a series of ritual performances designed to stimulate the gorillas into sexual frenzy. The first ploy was a kind of hide and seek played out behind the fruit bin, in the hay pile, and under the food prep table. They chased each other about, squealing and screeching in imitation of what they calculated to be erotic gorilla language.

At first the gorillas were stunned by their antics. They had never seen naked humans, much less a mating pair, and their noisy and tireless copulation had them all against the bars watching. But that was all they did—watch. No sexual activity followed so the scientists ratcheted up the excitement, performing in a makeshift trapeze suspended over the banana press. Back and forth they swung, the sounds of sexual ecstasy bouncing off the concrete walls.

Still nothing happened.

"It was disgusting," Alice reported. "Is that what humans really do to have children? No wonder you don't want to mate, Hoover. You could get hurt doing that sort of thing."

Human sexual behavior was as foreign to Hoover as it was to the gorillas; all he could do was shake his head in disbelief and hope the doctors of Captive Population Reproductive Behavior would tire of their game so life could go back to normal. And after a few weeks it did.

Time passed. There were deaths to be mourned and occasionally a new gorilla was brought in from another zoo to bolster the dwindling herd. But time and celibacy were clearly on the side of the gradual extinction of captive gorilla exhibits.

In 1982 Maria Kowalski died after a brief battle with some sort of cancer. A few years later, at 74, Lech suddenly died of a massive heart attack. The Kowalskis' Cape May home was sold, and Hoover put the money aside, though he had no particular idea of how he might spend it.

The recession of 1980 and stock market collapse in late 1987 took their toll on donations, the lifeblood of the zoo. Hard times meant that precious dollars were concentrated on the most popular exhibits, and in the ape house that also meant focusing on primates willing to capitulate to the reproductive demands of the administration. Hoover knew it was only a matter of time before the gorilla group either died off completely or was broken up and peddled piecemeal to other zoos. The director also began to hint to Hoover that he should begin thinking of his own retirement.

"You can't do this forever, you know, Kowalski," Hoover was told. "Sooner or later you're going to have to think about yourself. Make some plans. Florida might suit you. Get a place near the beach and forget about apes."

The idea depressed Hoover. Instead of dreaming about Pompano Beach, he became grumpy, distracted, and increasingly aloof from the other employees. He only spent a few hours a day in his apartment and took all of his meals in the feeding room. His diet changed, too. He had never been particularly fond of meat, but he gave it up entirely consuming only fruit and uncooked vegetables.

When the director found out he was spending his nights in the ape house, he reprimanded Hoover and forbade him to stay past closing time.

That's when Hoover took to the woods.

Directly behind the ape house there was a large patch of woods—fifty acres or so—used as a preserve with nature trails and a small picnic area. It was protected on the side against the Bronx River by a newly installed chain-link fence topped with razor wire put up to keep people from sneaking in at night. The woods had become a tempting place for nighttime drug users to gather, sometimes around a small campfire. The night watchmen did their best to patrol the area, but they had to do it in pairs, fearful of encountering drug-crazed interlopers.

The zoo had plans to expand the bird sanctuary into the woods, solving both the trespass problem and giving the popular bird displays more room. And down the road, when the gorillas were gone, the sanctuary could take over their enclosure as well.

Hoover often went to the picnic area to eat his lunch, and one day while poking aimlessly around the woods he found a manhole cover buried in a tangle of undergrowth, forgotten in the underbrush, the massive iron disc rusted in place. Curious about what was under the cover, Hoover worked his fingers into the clogged lifting holes, and after several minutes of pulling, he cracked the rust seal and moved the massive cover aside.

Below, a rusty ladder descended into a sort of brick chimney. Hoover came back with a flashlight, and making certain no one was watching, moved the cover and climbed down the ladder. About twenty feet below he found himself in a large storm drain perhaps 4 feet in diameter. He followed the pipe east, and several hundred yards later, it came to the end on the west bank of the Bronx River about twenty feet above the water. The opening, however, was blocked by steel bars set wide enough apart to allow the passage of water and leaves, but too close for even a skinny man like Hoover to squeeze through.

Hoover returned with a hacksaw and by removing one bar he was able to get through without scraping the rusty, slime-covered bars. The open end of the drainpipe was quite invisible on the bank, hidden as it was among old tires, sticks, chunks of plastic sheeting, and other city detritus. It was relatively easy to climb up the bank and walk south along the river to the ornate zoo perimeter fence on 180th Street.

Were it not for Hoover's climbing skills, the last part would have been tricky. The fence was fourteen feet high and lacked footholds. And the sight of someone struggling up and over the fence would have attracted unwanted attention. Hoover solved the problem by climbing an oak tree overhanging the fence. At night 180th Street is fairly quiet, and there is little foot traffic. Hoover simply waited on a limb over the fence until the sidewalk was clear and there was a lull in traffic. He eased himself out on the limb until it bent down over the fence then simply dropped five or six feet onto the sidewalk.

Nothing to it. The problem was *reversing* the trip. By order of the director, Hoover could no longer pass through the employee gate after hours, and scaling the perimeter fence, even at night, invited capture. He solved the problem by walking a few blocks south (away from the zoo) to the East Tremont Street bridge over the Bronx River. There he could easily climb down the base of the bridge, then work his way up the riverbank to the zoo. To anyone else it would have been a nasty hike through the debris, difficult in daylight, and totally impossible at night—even with the help of a full moon. But Hoover was agile, had excellent night vision, and even on the darkest nights easily made his way along the bank to the drain opening. Two minutes later he emerged from the manhole, replaced the cover and let himself in the back door of the ape house. Once inside, he enjoyed dinner and conversation with his family, spent the night, and slipped out just before daybreak. The only slight problem was avoiding the night watchmen, but they followed a precise schedule so it was easy to duck into a closet or hide behind the feed bins when they came along.

Hoover's schedule of work by day and visits by night grew increasingly important to him as the twin dreads of retirement and dispersal of the family grew inexorably closer. He tried to be cheerful around the family and pretend that all was well. But the gorillas knew perfectly well what was going on, and while they, too, were apprehensive, they did their best to hide their worry from Hoover.

"What can we do for Hoover?" they asked each other over and over. They were resigned to being split up, but they knew it would destroy Hoover.

The "answer," if you can call it that, came by accident and with a disturbing beginning.

When a watchman unexpectedly opened the side door late one night, Hoover was just emerging from the main cage only twenty feet away. The quick-witted Epstein threw a handful of dung at the man, plastering him dead-on in the face, distracting him just long enough for Hoover to dive into a pile of banana leaves. It was a very close call and Hoover decided it was time to change the system. But to do it required dealing with yet another obstacle, a dark side of the human persona he had never before confronted.

The fence protecting the woods behind the ape house had successfully discouraged drug dealers, but not groups of young people who frequently pushed under the fence to party in one of several hidden depressions where their small campfires and noisy antics were invisible to night watchmen making the rounds only a stone's throw away.

Hoover had seen evidence of their clandestine gatherings and naively decided to confront them, and guarantee nighttime security for himself and his family. Hoover, of course, had no experience with this sort of police action, and he walked straightaway into a hornet's nest.

He waited in a tree just above the most frequented party site, and sure enough, about eleven o'clock that night a group of a dozen or so showed up, cranked up their fire, and started to party. Hoover watched as they drank, smoked strange-smelling cigarettes, and shamelessly engaged in sexual behavior without the slightest concern for modesty.

That was enough for Hoover. He swung out of the tree, switched on his flashlight, and in the most authoritative voice he could muster demanded they immediately get out of the woods. To his amazement, no one showed the slightest flicker of alarm. Quite the contrary, several continued to rut, only momentarily distracted by the intrusion. The rest stood and began to hurl obscenities and threats at Hoover. Several snapped open ugly-looking switchblade knives.

Hoover did not readily grasp the danger. This was, after all, an entirely new experience, and he foolishly held his ground, raised his voice (though he didn't like being so confrontational), and continued to demand they leave. At that point a half a dozen of the group charged, catching Hoover flatfooted. They were on him like angry hornets, pummeling him with their fists, kicking, trying to stab him, all the while yelling and laughing as if this was grand sport. Hoover went down without throwing a punch or even trying to defend himself, perhaps clinging to some fragment of illusion that they didn't really mean him harm or would quickly stop when they realized what they were doing.

Not so. One of the group stabbed Hoover in the forearm with his knife, the blade penetrating deep enough to hit bone. The pain shot up his arm snapping Hoover into the instant realization he was fighting for his life.

The flashlight was immediately smashed enveloping the knot of attackers in darkness. That worked to Hoover's advantage because the attackers could not see him, but the tiny bit of light from the campfire gave Hoover all the illumination he needed to wriggle free from the group and make a break for the woods. Two of the group gave blind chase but Hoover seemed to vanish completely. He watched from his perch high in an oak tree as the group blundered about vainly trying to find their victim.

"That fucker is here somewhere! I know I fucking stuck him good. He ain't goin' far."

Indeed he was "stuck good," and the wound not only hurt but was starting to numb his arm and hand making it hard to move through the trees at all, much less do it silently. With considerable effort Hoover managed to get about fifty yards before he ran out of interlocking branches. He dropped to the ground and literally crawled back to the safety of the ape house.

"Dear God! Hoover! What happened to you!?" Hoover opened the door to the cage, his family surrounded him, and in halting, confused phrases, Hoover told them about the attack in the woods.

"First, let's fix his arm, then we'll deal with the other problem," Alice said calmly. Injuries of this sort are not uncommon in the ape world. Sharp unseen sticks are a frequent hazard to apes swinging through the tree canopy. Alice knew exactly what to do. She rubbed the wound with a combination of mashed banana, mango juice, and crushed bark. "The acid kills any infection, the bark stops the pain, and banana holds it in place," she explained. Sure enough, within a few minutes Hoover's arm felt better, and he could move his fingers without pain. Then he recounted the story more coherently, though still more stunned by the attack than concerned about his wounds.

"That's humans for you," offered Leonard. "They don't think, they just act. They're worse than monkeys, for sure."

"It has to do with mobs," said Josh. "They get crazy. It's like the mob does all the thinking. There's nothing scarier than humans when they get in a swarm."

"We'll have to deal with this," said Epstein, "We can't let them do this to Hoover. Besides, it'll never be safe for him to go back and forth if we don't."

Hoover protested, but it was in vain. Jenny stayed with Hoover, and the others—eight in all—went out the back door to set matters straight in the sanctuary.

Meanwhile, flush with victory, the party animals were in full tilt in the little hollow. No one heard the approaching posse or realized they were being surrounded

"Gotta piss," one of the revelers said unzipping his fly. He walked— maybe staggered is a better way to put it—into the woods, but just as he

PHILIP HIRSH

started to let go he felt two hands under his arms. Before he could utter a word, he was lifted into the tree above where someone, or something, seemed to put him under an arm and swing off into the black void. His cry of alarm was lost in the branches, and as suddenly as he was snatched up, he was dropped over the fence onto the sidewalk on 180th Street. He wobbled to his feet, dazed, his fly open, his nozzle hanging out, still dripping.

"Pervert!!" someone shouted from a passing car. He panicked and pulled his zipper up before stowing his gear, catching delicate flesh in the metal teeth. Screaming in pain, he was trying desperately to free his member when the squad car pulled up. He was bundled into the back seat and driven away still yelling and fighting with his zipper.

Things weren't going much better back by the campfire. Two more members of the group had vanished and the others were starting to realize something was going very wrong. Again the knives came out. A rock suddenly clocked one of the group, knocking him to the ground. Then another. And another. Then everyone ran for the fence, crashing through the underbrush, bouncing off trees. One by one they were picked up and either dumped over the 180th Street fence or literally thrown over the chain link fence. The ones who went over the barbwire rolled down the riverbank into the oily water of the Bronx River.

Back in the ape house Hoover was feeling better, assured by Alice his wound would soon heal, and by Epstein and the others that the party had been cancelled and they doubted any would dare return.

And so it was that the family started to meet in the woods at night. It was a novelty for the gorillas and less risky for Hoover. The watchmen never noticed anything was amiss. They didn't count noses, and as long as everything was quiet they simply keyed their watch boxes and moved along.

The family roamed carefully around the sanctuary watching for intruders and exploring the new environment. They were all mindful of Hoover's instructions to stay close and remain hidden from passersby. The large oaks, sycamores, and beech trees became an enormous playground, and the view through the street-side fence gave the gorillas their first real look at Hoover's living space.

"It sucks, Hoover," Epstein said when he first looked out on 180th Street. "No wonder you like it here with us." They agreed that while life in the ape house was confining, it seemed a whole lot less menacing than city streets.

Hoover's spirits improved noticeably. He could hardly wait every night to make his way into the woods with his family. But it all came

136

crashing down one Friday afternoon when Hoover was summoned to the Superintendent's office.

"Hoover, I've got some bad news and some good news. Which do you want first?"

Hoover knew from the Superintendent's sardonic smile and sarcastic tone that he wasn't going to like either one. "I don't care. How about the bad news."

"Okay, Hoover, here it is—we're shutting down the ape house."

The words slammed into Hoover like a giant punch. He had known for a long time that this was inevitable, but still, he wasn't prepared. "Why?" he whispered.

"Because a lot of asshole environmentalists are giving us a load of crap about the apes. They act like we're going out and actually catching the goddamn things. And, frankly, the public isn't as interested in large primates as they are in monkeys; you know, cute little fuzzy guys who at least have the decency to move around a little and act like they're having fun. It's too goddamn expensive to maintain your freaking pets, Hoover. Bottom line. We've got a grant to expand the bird house so we're going to tear down the big house, clear the woods, build a better facility for the monkeys, and spread the bird sanctuary all the way back to the river."

He leaned forward, lowered his voice, and staring coldly into Hoover's eyes said, "In about a month we're going to start sending the apes to other zoos, one at a time until they're gone. And we expect you to help, Hoover. None of your save-the-apes bullshit, understand?"

Hoover was silent.

"Now, Hoover," the superintendent said leaning back in his chair, "want to know the good news?"

Hoover was silent.

"Well, I'll tell you. And believe me, any normal human being would jump for joy over this. Since you're not old enough to retire on a full pension, in recognition of your many years of faithful service the Board has voted to give you a very fat severance package—in place of a pension, of course. You get the whole wad up front, Hoover. Two hundred thousand dollars!"

Hoover was silent.

"Shit, Hoover, I would think you could at least show a little gratitude. Two hundred K is a hell of a bunch of money. Frankly, I thought it was too much, but the Board outvoted me."

Hoover was silent. He was asking himself—*What would Alice do?* But the answer didn't come. He got up and slowly walked out of the office.

"You're welcome, Hoover," the Superintendent said sarcastically to Hoover's back.

That night he gathered with the family in the woods and told them the awful news. They had seen it coming and were prepared. They were, in fact, far more concerned about Hoover than they were about themselves.

Hoover did his best not to show his agony and even mustered a little hope saying he would use the money to visit the family no matter how widely they were separated. Their talk continued into the night, and about 1:00 a.m., Hoover fell asleep leaning against a log. Alice covered him with a blanket of leaves and the group moved further into the woods to talk.

"What are we going to do to cheer Hoover up?" they wondered in unison. Ideas were offered but nothing seemed to resonate, that is, not until Epstein came up with the Perfect Plan.

"I've got it!" he said. "Look, Hoover has to retire, right? And he hasn't ever gotten anything for himself. And you know what the other humans are always talking about—you need clothes and televisions and…I don't know…human stuff…those things we see in the stores in the human space across from the fence. Hoover will never get anything himself, but if we get it for him, then he can be retired and still come to see us."

"Just what are you proposing?" asked Alice, ever the cautious one.

"We'll go shopping! Look, it's dark, the humans aren't around; we can use the pipe. No one will be the wiser. Besides, what do we have to lose? They're getting rid of us anyway."

Alice didn't think much of the idea but finally gave in; after all, it was for Hoover. So at about 1:30 a.m. the group slipped out of the woods onto the river bank using the tunnel (after snapping off a few more rusted bars at the end), and crept up under the 180th Street bridge.

"We'll need disguises," Leonard said, "So let's hit a clothing store first." When there was no traffic they rushed out of their hiding place and moved down the street hugging the wall, doing their best to stand as erect as possible. They came to Abe's A&N, ripped off the front door, and fanned out across the store. Of course the alarm went off, but Jenny shot up the wall, and snapped off the clapper so they could shop at their leisure. The men selected camo pants and hooded raingear, while the ladies went for big hats, flowery dresses, and canvas pocket books.

They agreed to spread out, do their shopping as quickly as possible and meet back at the drain pipe. Before they could get going, however, the group was spotted emerging from the A&N—911 received a call about a Harlem gang destroying stores on 180th Street. "They're all on drugs, that's for sure," the dispatcher was warned.

By the time the police arrived the group was gone. But up the street a burglar alarm sounded at Vinnie's Sporting Goods, then another at Rafael's Gourmet Market. The People's Drug store was looted, and two streets over, part of the gang was seen fleeing Radio Shack. There were reports of vandals climbing light poles and scaling walls to escape police. Terrified residents reported monsters staring into upper floor windows. The doors at Bronx Electric were shattered and truckloads of high tech equipment were said to have been stolen. Hundreds of riot police swarmed into the neighborhood, blocking off all major roads. Helicopters circled overhead, their searchlights illuminating the chaotic streets. All the networks were there, along with the mayor and chief of police. Al Sharpton was on stand-by in case there were reports of police brutality.

But there was no one to brutalize. No one was caught, and no arrests were made. The rampaging horde of thugs seemed to evaporate. The police milled around for a while, store owners dealt with the mess, and the neighborhood settled down again.

"Hoover! Hoover! Wake up. We have something for you." Hoover slowly opened his eyes, then sat bolt upright stunned by the sight in front of him, an apparition made all the more bizarre by the shadows cast by the pale moonlight. The gorilla band stood in a semi-circle, a phalanx of masqueraders dressed in a hodge-podge of strange clothing. On the ground in front of them stood a pyramid of electronic gear, boots, hats, dozens of neckties, cooking pots, several hams, a plastic palm tree, and on top of it all—a bright red bowling ball.

"It's all for you, Hoover," Leonard said as he pulled a bag of golf clubs off his shoulder and held it out toward Hoover. "Now you have everything you need to retire." The woods became deadly quiet except for the sound of sirens fading in the distance.

"I don't know what to say," Hoover stammered, his mind racing to grasp what was happening. "You did this for me? So I could retire? I'm… I'm…thrilled," he said leaping to his feet. He hefted the bowling ball and gave it a practice swing. "I've always wanted one of these babies, I'll tell you that. And these clubs…how did you know? And they're the right size, too. Can I ask how you got them?"

"I knew he'd love them," Epstein said victoriously. They all agreed it was a good plan after all.

139

"We worried maybe you'd be mad at us for going out in the human space," said Jenny, pushing a flowered straw hat back on her head.

"Heck, no. As long as you all got back without getting hurt. But I think we need to store these things before someone comes along, just to be safe." They all agreed and the retirement gifts were stowed in the storm sewer. Hoover said he could take them out one at a time so no one would notice. Then they went back to the ape house to share a celebratory mango and pineapple snack. Just before sunup, Hoover sneaked back to his apartment, the bowling ball wrapped in newspaper.

Hoover made some coffee and sat down at the table by the window— the one he used to climb when he was a toddler—and stared across the street at the zoo. I need a plan, he thought, and I need it now. The family put everything on the line for me. I've got to do the same for them.

What would be the ultimate solution to all our problems? What is the one perfect conclusion and how do I get there?

At 8:30 a.m. Hoover was in the Superintendent's office.

"Hoover, I can't see you now, I've got a meeting."

"You will see me now, it will only take five minutes, and if you don't hear me out, I'm leaving the zoo today—right this minute. And I think you know what that will mean."

"Christ, Hoover, what the hell's gotten into you? Okay, five minutes."

"The transfers start one month from now. I can't stand the idea, but there's obviously no way I can stop it. So I want you to get my $200,000 in forty-eight hours. Here is my bank account number." The Superintendent started to protest but Hoover held up his hand and continued. "In two days I am officially retiring, but I will voluntarily work for you until all of the transfers have been made. At that time—and not one minute before—I will leave. There is no negotiating this. Tell the board if they don't agree to my demand I'll walk out right now and you will have chaos in the ape house. And I'll be sure to alert the press so they can watch you brutalizing the animals as you try to get them in packing crates. Maybe they'll get a picture of you holding a tranquilizing gun with one foot on a dead gorilla. I want your answer by 3:00 o'clock today. Oh, and one more thing, I'm taking tomorrow off."

Three hours later Hoover was informed the board had agreed to his terms and the money was being transferred immediately. The following morning Hoover went to his bank to discuss the financial part of his plan. The fact Hoover had $513,500 in his savings account ($200,000 from the zoo, money left from the sale of his parent's home, and years of unspent wages) meant he no longer had to conduct his financial affairs at a desk in heavy lobby traffic. Instead, he was escorted to an office to meet his Personal Funds Manager, Mr. Portwine, who greeted Hoover with unctuous concern for his comfort and wellbeing.

"I see you have been a loyal customer for many years, Mr. Kowalski. I'm sorry we haven't had a chance to talk before this. An oversight, you see. Won't happen again, I can tell you that. I see you have accumulated considerable funds, and I want to show our appreciation by offering you a chance to invest in the bank's own Gold Key Fund. It's something we only offer our best…"

"You can stop there, Mr. Portwine. I'll tell you exactly what I want to do with the funds." Hoover was firm but not unfriendly. Mr. Portwine was deflated but recovered quickly before too much momentum was lost.

"Of course, Mr. Kowalski. Our first rule: *always listen to the customer.* You were saying?"

"I want two certified checks: one for $10,000 made out to "VanZant, Parsons and Olinski," and the other for $500,000 made out to the Board of Directors of the Bronx Zoo. I want the remaining $3,500 in cash. I'll be glad to wait in the lobby."

"But Mr. Kowalski, that will close your account and from an investment perspective…"

"I'll wait in the lobby. Please don't be long, I have an appointment in Manhattan in just over an hour." Hoover left the office before Mr. Portwine could say another word. The cash and checks were delivered by a surly clerk who dropped three envelopes in Hoover's lap, spun on her heel, and walked away. Hoover counted the money, inspected the checks, and took a cab to Brooks Brothers on Madison Avenue. He had called ahead for an emergency appointment saying he had to have a suit fitted and ready in two hours, and he didn't give a damn how much it cost. He selected a shirt, tie, and a pair of shoes while he waited for the suit. He changed into his new costume and was in the lobby of the law office of VanZant, Parsons and Olinski by three o'clock.

"Good afternoon," Hoover said somewhat indifferently to the receptionist. "Mr. Vanderbilt to see Mr. Olinski. I have a three o'clock appointment." Hoover was immediately shown into Mr. Olinski's office.

"Mr. Vanderbilt to see you, sir," Mr. Olinski's secretary announced.

"Otis Vanderbilt, Mr. Olinski. Damn decent of you to see me on such short notice."

"Glad to, Mr. Vanderbilt. It sounds important. By the way, which part of the …ah…family are you from, if I may ask?"

"The impatient side, Mr. Olinski," Hoover said in a voice borrowed from Sister Angelica Mercy.

"Of course, right to it then. How can I help?"

"First of all, Mr. Olinski, I think this little project should take no more than an hour of your time. Here is a check for $10,000 to cover your services." Mr. Olinski mumbled something about it being overly generous but slid the check straightaway into his drawer.

"The Bronx Zoo is preparing to split up its gorilla population in advance of tearing down the ape house to make way for a larger bird exhibit and new space for its chimps and monkeys. My family has had a strong interest in the zoo for decades, as I'm sure you know, and we're delighted with the changes. Moreover, we're prepared to put some money where our mouth is, so to say. It's always been that way with our family, if you get my meaning."

"Oh, yes, I certainly do," offered Mr. Olinski.

"Good. Now, we're prepared to contribute a considerable sum of money to help the project along, and…"

"A 'considerable sum'?"

"Yes, ten million dollars, to be exact. But there's a catch—the Zoo has to agree to cancel its plan to send the gorillas one here, one there. Instead, I want them all sent back to the Congo to be released together into the wild. If the board agrees to do it, they get their ten million."

"Well, I'm certain they would love to have the money, but sending the gorillas back would cost a small fortune. They'd have to charter a plane, and…"

"You're quite right. Here's the rest of it. I will give them an additional $500,000 to cover their costs the instant they agree to the whole package. And there is one other condition. There's a fellow named Hoover Kowalski who has been taking care of the gorillas for years. They have to agree that Mr. Kowalski will be in charge of the transfer, and will accompany the gorillas to Africa."

"It's breathtaking, Mr. Vanderbilt. How do you want me to proceed?"

"Send them a letter by messenger outlining the deal exactly as I just told you. Don't make it complex, just a simple letter. When they endorse the deal you send them the $500,000. When the gorillas are safely in Africa, I will send them a check for ten million. No strings attached. Simple as that."

"I will take care of it immediately. But I notice these are cashier's checks. Your name isn't on them and you won't be able to satisfy the IRS without…"

"I don't give a rat's ass about the IRS," Hoover said standing up. "If I want a tax deduction, I'll give them some *real* money."

Hoover declined coffee and was back in his apartment by early evening. As soon as it was dark, he met with the family in the woods and told them his plan.

"Do you think it will work, Hoover?" they asked.

"We'll see. But I know how greedy they are for money."

The deal was accepted immediately, and three weeks later Hoover supervised the transfer of the gorillas to JFK, onto a 747 cargo plane, and once in the Congo, to the edge of the forest in several government trucks. There, Hoover ordered the soldiers to leave, explaining that when he opened the cages the gorillas were likely to run amok, and he didn't want anyone to get hurt. The soldiers were happy to leave, and when they returned in the morning the cages were empty and there was no sign of the gorillas or Hoover Kowalski.

THE LOST TARPON

Parsons opened the door on the wood stove with a pair of pliers, tossed in a log, and banged the door shut with his boot. He got a Coke out of the cooler and took his seat on the bench in front of the counter.

"Anybody want some?" he asked scooping a large pinch of shredded Red Man tobacco out of its pouch. No one answered so he stuffed the aromatic tangle into his mouth, using his tongue to wad it between his cheek and gum on the lower right side. The next wad would go on the left. Silence again fell over the four men gathered around the stove at the Mountain View General Store.

"Goddamned cold, I say," Parsons mused, maybe trying to stir up some conversation.

"Well…," said Russell Baynar, nodding in agreement, but no one else spoke. Old Man Morris was lost in his usual careful reading of the *County Register* newspaper. Tilson Edwards, the store's owner, was stuffing pennies into a paper roll.

Parsons tried again. "I said, it's damned cold, ain't it, Tilson?"

"Quit yappin' at me, I can't keep count."

"Ought to get you one of them automatic countin' machines like they got over to Wal-Mart."

"Don't be talkin' 'bout Wal-Mart. Sons of bitches'll be here in Mountain View 'fore you know it. An' that'd be the end of my store and everything else, 'cept maybe jobs. Think of that, Parsons. Maybe you could get you a good job and quit cuttin' pulpwood. You ain't cuttin' nothing nohow, cold as it is."

"That's what I'm saying, dang you. It's too damn cold."

145

"He's cuttin' pretty good, Tilson," Russell allowed. "Just look at that bandage on his leg. What they payin' for legs over to the mill, Parsons? You still got 'nother one."

"Shit," Parsons said spitting a jet of tobacco juice onto the hot stove. It instantly vaporized, releasing an acrid cloud of tobacco steam.

"Don't spit on my stove! How many times I got to tell you that?"

"Well, quit pissin' on my leg, then."

"Well, look at this," Old Man Morris said folding the paper over his knee. "Curley Boggs is goin' out of business. Got a big sale over to Cowers Gap on Saturday."

"I told you he wouldn't last past six months," said Russell, a tinge of triumph in his voice.

"True," said Tilson, "You did say that. But I ain't cryin'. He was taking my Cowers Gap business. I'll bet Molly don't last as long as his store, I'll tell you that."

"She'll stay through the sale," Russell said. "Then she'll go back to Charleston to her people."

"How you know that?" asked Tilson.

"A hunch is all."

"Well, all right, Russell, what you hunch on this?" Old Man Morris folded the paper again and started to read, "'State Game and Fisheries experts fear the lack of winter precipitation will result in an unusually dry spring which could force the closing of the spring turkey season.'"

"You reckon they'd really close the season down?" wondered Tilson. "I'll tell you what, if they close turkey season it's gunna hurt a lot of folks around here, starting with me. Come spring, don't nobody plant nothing no more, 'cept maybe a little garden, so I ain't selling seed and fertilizer like I used to. But I sure as shit sell a mess of licenses, shells, and lunch meat."

"Won't happen," said Russell, "Like you said, too much riding on it. If them game people shut it down, everybody'd blame the governor. Don't matter what he said, everybody'd blame him. Then he won't get reelected. Nope, turkey season's going on. Just might cut it to weekdays or something."

"You're probably right," said Parsons.

Again there was a long silence.

"Well, now, get this," said Old Man Morris. "They're fixin' on sendin' a casino bus through Mountain View every Thursday morning. Twenty-five dollars and they take you to the Lost Tarpon Casino up on the reservation."

"Yeah, but do they bring you back?" asked Parsons with a chuckle.

Old Man Morris ignored him. "And they give you ten dollars in quarters to play the slots."

"*Give* you ten dollars?" asked Tilson.

"It's what it says. Ten dollars in quarters."

"Them Indians would scalp you and snatch your quarters 'fore you got out of the parking lot. You might's well just stay home." Parsons seemed to be speaking for the group, but Old Man Morris persisted.

"'Ride in comfort to the Lost Tarpon and test your gaming skills in our ultramodern facility. You could be the next millionaire.' Damn if I couldn't use a million bucks, I'll tell you that."

"How far is it up to the reservation?" asked Parsons.

"It's about a hundred miles as the crow flies," Russell said, "But that casino bus ain't going to fly over Hanging Rock and Tullers Mountain. Take you three hours, for sure. You ain't thinking 'bout going up there, are you, Parsons?"

"Shit no, I was just wondering how far it is. Besides, I don't know nothing about gambling."

Russell laughed. "How can you say that, as many lottery tickets as you buy? And last time I looked it don't take no genius to pull the handle on a slot machine."

Old Man Morris finished reading the ad. "Looks like it might be a pretty nice three hour ride—six hours if you think both ways—'cause they got a toilet in the bus, and every seat's got a TV. They pick you up at eight in the morning in front of the Post Office and drop you back at eleven. Have you home by midnight with your million bucks. Think they give it to you in cash or you got to take a check?"

"Don't matter to me, just so's I get my money," said Tilson.

"You'll need a lot more than half a day at the slot machines to win that much money," offered Russell.

"I wouldn't fool around with them slots, Russell," said Tilson. "Ain't no big money in them things. If you want to win the big bucks you gotta play roulette or that poker you see on TV."

"He's right on that," Old Man Morris said. "You hit on that roulette wheel with ten bucks and you got at least four hundred."

"How you know that?" asked Parsons. "You ever been to a casino?"

"Sure have. I was stationed in L.A. during the Korean War and we used to slide over to Vegas after we was paid. I played roulette, twenty-one, craps, all that stuff."

"And how much did you win?" asked Russell.

"Not much, but we was usually so drunk we couldn't keep nothing straight. They give you free booze, you know."

Parsons was suddenly more interested. "They do that up at Lost Tarpon? Free booze and a roll of quarters? Where do I get a ticket?"

"They won't give free drinks to just anybody, Parsons. You gotta be a high roller like we was. You gotta show some green to get the drinks. You show up with a roll of quarters and you'll be lucky to get a Dr. Pepper."

"You're right. I'd just lose my quarters and have to sit on the damn bus all day waiting to go home. Screw it. I'll stick with cuttin' pulp wood. Weather's gotta break soon anyway."

"Well, now hold on just a minute here," said Old Man Morris. "Maybe there is a way to do this. I mean, if we was to go there with an edge, you know, a secret weapon kind of thing. Then maybe we *could* win some serious money."

"You fixin' on robbin' the place, Old Man?" asked Tilson.

"Maybe, but not with no gun."

"No gun," said Parsons. "I'm glad to hear that. So what's your secret weapon?"

"Well, all right," Old Man Morris said leaning forward and lowering his voice even though there wasn't anyone else in the store. "We take Russell."

"Me? What do mean, 'we take Russell'?"

"It's simple. You're the best guesser we ever knowed, and with you guessin', we'd know just what to play."

"That's the dumbest idea I ever heard," said Parsons. "I'll give you that Russell is the best guesser I ever seen, but if he was that good why don't he just save us a trip and buy four lottery tickets?"

Russell was silent, but Tilson took up for him. "He don't buy lottery tickets 'cause he don't believe in the lottery. Russell ain't one to abuse his gift, know what I mean?"

"Ain't so," asserted Parsons. "I seen Russell buy a chance at the horse pull last summer. And he won it, too, come to think of it."

Russell tipped his chair back against the soft drink cooler, an amused smile on his face.

"He done that because it was for charity, ain't that right, Russell?" asked Tilson. Russell was silent.

"All right, what about the time he took two hundred dollars off that gypsy down at the fair. Remember that? Guy damn near hit Russell when he guessed the right card. Remember? That was gambling. Weren't no charity in it." Parsons rested his case.

"Weren't nothing of the sort," retorted Tilson. "He done that 'cause the bastard was cheatin' everybody, and Russell wanted to screw around with him, show him up. That's what it was."

The group turned to Russell. Tilson was the spokesman. "What about it, Russell? You *are* the best guesser in these parts. Would you go with us? I mean it's not all about money, it'd be about havin' some fun. It'd be good if all we was to do was win enough for a good dinner. I hear they got good food up there."

"I don't know. Sounds like you got your heart set on winning some real money, and I ain't likely to be part of that."

"Not at all, Russell. We understand how you feel about that—really—but it'd just be fun to go. And if we don't win nothing, who cares? We'd be out fifteen bucks. Hell, we'll even buy your ticket."

The debate went on for a while, but in the end Russell gave in and the group decided to go to the Lost Tarpon. Two weeks later, on a cold and drizzly Thursday morning the four men gathered in front of the Post Office just before 8:00 a.m. The casino bus pulled in ten minutes later, and they climbed on. Let the fun begin.

"Where is everybody?" Old Man Morris asked the driver as he handed over his twenty-five dollars. Indeed, the bus was empty.

"Looks like you fellows are the only customers today. Nobody wants to go out in this kind of weather, and the radio's callin' for sleet later on. Good day to stay home, if you ask me," he said closing the door.

Most of the TVs weren't working, so the four gamblers had to spread out to find the few that still had reception. Parsons went all the way to the back, settled in, and took a tug on the pint of Sleepy Hollow bourbon he brought along to ward off the cold.

The ride up through the mountains to the reservation took almost four hours. By the time the bus pulled up in front of the Lost Tarpon, Parsons was crocked and passed out. It took a while to get him going, but the group finally walked into the vast and nearly empty lobby. Through the open double doors beyond the restaurant they could see what appeared to be a thousand slot machines, and beyond them, dozens of gaming tables.

"Where the hell is everybody?" Tilson asked the attendant who took his bus ticket and returned a roll of quarters.

"Weather. Folks are happy to bet their money, but they don't like to gamble on the weather. Happens a lot in the winter."

"Look at the good side," said Old Man Morris. "We got the whole damn place to ourselves. We don't have to hurry, and we can pick a table that's got the right feelin'. Ain't that so, Russell?"

"I'm hungry," said Russell, ignoring the reference to his best-guesser status. He veered off course into the restaurant without waiting for a response. The others had no choice but to follow. Parsons grumbled and said he had to go to the restroom.

"Must have somethin' left in that bottle," observed Tilson. "He really ought to save some for the ride home, don't you reckon?"

"Let him finish it," advised Old Man Morris. "Maybe he'll pass out again and we can concentrate better."

The cafeteria only offered meat loaf or spaghetti, but the price was right—$3.00 for all you could eat—and just shy of one o'clock, the group was ready to do some serious gambling. Well, three of the four were ready. That would be a better way to put it.

There were only a few dozen customers scattered around the vast gaming room. Twenty or so dealers stood behind empty tables looking bored. A few were reading. One twenty-one dealer was playing solitaire.

"I like that one," said Russell, pointing to the solitaire player. "Looks like he's losing, we'll start there."

Old Man Morris agreed and cautioned Russell that he would make the plays until he got stuck. "They don't take kindly to it when someone's coachin', so I'll make the plays, but if I get stuck, I'll give you the code and you can poke me in the back so's the dealer don't see it. One poke is stay, and two is take another card. Three is double up. Got it?"

"Yeah, got it. But what's the code?"

"I'll ask Parsons what he'd do. So if I ask Parsons, you poke, got it?"

"Got it. That'll fool the dealer for sure."

The group approached the table, the dealer gathered up his cards and flashed a friendly smile.

"Good afternoon, gentlemen. Are you ready to warm your pockets with some money on this cold and gloomy day?"

"Could be," Old Man Morris said cautiously, doing his best to look like this was something he did every day. The men took their seats at the table. "Now give me your quarters," he said to the others as he dropped his own roll on the table. Tilson added his, but Parsons seemed immobilized. He poked Parsons in the side. "Put up you quarters, dang you." Parsons still didn't seem to hear the instructions.

"Is he all right?" asked the dealer.

"Sure is. Just a touch of the flu, is all." Tilson rummaged through Parson's pockets, found the roll and banged it on the table triumphantly. "Where's yours, Russell?"

"I'll hold it in reserve, just in case we need it."

"Good idea," Old Man Morris said, then added *sotto voce*, "Always good to have an ace in the hole, so to speak."

It was clear that Old Man Morris was in charge so the dealer stacked thirty one-dollar chips in front of him. "Ready, sir?"

"Yep, but maybe you should go over the rules—for my friends, of course—'fore we get rollin', so's they know what we're doin'."

"All right," the dealer said. Then, looking at Parsons, he added, "Is he going to pass out or get sick or something?" At that point the only thing that seemed to be holding Parsons upright was the edge of the table.

"He's fine," said Tilson, impatient to start the game. "He's concentratin'. Does his best when he's quiet like that."

The dealer was apprehensive, but explained the rules and dealt the first hand to Old Man Morris.

The dealer's up card was a ten, Old Man Morris had a seven in the hole and a five showing. "Shit," he said under his breath. "Gotta go for that. Hit me." He drew a two.

"What you think, Parsons?" he asked. Russell poked him twice. Old Man Morris turned to Parsons. "You sure about that?" Russell again poked him twice.

"Do you want another card, sir?"

"Well, yes," he said firmly. He drew a three. "Okay, I'll stick."

The dealer turned over his hole card. It was an eight. He scooped up Old Man Morris' dollar.

The next hand was not much better. The dealer showed an ace while the consortium's hopes rode on two fours. Old Man Morris drew an eight, stayed, and watched in dismay as the dealer turned a nine. Two dollars down. And so it went, hand after hand with no break. Well into their second roll of quarters, the dealer showed a queen and Old Man Morris had a ten in the hole, and eight on the table. Before he could say "I'll stay," Russell poked him twice in the back, paused and poked him three times.

"What!?" Old Man Morris said turning to Russell. Catching himself he said, "Did you say something, Russell? I thought you said something?"

"I said you ought to double up and get another card, is what I said."

"Now that's just plum crazy, Russell."

"Sir, do want another card or not?"

"Well, okay, yeah, another card and I'm doublin' up." Then he added under his breath, "Some guesser he is. We'll be outa here in another ten minutes."

The group's card was a three. "Twenty-One!" yelped Tilson. "Goddamn!"

The dealer turned a jack and paid back four dollars. At that point things seemed to turn around, and with a steady series of back prods and many doubles, in less than twenty minutes the group was ahead by sixty dollars. They swapped their dollar chips for two-dollar chips, and after an hour of seesawing back and forth, they were ahead by $240. At that point they started to play five dollar chips, and by four o'clock they had amassed $840. Parsons woke up somewhere between five and six hundred dollars, and was fully animated by the group's growing fortune. It was time for a strategy session so they scooped up their winnings and retreated to the bar for a beer and an enormous plate of nachos.

Russell excused himself to go to the man's room while the others worked on the next step.

"At the rate we're going we won't have more than a couple a thousand by the time the bus leaves," said Tilson. "So we gotta speed things up, change our strategy, if you get my meaning. I say it's time to hit the roulette wheel. Didn't you say you could really roll up fast on that thing, Old Man?"

"Sure enough, but you can wipe out damn fast, too."

"Don't matter a bit," said Parsons starting on his third beer. "Don't forget—we got Russell." He took a long pull on his bottle of Iron City. "And he's hot!" he added in a near whisper.

When Russell returned, the group told him about the New Plan. "I got a better idea, boys."

"What's that, Russell," Tilson asked eagerly. "You going to play craps? That's it! Craps, ain't it, Russell. Dang!"

"Nope, ain't craps. It's leaving. Time to go. Weather is turnin' real sour, and the driver says we got to be out of here in half an hour—tops."

"Well, he can kiss my ass," declared Parsons wobbling to his feet. "We're just getting' goin', and we ain't leavin' till we got our money."

"Shut up, Parsons," said Tilson. "Look, Russell, we can't go yet. You're hot and we're right on the edge of winning a lot of money. Please, Russell, be reasonable. We didn't come all this way to go home with no two hundred each." Old Man Morris agreed with Tilson's soft approach, and added, "Just a little while on the roulette wheel, Russell. Then we go, okay?"

"Look boys, I told you at the start we come up here to have us a little fun, and if we was lucky, well, then we might go home with a good story and a few dollars. But I'm telling you, I ain't doing this for the money. I told you that. Now, we had our fun, we got our money, the bus is ready, and it's time to go. Simple as that, time to hit the road."

They tried to bend Russell around, wasting fifteen of their precious minutes. Finally Russell broke.

"Okay, all the money. One spin. Then we go, no matter what. But I'm changing the rules, 'cause I told you I wouldn't do no guessin' for anything but the fun of it. And I'm stickin' to that, so *you'll* have to decide which number to bet. I'll just help you with the odds."

"Shit, Russell," Old Man Morris said smacking his hand on the table, "odds of us guessin' it is like thirty-somethin' to one. With you guessin', odds go to fifty-fifty. The only way you get fifty-fifty is bet red or black and that just doubles your money. We need to hit one number to put us in the big money. And we're wastin' time, in case you ain't noticed. "

"So you're okay with fifty-fifty on hittin' one number, right?"

They all agreed, fifty-fifty is fine odds for hitting one number, especially when the payout is thirty-six to one. "But how we goin' do that with us guessin'?" asked Tilson.

"Come on, I'll show you." Russell picked up two Lost Tarpon matchbooks, and led the group to the roulette table. The dealer brightened to see he had customers, though he was a bit leery of Parsons. Maybe it was the fact he only seemed to be using one eye, or the way he leaned over the table, like he might fall over. Hard to say, but he looked like trouble.

Russell studied the wheel, hand on his chin. Russell usually rested his chin in his hand when he was doing his toughest guessing. The others watched Russell in silence. Tilson and Old Man Morris wedged Parsons between them to keep him upright. They didn't much care if he fell on the table, but they sure enough didn't want him to distract Russell while he was working. After all, this one was for the Big Money.

Russell scribbled something on the inside cover of both matchbooks, closed the flap, and put them on the table.

"Okay, boys, here's how it works. You can take the money we got, get on the bus and leave right now. Or you can pick one of these two match books. I've wrote a number inside each one. You got to pick one of 'em. One's got my best guess, and the other is just any ol' number. You pick."

"Oh, shit, Russell, that ain't fair. How we gunna know which…"

"You're wastin' time, Tilson. It's Pic or Git, that's the game."

Tilson and Old Man Morris argued about which one to pick—there was no discussion of leaving.

"I like this one," said Parsons, reaching for the matchbook on the left.

"Can't have no drunk pickin' our bet," said Tilson. "What do you think, Old Man? One on the right?"

"Yep, one on the right."

"Okay, then," Russell said, picking up the rejected matchbook. "I'll see you on the bus."

Russell settled into a seat with a functioning TV, the driver warmed the engine, and they waited for the others to return.

It didn't take long. With Tilson pushing and the driver pulling, they managed to get Parsons onto the bus and into a front seat. It was clear from the look on their faces that things hadn't gone well at the roulette table. With everyone seated, the driver closed the door and the bus started to move. No one said a word.

The weather was rapidly deteriorating. Rain had turned to light snow, then back to rain, and as the bus cleared the parking lot, sleet started pelting the roof.

"Don't look good, I'll tell you that," the driver said loudly over his shoulder. "We'll be lucky to get back before 1:00 a.m."

More silence. Finally, Old Man Morris got up and walked back to where Russell was sitting. "Lost it all, right, Old Man?"

"Yep. Every goddamn cent. I think I got eight dollars left."

Russell answered with his usual, "Well…"

"Let me see that other matchbook, Russell. I just gotta know."

Russell handed him the matchbook. Old Man Morris took a deep breath and opened the book.

"Son of bitch! Four! Son of a bitch!"

He returned to his seat, mumbled something to Tilson and Parsons followed by a son-of-a-bitch chorus—then silence. They rode along for the better part of two hours, and as they approached the top of Tullers Mountain, Russell walked up to the driver.

"There's an exit in about two miles, just before you head down the other side of the mountain. Pull off and let me out at the fillin' station."

"Let you out? Are you crazy? That ain't a regular stop. If you want to get out you gotta wait 'til we get to Uniontown. That's twenty-two miles."

"I said, pull off and let me out. If you don't, I'm gunna open that damn door and jump."

"Man, you are one crazy son of a bitch. Fact is, you're all crazy. I wish to hell I never met any of you bastards."

"Don't matter how crazy we are. Just let me out."

"What's goin' on?" demanded Old Man Morris as the bus slid up the exit and stopped in front of the Mountain Top convenience store.

"I'm getting' off is what's going on. And I advise the rest of you to do the same. I just don't like the weather."

"Well, I don't like it, neither," said Tilson. "But I damn sure want to get my sorry ass home tonight. Just how you fixin' on getting home from here, anyway?"

"Don't know. Don't care. I just ain't going down that damn mountain in this tin can."

"I ain't never had an accident since I been runnin' this bus," the driver said defiantly. "You're safer in here than in a damn car. And look at all them cars drivin' along out there. They sure as shit ain't stoppin'."

"If the bus was full, I'd stay. You just don't have the weight. But I ain't gunna argue with you." Russell opened the door himself and stepped off. The door closed and the bus started out of the parking lot toward the highway. Then it stopped. The door opened and the other three got off. Parsons was cussing a blue streak, and Old Man Morris and Tilson were literally dragging him across the icy parking lot toward the store.

Inside, a lot of the customers were crowded around a small television listening to the news. It was all about the weather. Russell sat down at one of the several tables in what was grandly called the Dining Area. Folks in heavy parkas and lined overalls were eating microwave pizza, burrito sandwiches, and chicken nuggets. Russell's companions took seats at an adjacent table, but no one spoke to Russell.

"Just what in the hell reason you got to drag me off that bus?" demanded Parsons. "I was sound asleep, warm, and dreaming of getting' home, and you up and run me in here. Jesus H. Christ! What was I thinkin' when I set off with you crazy bastards!"

"You was thinkin' like we was," answered Old Man Morris. "You thought we'd make some money, have some fun, and git home on time. And we damn near done it, too. We come within a damn inch of winning it all." He and the others looked over at Russell at the mention of just how close they were. Russell didn't seem to notice. He was reading a used truck catalog.

"And another thing," said Parsons. "Just what do you have in mind for food? That ain't even countin' how we get home." He looked around at the other diners. "Maybe I got an idea about the food part." Raising his voice he said, "We send Russell out to root around the dumpster for Burrito scraps. He'll know just which one to go divin' in. Won't take a good guesser like him no time at all to smell out a pile of scraps. Why, we'll be eatin' like kings. Maybe he'll find me a beer and some bus tickets while he's in there."

Russell didn't take notice.

"Oh, shut up, Parsons," Tilson said. "I'm tired of your complain'. If you hadn't opened your stupid mouth at the roulette table we'd be riding home in a limousine. It ain't all Russell's fault. We could of quit."

The group lapsed back into silence. Outside the wind picked up, driving the sleet into the windows. Two police cars, blue lights flashing, sirens wailing, sped by on the highway.

"You got any money, Tilson?" Old Man Morris asked.

"Two dollars is all."

"How 'bout you, Parsons?"

"I ain't got shit. But I'm damn hungry. I could eat the ass out of a bear. How about you, Old Man. You got any left?"

"I got eight," he said counting a fist-full of crumpled ones. "How much is a pizza?"

"Twelve dollars with toppings," said Russell without lifting his head from the truck catalog.

"Who asked you?" said Parsons.

"Just tryin' to help is all."

"You done enough helpin' for one day, right boys?"

"Just shut your goddamned mouth, Parsons," Old Man Morris said. "It weren't his fault."

Two more police cars and a fire truck went by.

"What the hell is going on out there?" Tilson asked no one in particular. A man passing the table said, "Truck jack-knifed on Tullers. Got all the traffic backed up. It's on the scanner." Several of the customers crowded around the counter listening to the police and rescue traffic. Old Man Morris and Tilson joined the group. Parsons slumped over the table, put his head on his arm, and appeared to be asleep.

"Truck went clean over the embankment," someone close to the scanner said. "Driver's hurt, and they're havin' to cut him out. Hold on, now. Shit! Weren't no truck at all. It was the casino bus." Tilson and Old Man Morris stared at each other for a long minute, then went back to their table.

"Weren't no truck, Russell," said Tilson. "It was the bus." He paused. "But I suppose maybe you knew that?"

"I had an inklin'," said Russell.

156

A few silent minutes passed. Parsons raised up, clearly aware of the news. Finally, Old Man Morris said, "Want to join us over here, Russell? We got a little money. Maybe we could get us some crackers and soda."

Russell moved over, reached in his pocket, and put his roll of quarters on the table. "Always good to have a reserve, know what I mean?"

"Damn!" exclaimed Tilson with a chuckle. It was the first time any of them had laughed in several hours. "Looks like we get the Special with pepperoni and Mountain Dew all around!"

Tilson picked up their order and put it in the center of the table. "Scanner says they got the driver out. Busted his arm, cut him some, but he's okay."

"That's good," said Russell. "Now, let's eat."

About half way through his second slice, Parsons picked off a disc of pepperoni, chewed it slowly, and said, "That there is the best damn pizza I ever ate in my whole life!"

THE WISDOM OF CAPTAIN YU

"It's hopeless, Morris," Emily said as she skillfully guided the little paint brush across her toenail. "Therapy for you is a waste of good money. It would be easier to show an orangutan how to take out an appendix than teach you what being a responsive husband is all about." She spoke with resigned disappointment, her tone flat and dismissive. It was her most annoying voice, one she learned note-for-note from her mother, Rachael Edelman, though she would never admit it. Mrs. Edelman certainly had a wider range, and was even faster off the mark at the first hint of male assertiveness. At her best, she could wilt a cactus with two or three words and a slight wrinkling of her upper lip.

It was probably the reason Mr. Edelman jumped off the upper deck of a White Plains mall parking garage. But why he was wearing a French maid's outfit was a complete mystery. He had a gardenia behind his left ear, and his bra was stuffed with two bags of Raisinets. It was a terrible embarrassment for the family, and after a small private funeral, he was buried (in a suit), and no one spoke of him again.

Captain Yu understood it right away, though, and in one short, garbled sentence made sense of the whole thing. It was one of many insights Morris gained from Captain Yu before he decided to kill him.

"Change isn't instant, you know, Emily. It's like making a good wine—it takes time. You don't sort out your issues overnight."

"Morris, good wine starts with decent grapes. You're not making wine, you're making vinegar."

It was damn lucky Dr. Gold agreed to a temporary shift away from analysis to Problem Focused Therapy. They had been doing some important work on Morris' early fantasies about pubic hair. But that would have to wait; the conflict with Emily was getting out of control.

"There's no pleasing her, Dr. Gold, and God knows I've tried. I thought four crowns and six or seven fillings a day would make her happy. That's a new SUV every two years, a golf membership at Rochelle, and enough left over for her to take her mother to Italy for two weeks every fall.

"But that wasn't good enough. Now I'm averaging *six* crowns a day—that's where the money is, if you want to know the truth. Do you know how exhausting six crowns a day is? Your fingers cramp, your vision starts playing tricks on you, and you worry one of them will bite you. I should have been a gynecologist."

"You talk about your anger, Morris, but you're still holding it at mind's length."

"That's what you said in your book. Incidentally, I still think you could autograph it without compromising our transference relationship. I did buy the goddamn thing, you know."

"One battle at a time, Morris. Remember—you won't solve the problem as long as you think your mind is a lock that needs to be opened. When you can become the key, and let your feelings explode in the lock, *then* you'll be in control."

"I'm just not comfortable with that image, Doctor Gold."

"Reread Chapter Six, Morris. Ah! I see our time is up. See you Thursday."

On the way home Morris decided it was time to stick his angry key in the lock. No rehearsal this time. Right to the point—Emily, something has to change. I'm doing my part. What are you going to do to solve our problem?

"You know, Morris, I can always tell when you've just seen Doctor Gold. You come charging through the door dripping with self-pity, ready to assault me with your inadequacy and project your misery onto me. You don't know how to use therapy any more than you know what my real needs are.

"I'm sick of waiting for you to get past your infantile need for constant external validation, Morris. You need an exoskeleton, and I need a divorce."

"That's in Chapter Four of *Couch Coach!* Have you been reading Doctor Gold's book?"

"Never mind Doctor Gold. Here, read this and sign in two places on the last page." Emily handed her husband a thick sheaf of legal-length papers.

"It's a separation agreement, Morris. I told you I've had enough. And sign this, too. It's your resignation from the club."

"What?" Morris said in a near whisper. "Separation! What about Rebecca? And why do I have to resign from the club? What the hell do you think you're doing? I have something to say about this, too, you know."

"Cut the crap, Morris, sign the damn thing. Right now Rebecca is in her dorm room three hundred miles from here *shtupping* her idiot boyfriend. She could care less what we do. And as far as the club is concerned, it would be ridiculous for both of us to stay members."

They were interrupted by the movers bringing Morris' bureau down the stairs. Emily had thoughtfully packed his clothing and boxed his dental books.

"I put the stuff from your desk and our safety deposit box in a garbage bag on the back seat of the Honda. I signed the title and put it in the glove compartment along with your precious *Couch Coach!*

"Time to be off, Morris. Oh, and don't forget, I expect those papers back in the next week. Signed."

Morris stood mute in the driveway, papers in hand, as the movers closed the door on the van.

"Yo! Tooth Man—where you want us to take this shit?"

Without answering, Morris walked over to the Honda, spread the documents on the hood, and signed next to each red sticky arrow. Leaving the papers on the hood, he walked to the driver's door, his pace quickening. He got in, started the motor and backed down the driveway.

"Hey! Where you want this stuff to go?" shouted the mover.

Morris backed into the street, stopped, and buzzed down his window.

"Take it to Italy," he said loudly, and drove away, scattering the legal papers down Happy Hollow Lane.

Morris stopped at an ATM, but the screen told him their joint account had been closed. The machine kept the card and promised severe penalties if he ever tried to use the account again. He drove to his office and emptied the petty cash box—$320.00.

It was getting dark when he got to the club. He drove across the fairway to the seventh green, parked next to the flag, got out, and urinated in the cup. By midnight he was in Philadelphia, and by noon the next day he was approaching St. Louis. He checked into a motel, caught the second game of a Cardinals double header, and had a rack of ribs at Black Charlie's.

He was on the road again early the next morning, but by mid-Kansas he was running out of money. He left the interstate at Elgin and found a used car lot. Rudy told him times were slow and the best he could do for the Honda was six grand. Morris accepted, but the deal fell through; unfortunately, Emily had signed the title as Buyer, not Seller.

"You'll have to go to your DMV," Rudy advised.

"Not necessary," said Morris. He drove to a pawnshop and swapped his Rolex Oyster for $250. Times were slow there, too, the owner apologized, but it didn't matter a bit to Morris. He had a plan.

From the pawnshop he drove across the street into McDonalds and parked by a dumpster. He threw away everything except his passport, some clothing, and the book.

The car was almost out of gas and was starting to sputter. Morris locked the door and threw the key in the dumpster.

He walked to the Amoco station where the Greyhound stopped and waited six hours for the bus to San Diego. He settled into a seat at the back of the bus and fell asleep. He could sleep easily now; the plan was taking shape.

As the bus approached San Diego, Morris went into the bathroom, locked the door, and carefully lowered his pants just enough to sit down, but not enough to blotter up anything from the slippery wet floor. The toilet was directly over the engine causing it and the water in the bowl to shake, occasionally splashing his nether parts. The combination of exhaust fumes and *sufflance* from the backed-up toilet was overpowering.

But Morris didn't seem to notice. He opened *Couch Coach!* to the title page, uncorked his Waterman Paris, and wrote in bold script: **You are where you sit.** He signed it **Best Wishes, Ira Gold, MD, FAPA,** put the book on the small shelf under the sink then returned to his seat

Once in San Diego he made his way to the docks and inquired about working on a westbound freighter. He quickly found out that members of the Merchant Marine Union filled all the jobs. But Morris had a plan, and that gave him momentum. He kept asking, but the story was always the same: no union, no experience, no job.

Unless, of course, he wanted to sail with Captain Yu. It was quite a joke on the docks, but Morris felt he was following an invisible but utterly certain trail, and he boldly climbed up the rusty ladder of the MoJoHa.

Standing on the deck smoking a Camel under the faded NO SMOKING sign, an Asian man wearing khaki pants and shirt with shoulder epaulets eyed Morris briefly and said, "Go away. No job for you."

Ignoring the rebuff, Morris asked, "I would like to see Captain Yu. I'm told he is hiring."

"I am Captain Yu. And, ah, yes I hire. But not you. Go away."

"Why not me? I can work, I don't much care about wages, and I love the sea. My name is Morris, by the way."

"Well, Misser Morris, I hire man who chase dream of sea, not man running from nightmare."

"How do you know that?" asked Morris.

"You carry belongings in plastic bag, not shave, and smell bad. Yet your fingernails trim and clean. You have fine clothing, but many wrinkle speak of desperate flight. You are professional man on run. Trouble, Misser Morris, trouble for Captain Yu."

"Well, it's true, I did leave a 'situation' rather quickly, but I assure you I am not a criminal. I am simply seeking an alternative way to find peace."

"Man who look for peace never find it. Peace find you when your mind is prepared to receive it."

"That makes sense, Captain Yu. Perhaps I will become more receptive at sea. And either way, I'll do whatever you ask."

"Promise made in haste seldom last. Can you paint?"

"Yes, actually, I can."

"Okay, Misser Morris. I try you. If you fail, I put you off at first stop. No pay."

So Morris went to work chipping, scraping, scaling, and sanding the rusted walls and decks of the MoJoHa. It was an utterly impossible task, of course, because the forces of oxidation made a fool of anyone who tried to move faster than rust. He pointed that out to Captain Yu.

"You think in terms of race, who going to win. Rust ahead, rust behind. But you ignore beauty of paint at your fingertips, Misser Morris. You not able to see that at all."

So Morris went back to painting. It was tough on his hands, of course, and gloves weren't part of the scheme, but Morris didn't seem to notice. The plan was taking shape and the job gave him time to think. But Captain Yu was right—what he needed was right in front of him, not part of the failed past or anxious future. No, right there. It made him feel immensely more relaxed.

After a week of waiting, the MoJoHa finally loaded enough cargo and limped out of the harbor as the morning fog lifted. The invisible sun cast long shadows on the soldier's and sailor's graves on the point below the lighthouse. Morris watched from the stern, his mind clearing in the chilly ocean breeze.

"Back to work, Misser Morris!" Captain Yu shouted from above.

That night the crew was allowed to dine with the Captain, a tradition to bring luck to the voyage. There was some muttering about an apparent list to starboard, but Captain Yu dismissed it as cargo imbalance.

"Tell me, Misser Morris, you find your first day on ocean bring you peace?"

"Yes," said Morris, mindful of the plan crystallizing in his brain. *Just a few more days and the MoJoHa will carry me—and the rest of you, sorry about that—to a better place. Just a few more details to work out, then freedom.*

"Very fast work, Misser Morris. Tell me, you ever know anyone who find peace so fast?"

"Maybe. My father-in-law. He committed suicide." Morris told the story, minus the reference to Raisinets.

"Ah! I think you right, but as usual you wrong. You think he find peace by being dead. Not so, Misser Morris. He find peace by say everything he ever not able to say before in one final moment so powerful his mind explode with joy. He never know he die, Misser Morris, so his last joyous thought remain with him forever. Very wise, lucky, and honorable man."

"Thank you, Captain Yu. That fills in a blank for me. By the way, where did you learn so much? You didn't get it watching Charlie Chan movies."

"I am descendant of Yu the Great of the court of the Emperor Shun, China's first magician. Not related to Sidney Toler."

That night Morris slipped down to the boiler room. The chief engineer was passed out on a pile of oil rags, an empty bottle of *oomie* wine clattered back and forth on the metal floor. Below, in the bilge, Morris searched for the seacocks, though he had no idea what one might look like. It amused him to imagine tiny sea horses swimming about sporting huge erections.

What did one sea horse say to the other? Go fuck yourself.

What he did find was water, a lot of it sloshing around as the vessel pitched and rolled. In a few minutes Morris was soaked, but it didn't trouble him a bit. Finally, he found what he assumed to be a seacock—a large valve welded to the hull. It was entirely covered with a thick coating of rust, and in spite of his best effort, Morris couldn't crack the valve.

He returned to the boiler room the next night with a large wrench, determined to make short work of the rusted valve. If the engineer tried to stop him it would be at his peril.

But the engineer was nowhere in sight and Morris made straight for the bilge. Unfortunately, the water level had risen and the seacock was only visible when the vessel rolled to port. He struggled briefly with the valve, but lost the wrench and returned to his cabin soaked with greasy bilge water. Time to think this over, he reasoned.

As usual, you're fighting it, he thought. What is it that Captain Yu always says? Strongest opponent man ever face is self. Look at your fingertips—the forces of Nature are with the plan. Relax, let it happen.

The next morning his plate slid off the table, and by midafternoon it was clear even to Captain Yu that the MoJoHa was going down.

The ship's one functioning lifeboat was floated as the starboard rail went under. Captain Yu stood calmly holding a cleat with one hand, a Camel in the other as the crew clambered aboard.

"You not join us, Misser Morris." It was a statement, not a question.

"That's right, Captain Yu. I think I'll just stay here and enjoy the sunset. You don't seem surprised, by the way."

"No, Misser Morris, I always know you be trouble for Captain Yu."

"I'm sorry, Captain Yu."

"Not be sorry, Misser Morris. You not only one who seek peace on ocean."

Captain Yu stepped aboard the lifeboat, lit a fresh Camel, and ordered the crew to row.

Morris made his way to the bridge singing:

> My bonnie has tuberculosis;
> My bonnie has only one lung.
> My bonnie can cough up raw oysters,
> And roll them around on her tongue.

By sunset, only the MoJoHa's bridge was above water. The ship, having filled completely with water, had leveled itself for the first time since the voyage began. Morris sat in the Captain's chair and continued to sing.

> The most chivalrous fish in the ocean,
> To ladies forbearing and mild,
> Though his record be dark,
> It's the man-eating shark,
> Who would eat neither woman nor child.

By midnight the bridge was awash, Morris was tired, happy, and out of tunes. He fell asleep in the chair.

When he awoke, the sun was up, but the MoJoHa was still on the surface. At first, Morris was upset, but then he realized it was all part of the scheme. What's the rush? Why ruin a perfectly lovely voyage?

But the voyage became less lovely over the next few days as the MoJoHa refused to go down, the drinking water ran out, and Morris' euphoria dissipated in his emerging dehydration delirium. Then he passed out.

The next sensation he felt was a needle being maneuvered into a collapsed vein in his arm.

"Rough time, eh, partner?"

"Who the hell are you?"

"Harvey Cathcart, ship's surgeon on the Sunset Lines luxury liner *Dancing Mermaid*." Dr. C (as the passengers knew him) recounted the rescue.

"You're a damn sight luckier than the poor bastards in the lifeboat, my friend. Found it upside down a day before we found you. Like the old proverb says—good luck is usually better than good planning."

Oh, shit, Morris thought, realizing that not only had peace escaped him one more time, but he was in the clutches of another damn philosopher.

The Captain came by to see how he was doing. The passengers had enjoyed the drama, but the Captain was obviously quite cross over the schedule delay. He told Morris he would be confined to the dispensary until he could be put ashore at the next stop.

Over endless games of gin rummy interrupted occasionally to dispense some Dramamine, Dr. Cathcart described the *Dancing Mermaid*. Four thousand passengers were busy taking calligraphy classes, gambling in the casino, drinking, or attending the big seminar. Seems some famous mind maven was teaching an adoring throng of worshipers how to live longer, better, happier lives.

"Who's the guru?" Morris asked picking up a discarded queen.

"Some guy named Doctor Gold. In fact, he's due in here in a minute. Called and said he had to see me right away." Morris froze, holding the queen in midair.

The nurse came in to announce Dr. Gold was on his way in.

"Shit," said Dr. Cathcart. "Stay here a minute and keep quiet. I'll get rid of him and we'll see what's so great about that queen." He pulled the curtain around Morris' bed and walked toward the door just as Dr. Gold rushed in.

"Hello, Doctor Gold, it's very nice to…"

"Yeah, sure. Look, Doctor Cathcart, I only have a minute. Gotta get back to the seminar. This is just between us physicians, right?"

"Of course, Doctor Gold. What is it?"

"It's a little embarrassing," he said lowering his voice, "But my fiancée and I are, well, I'm having a little trouble with my, er, sex thing. You know, my, er…"

"Erection?" said Dr.Cathcart.

"Yes," Dr. Gold answered, wincing. "She suggested you might have some Viagra. Just temporary, of course; you know, the stress of being on stage all the time."

"No problem, I understand." Dr. Cathcart dumped a dozen blue pills in an envelope. Dr. Gold thanked him and darted out the door.

Morris was still holding the queen when Dr. Cathcart pulled back the screen.

"Well, so much for the great one, eh, Morris? You gunna play that card or what?"

It took a while for Morris to recover. When he did, he asked Dr. Cathcart if he might go out and mingle with the passengers for just a little while. Cabin fever.

Harvey didn't like the idea; after all, the Captain had given orders. But he finally relented, provided Morris would take the blame if he got caught. He gave Morris a hall valet's suit and made him promise to go out during dinner when the Captain would be occupied entertaining that night's lucky passengers at his table.

Morris scanned the crowd from the pantry door. Then Dr. Gold and his fiancée walked into the dining room. People clapped, and he waved to his adoring fans. As they walked by the pantry he heard a familiar voice.

"Christ, Ira, you'd think you were a frigging king. I'm getting sick of this shit," said Emily.

Morris was back in the infirmary on time.

"See any mermaids, Morris?"

"Nope, couple of kippered herrings, but no mermaids."

"Well, try again tomorrow night. It's the costume ball, and everyone gets really dressed up for that."

"I can't wait." Another plan was forming. Tomorrow is the seventeenth, Emily's birthday. Perfect. He asked Dr. C if he would indulge him one more time. He was having a terrible craving for Raisinets, would he mind going to the gift shop and getting him six or so bags?

Then he set to work on the piñata using plaster and gauze from the infirmary's cast room. It was dry by morning, and he used various magic markers to paint it. By afternoon it was done—the figure of a bare-busted French maid with purple breasts topped with brick-red nipples wearing a gauze apron which hardly concealed the black suture thread tangle of pubic hair. He poured the Raisinets through a hole in the back.

That night, while everyone—including Dr. C, dressed as a satyr—was at the costume dance, Morris put on his valet's suit, and with the piñata in a bag, made his way to the upper deck.

"Who are you?" asked the hall maid.

"They took me off tables and said I should come up and help you with turn-downs."

The maid was pleased. "I've unlocked the doors, you start at this end and I'll start at the other. We'll be done in time to watch the costume promenade!"

Morris entered the Gold suite, closed the door and took the piñata out of its bag. Standing on a chair, he tied it to the ceiling light, and using a probe he had borrowed from Dr. C's surgery, made a hole about where the maid's anus should be. Raisinets droozled out forming a small brown pile on the floor. He taped a HAPPY BIRTHDAY EMILY sign on the maid's foot, admired his work briefly, and closed the door. He finished the other turn-downs and returned to the infirmary to wait.

About 2:00 a.m. Dr. C burst into the dispensary, still wearing his satyr's costume.

"What's wrong, Harvey?" asked Morris in a sleepy voice.

"What I hate the most is going on, Morris. A goddamn psychiatric crisis, and you won't believe who it is. The great Doctor Gold's girlfriend, that's who. She's gone nuts, screaming like a banshee and ripping up their stateroom."

"What set her off, Harvey?"

"Who freaking knows? Where the hell is that Thorazine?"

"Maybe it was too much Viagra. What do you think?"

Dr. C finally found the syringes and drugs he needed and headed for the door.

"Might be a good idea to take along some restraints if you have them, Harvey."

Morris went back to bed and slept like a lamb. The next day a rescue helicopter from a passing military ship headed for Hawaii landed on the *Dancing Mermaid*. Dr. C and Morris watched from the crew's deck as

Emily, firmly tied to a stretcher, was loaded on board. In spite of heavy sedation she continued to struggle and make noises like a dog whose collar is cinched too tight.

"Sad business," said Dr. C shaking his head as they watched Dr. Gold being pushed onto the chopper. He was yelling something about his bags when they slammed the door and took off.

"Depends on how you look at it, Harvey. Want to play some more gin?"

Mystery in Morse Code

It didn't take much to get Harold Newcomer into a fight, no surprise when you consider the way he grew up. His dad was an alcoholic lobsterman working out of the port of Rockland, Maine, irritable when he was sober, downright dangerous when he was drunk. Harold was the youngest of four boys, all well-schooled in fending off their father and looking out for themselves. Their mother was a passive, despondent woman who did her best to keep the peace, often giving up her food for the others or taking a blow aimed at one of the children.

Times were tough in the early 1890s when Harold came along, another mouth to feed, another kid to see through the many untreatable diseases that stalked impoverished homes, another reason to have a few more drinks. Lobsters weren't considered gourmet food in those days. They were prehistoric looking bottom feeders living on dead fish, food fit for prisoners in local jails and the large state prison in nearby Thomaston, not something regular folks would buy. Even the Newcomers avoided them. They lived on cod and other fish inadvertently caught in the lobster traps.

As if being the youngest as well as his father's least favorite kid wasn't quite enough, Harold was also the shortest member of the family. At five feet nine inches, he was eyeball to eyeball with his mother and three inches shorter than Patrick, the shortest of the other brothers. His brothers found great sport teasing and beating up their weaker sibling. Harold always fought back, never allowed himself to cry in front of his abusers, and made it a point not to whine or complain to his parents, though it certainly wouldn't have done any good if he had.

Around the age of twelve, as puberty began to advance, Harold started a secret training program, determined that being the shortest son didn't have to translate into being the weakest. He spent hours in the woodshed doing pull-ups on a rafter, endless pushups, and weight lifting using bags of trap weights and bricks tied on both ends of an axe handle. Over a two year period he put on weight and muscle, lots of muscle. His brothers quickly caught on to his secret workouts but were dismissive of the possibility Harold would ever be anything beyond an irritating "shrimp," their father's favorite name for Harold.

Then the inevitable happened. One of the brothers tried to push Harold off the dock, but Harold was ready, ducked, and it was the brother who ended up in the drink. The other two went after Harold and paid the price, one with a broken nose and the other lost a front tooth. Harold wasn't hurt, and even though his father gave him hell about the incident, it was clear to all that a tectonic shift had taken place, a new dynamic that ended Harold's physical torment.

It was a heady moment for Harold, one that was also noticed at school. The cautious, defensive scrapper was slowly evolving into a more confident, even friendly, kid. The sports coach got Harold interested in boxing, and on his eighteenth birthday, he fought in a regional Golden Gloves match, beating his opponent soundly. He advanced to the semifinals before giving up a decision to an older, faster fighter with a three-inch reach advantage.

The loss meant nothing to Harold. In his mind, it was a triumph, a surefire sign he could do anything he wanted and never have to follow his father and brothers struggling to pull a living out of the stormy, ice-cold water in the Gulf of Maine.

Harold joined the Rockland police department the day after he graduated from high school. Rockland was a tough place to live and work in 1915, even tougher for a cop trying to keep the peace in a seaport filled with bars and whore houses offering intoxicating comfort and mayhem to sailors and area watermen, lumbermen, limestone quarrymen, and boat builders. Harold thrived on it; after all, there was nothing in the town's underbelly he hadn't known before. He quickly gained the reputation of a flinty, no-nonsense, honest cop, respected by anyone who made the mistake of challenging him, resented only by those who couldn't turn him with a juicy bribe.

In the spring of 1917, two years into his career, the United States entered the Great War. Harold immediately joined up, trained as an artillery officer for six months then shipped out for England on a freighter grandly named the *Coastal Puritan*.

The *Puritan* sailed straight into a fierce North Atlantic storm, the sort of weather Harold was used to experiencing in a far smaller, vulnerable boat. He was one of only a handful of soldiers who weren't devastated by seasickness, so when the radio antenna went down, Harold volunteered to climb the icy rigging to repair it. The radio operator was grateful and invited Harold into the sanctuary of the radio "shack," one of the only warm places on the boat that didn't reek of stomach contents.

Harold was fascinated by the radio apparatus and the speed with which the operator both sent and read messages in Morse code. In radio language, fast, uninterrupted messaging is called having a "good fist." To Harold it seemed impossible to tell the difference between a dot and a dash, or sense any space between clusters of dots and dashes spelling individual words. But like any language, over time one's ear starts to pick up the distinctions, time intervals called "units." A dot is one unit long, a dash is three and a space is one.

Harold quickly became absorbed in the cadence of Morse code and set about learning the letter codes and abbreviations (prosigns) that shorten messages. By the time the *Puritan* reached Southampton, he was able to spell three words a minute on the practice key, far from the forty a good operator could average, but still an impressive start. He also had a working knowledge of the radio equipment itself and was determined that if he was lucky enough to survive the trenches, he would build his own HAM radio and become an amateur radio operator. HAM, by the way, is not an acronym, and no one has any idea how or why amateur radio picked up the name.

Harold did survive the war, though he was badly wounded when one of his own shells accidentally exploded. Surgeons saved his leg; he returned home on a hospital ship then spent six months in a Long Island military hospital. During his convalescence he studied everything he could find on the emerging science of radio transmission as well as the life stories of his new heroes—Marconi, Hertz, and, of course, Morse.

Back in Maine, he rejoined the police department, doing his best to conceal lingering pain and walk without a limp. Unfortunately, it quickly became obvious he could no longer chase drunken sailors around the cathouses and docks of Rockland, so he was reassigned as an investigator. He missed the rough, dangerous life of a seaport cop and deeply resented spending his time looking into petty crimes and burglaries. He hung on until 1931 when an infection settled into his old wound, festered painfully for several months then invaded the bone in his leg. This was more than a decade before penicillin so there was no alternative to amputation. Worse, the infection forced the surgeon to remove his leg just above the knee preventing use of a prosthesis that would have allowed Harold to return to work.

Though devastated, he accepted a small pension and retreated to "Coffin House," the name he gave his cottage on a hill overlooking the harbor. His parents were both dead, one brother was permanently institutionalized with a brain injury suffered in France during the war, and his other two brothers had moved away to heaven-knows-where.

Even though he lived less than a mile from his old precinct, Harold cut off all of his old friendships, instead turning for solace to his only companion, the radio set in the attic and the friends he gradually accumulated in distant places—people known only by their call signs, their words nothing more than fleeting electrical sounds piercing the night skies.

Radios weren't available off the shelf in those days. A HAM operator built his own "glowbug," as early homemade sets were called, often spending days winding armatures and finding just the right spot to string one hundred feet of antenna wire. Vacuum tubes and other components were bought, scrounged from discarded sets, or traded with other operators. It was a delicate, highly technical, and painstakingly slow process, but Harold already had a modest receiver, and when he was forced to retire, he set about building a larger and far more powerful set, one that could reach across oceans, and by bouncing signals off the moon or aurora borealis, literally anywhere in the world.

Then as now, every operator had a unique call sign, a three-part signature with prefix, center, and suffix. Harold's call sign was W1HAN. The prefix letter identifies the country of origin, the number represents the subdivision within the country, and the suffix is usually the operator's initials. An operator in England (ZQ) would know W1HAN was in the USA, in the state of Maine. Operators quickly came to know each other's call sign with the same easy familiarity they would using each other's first name.

Operators also used abbreviations, the most common being "CQ," meaning "seek you"—"I am trying to contact you." Messages always used the shortest words possible and skipped nonessential words and letters in much the same way people today "text" using cell phones. For the sake of clarity and comfortable narrative, I am going to quote conversations in conventional English and non-metric units. They weren't originally transmitted that way, but a literal translation would be too distracting.

The challenges of long distance communication were formidable, and when contact was successfully made, the operators on both ends collected and bragged about new call signs like kids on a long car ride being the first to spot a Montana license plate.

Certain places were so difficult to penetrate, and operators so few, that a successful transmission was reason to celebrate. By 1930, HAM radio had become so popular that "derbies" or "field days" were started, contests to see who could collect the most call signs in a specific period of time. There were also transmission speed challenges to see who could rattle off the greatest number of five-letter words in one minute while still maintaining a "good fist."

Because transmission was poor during the day, truly dedicated operators spent long hours at night trying to find just the right combination of weather, sun spot activity, sky conditions, proximity to the moon, and myriad other subtleties to lance the sky and score a single long distance contact.

Harold's hobby quickly became an obsession, obliterating his disappointing circumstances, painful stump, and limited income. He tossed his prosthesis away and went everywhere on homemade wooden crutches, no longer bothering to roll up his empty trouser leg. Even in public, he hobbled along on his crutches, oblivious to the filthy pant leg dragging behind.

He stayed up most of the night and slept during the day. To his neighbors, Harold was an oddity, a mole-like eccentric, nice enough if you happened to run into him, but Great Goodness! Don't ask him what he's been up to; that is, unless you know a lot about electronics or think that a few words exchanged with a stranger three thousand miles away is something to get excited about.

Harold's enthusiasm for HAM radio never flickered. Over the next decade he became an expert, and though he rarely met with other operators, he was well known, someone to contact for advice and technical expertise. He had many friends around the world, some he talked with in long daily conversations. Harold's fist was solid, and he could convert code as easily as one would read a newspaper.

February 14, 1932, 3:44 a.m.:
Harold would not have known or cared it was Valentine's Day. Even if the thought had occurred to him, it would have been blown aside the instant he heard the scratchy transmission: "CQ, CQ ZQ2ENO." There it was! Harold had been working for weeks to pick up ZQ2ENO, a call

from England he thought he heard intermittently through the static, one he had answered countless times without a response.

"W1HAN, W1HAN. Receiving your signal. Where are you?"

"ZQ2ENO. I am in Lyme Regis on the south shore. And you? In Maine?"

"W1HAN. Yes, Maine. Like you, on the coast. Receiving you well, what are you using?"

And that was as far as the first contact with ZQ2ENO went. Harold sent CQ after CQ into the ether, but nothing else was heard. But it didn't matter to Harold. This was what he lived for. All of the skill building his system, his antenna configuration, augmented power box, and tube boosters—everything came together in that brief moment. And Harold was happy, so happy he could hardly sleep after he finally gave up trying to contact ZQ2ENO.

And so it went for weeks. Every few hours Harold would try again. CQ CQ. Then, clear as can be, an answer. "ZQ2ENO. I have been trying to get through but the weather here has been awful. Glad you persisted."

That simple conversation was the start of a deepening friendship between two people three thousand miles apart who would likely never meet. ENO's real name was Eric Norton Obstervent. He was a long time HAM operator recently retired from a career as a signal officer in the British army. He, too, had been injured in the war, mustard gas in his case, but he managed to stay on in spite of some chronic shortness of breath.

Eric was dismissive of his problem. "If they canned everyone who had mustard lungs, they wouldn't have enough soldiers left to fill a latrine." Harold told him he, too, had fought in the war, and eventually, after a year of talking back and forth, told Eric about his leg and forced retirement from the police force.

There were often frustrating lapses in their exchanges, some as long as six months. Eric was vague about the reasons, but Harold began to think he was not as well as he pretended. A few cryptic references to treatment in a hospital outside London, complaints about the cost of medicine, and jokes about putting a "wheezer" on the third floor of his boarding house, all painted a picture in Harold's mind of a proud man doing his best to conceal his limitations, familiar territory for Harold.

MAY 9, 1933–JUNE 2, 1933:

Harold hadn't heard from Eric for several weeks, then suddenly he was back, clear as ever, and apologetic for the lapse. Over the next several weeks they exchanged numerous messages, but summer skies in the northern hemisphere are notoriously fickle and frequent interruptions drove Harold mad with frustration, particularly toward the end as the pieces of an evolving puzzle started to fall into place. I will present the conversations as far more contiguous then they actually were.

"Sorry, bad weather and other distractions kept me away."

"Never mind, glad you're back. What has been going on?"

"Ghastly story, Harold. There has been a murder here in my boarding house. No! Two murders! Can you imagine that? Here on the quiet shores of Lyme Bay, two innocent people have been killed!"

Harold was stunned but the nascent detective immediately kicked in. "Two murders at the same time? In a boarding house? Did they catch the killer? "

"No, not yet, but they are hard at it."

"Details, give me the details!"

"Oh, yes, I forgot for a moment you are what that wonderful new actor, James Cagney, calls a 'copper.' Okay, I'll do my best, but I don't want to get your blood up over this. The chief constable says it was a robbery gone wrong all the way."

"A robbery? Robbers try to avoid confrontation. Did someone surprise him or them? More detail, please, Eric."

"Well, for starters, it happened late at night. There was a hellish rainstorm going on, thunder and all that, everyone was buttoned down, so I guess whoever it was thought it would be a good time be on the prowl."

"Burglars hate bad weather, Eric. People are always home, confrontation is more likely, and it makes everything more complex, most especially the getaway. Bad weather takes people off the road, particularly at night, so cars stand out. Increases risk. But continue. Sorry to interrupt."

"Well, perhaps I should describe the house where we live, all eleven of us, counting the landlady and her daughter. That will give you a better picture of just how this happened. It is a large Victorian thing, a mansion really, facing south across the road from a salt marsh. The ocean is about a quarter mile further on. The house is shaped like a square box with a smaller box stuck on the east side, so if you are facing the house, marsh and sea to your back, facing north, you look up a wide set of stairs to a big porch that runs all across the front and turns the corner about twenty feet on both the east and west sides.

"The porch is the most important room in the house. It's huge, really, at least ten feet wide and stocked with plenty of rockers and tables for us to have a tea, watch the birds in the marsh, smell the ocean, and enjoy the sea breezes. The people who were killed lived in the only two bedrooms downstairs, right next to one another. They each had two windows onto the porch. That's how the lifter, or burglar as you call them, got in. Is this too much detail?"

"Not at all. I can picture it. How is the first floor laid out? And what did you mean by the box on the side. Is that an annex? Attached?"

"Yes, an annex, two floors, attached. It's where the owner, Mrs. Dauthington and her daughter, Elsa, live. They run the house, serve all our meals, and mother us, if you know what I mean. The front door is on the left side of the porch. You enter a vestibule—a small room, really. It's where we leave our jackets, boots, and the like. Then you go through another door into a parlor with chairs, sofas, and a coal stove. The stairway is hard on the left wall, goes up to the second floor where there are four rooms. The stairs to the third floor are over the lower stairs. There are two of us up top here in the 'perch,' as we call it. I'm up here because it gets me closer to my antenna, you understand.

"The dining room is through the parlor to the back of the house, a big room with a table that seats all quite comfortably. The pantry and kitchen are off the dining room to the right in the back. There is a back stairs up to the second floor but not for us, it's for Elsa when she cleans. In the front, there is a hallway to the right of the parlor leading to the annex. The two victims lived on that corridor."

"Are the stairs carpeted?"

"The front stairs going to the second floor are, but not the back stairs or the stairs to the third floor."

"Who were the victims, how old were they, and which room did each have?"

"Miss Kinsky and Mr. Bartles. I'd say she was close to eighty, he was maybe sixty-five. She had Room 1 immediately off the parlor. His was just down the hall, Room 2, as you might guess. Her room is a bit larger than his and is *en suite*. His is smaller, and his bath is directly across the hall. Quite convenient, really."

"*En suite*? What is that?"

"Sorry, 'with bath.' She had her own bath. There is only one other *en suite* in the house. A young couple, the Trents, have that one. It's on the second floor at the top of the stairs."

"You say it was a robbery. Any idea what was taken?"

"We all peeked in while the police were there, couldn't help ourselves, really, a kind of morbid curiosity or something. Anyway, Miss Kinsky's room was quite orderly, just her bottom bureau drawer was open, and there was a Gladstone bag open on the floor with a small wooden box open next to it. The chief constable says it's obvious there was something in it that the thief wanted."

"What did the box look like?"

"Quite ornate, dark wood with narrow metal bands all around it. I couldn't see the top very well, but it was open and there was a key in the lock. I remember the key, very fancy, it was."

"Did you see the body before it was taken away?"

"Oh, yes, at least the top half. There was a blanket over the rest of her. It was awful. She had bruises on her face; you could see the blotches ten feet away. Her nose was bloody, as well. There was blood on her nightgown and in her hair."

"Was she lying on her back? Near the bed?"

"Yes, just so. A few feet from the bed. The police had pulled the curtains back and we could also see one window was partly open. The chief constable thinks she was strangled, poor soul."

"Anything else?"

"Well, yes, her hand. I noticed her left hand. The pinky finger stuck out at a strange angle, and it was almost purple. She must have fallen on it."

"And the man, Mr. Bartles?"

"Oh, horrible. He was stabbed straight through the heart. He was lying just inside his door, on his back, too. I'll never forget the sight of that knife sticking up out of his chest, blood all over his pajamas, and a big pool of it on the rug. Awful."

"What kind of a knife, could you tell?"

"Oh, yes, no mistake about that one. I've seen lots of them here on the coast. It was a fish filleting knife with a wooden handle. As I said, quite common here on the coast where every soul makes his living selling his soul. Sorry, local joke."

"Was his window open, too? And how tall was Mr. Bartles?"

"Goodness, such questions. Well, the easy one first—yes, the window was up slightly. As to height, I have to guess he was about six feet, maybe a hair more. What does that tell you, detective?"

"With most stabbing, the thrust is either up or down. The most common way is up. The perpetrator has his hand wrapped around the handle with his thumb at the top of the blade, at the ready, knife held low, ready to strike, but the stab has to be upward, usually through the abdomen into the chest. If you hold the knife with your thumb at the end of the handle away from the blade, you have to strike down, usually through the shoulder or upper chest. Straight in is a thumb-by-the-blade grip, but the elbow has to be well up to make the move. No one walks around in that position unless he is about to deliver a calculated death stroke. But tell me more about the windows. How did the thief manage to get in? I can't imagine he broke the glass. Even in a storm that would make one hell of a noise."

"Exactly so. After they removed the bodies, one of the constables showed us how it was done. Seems all you need is a really stiff, thin piece of metal like the filleting knife to stick up between the upper and lower window casements. Then you push against the latch and it opens. He did it in seconds, stepped in from the porch, and from there it was only two steps to her bed. Poor dear never knew until it was too late."

"Tell me more about Mr. Bartles' body. How was he lying? Facing the door? On his back, you say?"

"Yes, on his back, feet toward the door. Mrs. Dauthington discovered the body. Such a scream you have never heard. It was still pouring rain, but I could hear her clear up here in the perch. Woke me up. By the time I got down there—it was about six in the a.m.—Mrs. Dauthington and Elsa were both screaming, and all of the others were there, too. We found out later, when she came through from the annex, his door was open a bit—opened in, it did—and she saw his foot right there. She called his name, knocked, the door opened a little more, and there he was.

"At first no one thought about Miss Kinsky, then we all sort of realized at the same time she hadn't come out in spite of all the ruckus. We knocked but she didn't answer, so we waited for the police to open it."

"Was it locked?"

"No, it wasn't."

"Do you remember anything about the rugs in the room or in the hall? I'm wondering if they were wet or if there were wet footprints? And Mr. Bartles' rug, was it twisted or messed up like there was a struggle?"

"Can't remember anything about the rugs except the police asked each other the same question. I don't think they found any water or footprints."

"Strange, don't you think? The storm had to have blown water all over the porch facing the sea as it does, and the killer had to walk from the street, all the way up the stairs, across to the window, stand on the wet porch while he checked inside both rooms before he made his move. He had to stand there for some time because there were curtains, probably thick ones to give privacy right there by a public area. That had to slow him down.

180

"How do the police read it? Surely, you've heard their idea of how it went."

"Yes. They think it was one man, a bloke who knew the house and struck in the middle of the night, on purpose at the height of the storm. They think he went to Miss Kinsky's room first, felt the window crack, stuck in his knife, popped the latch, stepped in, probably turned on a small torch, put his hand on her mouth, pulled her off the bed, and strangled her, then searched the place, found the key and the box, opened it, and took the cash and jewelry. They think he heard Mr. Bartles stirring about, maybe opening his door, so he went out into the hallway, encountered Mr. Bartles, stabbed him, pushed him backwards into his room, grabbed his wallet and whatever else was in easy reach, opened the window, and left.

"And before you ask, the reason the windows were both almost shut is he closed them both from the outside to keep the storm sounds down, 'to delay discovery,' they said. Then he went down the steps into the night. Cold and quick. No more than five minutes total according to the chief constable."

"Have there been other burglaries in the town recently?"

"None I've heard about. And absolutely no murders. Proper Englishmen don't do that. We leave it to you Yanks."

"Tell me more about the victims, most importantly, was there a relationship between the two, and if so, what was its nature?"

"Why do you want to know all of that? Surely, you don't think someone in the house did this, do you?"

"Maybe, maybe not, but absent a ripe suspect, a good detective never passes up information, no matter how farfetched, especially when it's fresh. You have two dead people right there, Eric, and you may be the only one thinking this through. Sounds like the police have made up their minds to look elsewhere. I'll bet they didn't even question the guests, right?"

"True, but realize, we were all in bed at the time. What is there to question?"

"Bad assumption, Eric. Perhaps one of your neighbors was not asleep. If you allow just that one possibility to enter your thinking then the entire picture changes, doesn't it?"

"Quite so, Harold, I take your point, but surely the police know these matters, and if there was the slightest chance the murderer was in the house, wouldn't they be on it right off?"

181

"The police may have their own bias, Eric. And they play the odds. It looks like a robbery gone astray, the evidence seems to point to an outsider, so the conclusion is it's the work of a bungling thief. Go have another cup of tea and wait for someone to turn him in.

"So, back to the two victims, what do we know about them?"

"I can't tell you anything about either one. They arrived at the same time about three years ago taking the two downstairs rooms available when two sisters moved out. This is a popular house, and it didn't seem odd at all that two new boarders would arrive simultaneously. They were proper enough, polite to a fine point, but not chatty at all. Mr. Bartles was the more talkative of the two, quite up on affairs of state, the economy, all that. But a relationship? I don't think so, though it was certainly true that Mr. Bartles seemed to be intensely respectful of Miss Kinsky. After all, they were first floor neighbors, and he had been in service previously."

"Service? You mean the army?"

"No, meaning he was a butler or senior footman or the like. He never talked about it, but there were hints he used to serve in high places. Talk in the house was he got a nice inheritance or bequest and was able to retire to a quiet life by the sea. Let someone else do the cooking, if you take my meaning.

"Now that I think about it, they always arrived for meals together, usually the last to sit down. He held her chair like a proper gentleman. They took tea together, and if she left for a walk, he always went along. Beyond that I can't say much, but she was reserved to the point of being rude. No one really had much to do with her because she was standoffish, spent most of her time in her room, acted like we were beneath her or she couldn't be bothered. But mostly she was quiet. Smiled a bit but quiet. Had an accent, though."

"Accent? That's interesting; what sort of accent?"

"Hard to say, very proper English, to be sure, but she did have a way of putting a "yuh" sound at the end of some words. You sure do like details, Harold."

"They solve crimes, my friend. Any hints about her life? What brought a refined snob with an odd accent to a boarding house in Lyme Regis, and what did she bring with her that attracted a killer?"

"I have no idea."

"Okay, then let's move on to the others, starting with you, though I certainly know a lot about you already. Have you been particularly close to any of the others?"

"I don't think Miss Kinsky spoke ten words to me, though Mr. Bartles was friendly enough. The ones I talked to the most were Mr. Litton and Mr. Dickens. Dickens lives in the perch with me, and we share a bath. He's from London, a former banker who lost his money when the depression hit. He's been here about two years. He's about six feet, wears thick glasses, and talks endlessly about the rich old farts whose accounts he used to service. Lives in a dream world, really. He thinks he'll get called back some day, but he's at least sixty, and from a few things he's said, I think he got sacked for borrowing a little cash from the register, if you get my meaning.

"But he's a nice enough fellow, very tidy—good when you share a bathroom—and he stays fit by walking all bloody day, and on the wet days he can't walk, he does pushups and the like for hours. He's a bit daft, talks like he's on a bank holiday not retirement, but he's tough as shoe leather, I'll tell you. The only problem we have up here is he's a light sleeper, anything wakes him up, so I have to keep my volume down in the night hours or he complains.

"Mr. Litton lives on the second floor across from the Trents, the young couple. He's about forty or so, disabled in a factory accident in the north. I guess he's on pension. He's about five feet ten or eleven inches tall, came here about six months ago. He looked like hell when he got here, I guess he was still getting over the injury, but he's doing quite well now, I think."

"What is his disability? And what do you mean, 'he looked like hell'?"

"He was pale, washed out looking, jumpy, nervous, that sort of thing. Took him a couple of months to settle down. He has a badly injured right shoulder, wears his arm in a tight sling. Unfortunately, he's right handed and still has quite a time doing things with his left hand. If he doesn't wear his sling, he says he'll reach for something without thinking and quick as that pull his arm out. It's no joke, I'll tell you. I've seen it happen a couple of times. It makes a 'pop' sound, his arm seems to grow three or four inches and he has to sit down and twist it a certain way to get it back. Hurts like hell, you can see that. But he's stoic, doesn't complain, and is polite to everyone, not friendly, really, but proper. I think Elsa is sweet on him. I've seen them out walking together, but her mother doesn't approve. It's not Mr. Litton's fault, she just doesn't think it's proper to be too friendly with the boarders.

"The thing I like about him is his interest in radio. He sits up with me some nights, and he's learning Morse code. Pretty good at it, too."

"Let's see. Next we have the Trents, Connie and Mic, both maybe twenty-five. She's about five feet, six inches and he's not much taller. He's a fisherman, mate on a good boat for the last two years. Connie works in the fish factory. They're nice enough though they argue a lot. Hard to hide that in close quarters."

"What do they argue about?"

"Money, mostly. And smell. Connie hates the smell of fish, and with two of them up to their elbows in fish guts all day, they never quite get rid of the odor. She wants to move inland and get work on a farm, have pets and kids. He likes being at sea and thinks he'll get his own boat someday. I'm not sure I'd bet much on that marriage."

"Who are the other two on the second floor?"

"Old Colonel Proctor, a curmudgeon if ever there was one, and Mr. Blivens, bit of a mystery man. He's about thirty, maybe just shy of six feet tall, skinny as a rail, and his eyes dart around all the time, like a mouse living in a house full of cats. He says he has a government job but I don't believe him. He leaves every day about eight in the a.m., comes back about five, but he never quite says what he does. Best I can tell from his dinner talk, he's a sort of postal inspector who investigates crimes involving the mail. But I've seen him in town during the day coming out of a pub. And I know for sure he sometimes comes to the evening meal tipsy. You can tell because he splashes cologne all over himself to cover the smell. I don't know who smells worse, Mic, Connie, or Blivens. Anyway, that's all of them. Does it give you any ideas?"

"Not yet. What about the Colonel, what's his story?"

"Being bloody nasty is his story. He's fat, has terrible manners, and hates everything and everyone. The food is never to his liking, and he won't shut up about bloody India and how many *kaffers* he killed in this skirmish or that assault. Cashed out after twenty-five years, on the early side because he said the army was festering with cowards and communists. He's got a gun, too, a Webley. He's not supposed to have it, of course, but he got drunk at a Christmas party and had it in his belt at dinner. Scared the hell out of all of us.

"Funny, I can only remember one time when Miss Kinsky spoke to him. Terrible scene, really. We were at dinner and as usual he was going on about how the government is infested with this crook or that communist, and right when he said 'communist,' up jumps Miss Kinsky and she yells at him, 'What do you know about communists, you damn fool?!' She stormed off to her room and slammed the door. Poor Mr. Bartles made an apology, but as I recall, he stayed at the table.

"Does any of this help?"

"A lot. And Miss Kinsky is right; he is a damn fool and a liar on top of it. I have no idea who your 'Colonel' is, but for starters I'd bet he's never been to India. '*Kaffer*' is South African slang, not Indian. I heard it a lot during the war. Maybe he's an Afrikaner pretending he's a Brit. We need to know more about him.

"But right now I need a couple of other details. How many keys do you all have to your rooms? And do you know if Miss Kinsky locked her door at night?"

"We all have two keys. And, yes, she did lock her door."

"How do you know?"

"Because I have seen Mr. Bartles check it after she retired. He would knock, give the knob a twist, push on the door then retreat to his room. Funny, I had forgotten that. I don't lock mine unless I'm going to be away for a while. That's pretty much what everyone does."

"Okay, Eric, it's time for you to do a little investigating. I assume you're willing?"

"What sort of investigating?"

"For starters, we need to know who Miss Kinsky really was. Same for Bartles. What happened to their bodies? Was there a funeral, burial? If so, that means someone stepped forward to pay the bill."

"Not that I know of. The police took them, and I assume they still have them somewhere unless, as you say, someone took charge of the situation."

"The best way to begin is at the police department. Talk to one of the investigating constables, he'll know or he can find out. If no one has claimed the bodies and he's reluctant to give you any information, tell him you're getting some funds together to get them buried. I'm sure whoever has their bodies would like to get them out of the refrigerator into the ground. They will want to cooperate. Same for Bartles, of course. Once you have that, press the police about the others, see if they know any of them.

"Then go to the library and look up the census records. Go to any employment agencies around there and ask if they know Bartles. That ought to get you started."

Two weeks later Eric was back on a clear night with his news.

"You were right, Harold. The constable was glad to talk. Seems our Mr. Bartles was collected by a niece from Brighton. I sent her a letter of condolence and asked about Miss Kinsky. I got nothing back. Miss K, by the way, is still "on ice" as they say. The police tried to find relatives and even they failed. They will hold her one more month then put her in a pauper's grave. What a terrible ending. We don't have employment agencies so that's a dead end. Higher-class servants move about in an invisible social network.

"By the way, the police said they know all about Mr. Blivens, well known to have no visible means of support except what he can make as a tout and petty con man. Who would have thought! Mic Trent is no stranger, either. Seems he has been arrested several times for fighting, once for pulling a knife on a fishmonger over the price of his catch.

"And there's more—Mic and Connie are not married! How about that! They said they would look into Mr. Dickens, the banker, but nothing so far. The rest didn't seem to ring any bells but remember, most of the lot come far away from this little hamlet. Anything is possible.

"The census records showed nothing about Blivens, Colonel Proctor, or Miss Kinsky. In 1925 Bartles was 'in service' in London, and Dickens was married and living in London. Seems like he lost his wife as well as his money along the way. Anyway, Connie and Mic were too young to pick up, and there are too many Thomas Littons to say anything about him. And I never would have picked up my own name if I didn't know the address. Like Litton, too many Obstervents. I never would have guessed that!"

Eric faded out again after that last communication. Even with favorable weather, it took another week to raise ZQ2ENO.

"More news, Harold. Connie has left Mic and gone off somewhere, no one knows where, and Mic won't talk about it. It happened about three days after the murders. They got in a terrible row, she packed a bag and stormed out. Mic is fuming mad, stays out, and closes down the pubs. Mrs. Dauthington told him he has to take Mr. Bartles' room or get out. My guess is he'll leave.

"That's not so bad, I mean, I really don't think Connie killed anyone, and Mic doesn't seem smart enough to plan anything, assuming one of us is the killer.

"But here's the bad part: that shifty-eyed bastard, Blivens, is gone, snuck off in the middle of the night, Harold. Took a suitcase full of his possessions but left a lot of clothes behind. What does that tell you, detective? And if that's not bad enough, the Colonel said at dinner that he has given notice and plans to leave within the week. He said he feels like his home is falling apart, and he wants to go somewhere more peaceful."

"Interesting, but in some ways helpful, Eric. How about the others? Are Litton and the banker sitting tight?"

"So far, yes. Dickens is still going on about the bank calling him back, and Litton is courting Elsa right out in the open. He says he hasn't got anywhere to go and thinks it won't take long for the place to fill up again. I think he'll move downstairs if Mrs. Daughington will let him, but I don't think she will because it puts him too close to the annex and Miss Elsa, if you see what I mean."

"Got it. And anything from the police?"

But that was the end of that batch of messages. Harold grew more agitated as the days went by, his CQs going out literally every hour, even in the daytime.

FRIDAY, JULY 16, 1933:

At 10:45 p.m., Harold finally broke through to ZQ2ENO.

"Christ, Eric, where have you been? I've been worried to death about you. I think you are in danger! Do you read me?"

For over an hour there was nothing, then, "CQ W1HAN, do you read? Bad weather, sorry. Do you read?"

"Yes! For God's sake, Eric, stay with me."

"Right. Let me tell you fast what has happened. It has me worried. Need advice."

"Yes, man, tell me!"

"The Colonel didn't wait a week, he's gone. Just like that ferret Blivens, he just left. So I went to the police and talked to the chief constable and told him everything, all about our messaging and your worry this is what I think you called an 'inside job.' I thought it would be helpful, maybe spur him into action, but he took it all wrong, went berserk, yelled at me, 'Are you a bloody detective?' He called me a troublemaker and said he didn't think there was any Harold Newcomber, and for all he knew, maybe I was just trying to create a smoke screen for my own crime.

"Then he showed up at the house and stormed in during lunch with two constables and searched my room! Told everyone at the table I was bloody Sherlock Holmes and left me sitting there with everyone looking at me like I was a traitor or some kind of saboteur."

"Quick, Eric, who was there?"

"Mrs. D. and Elsa, Litton, a new boarder named Krebbs, and the banker, Dickens."

"Listen to me, Eric, I'll spell this out for you. Don't interrupt, just write it down then get out and go back to the police. No matter what, don't stay in that house. Are you there?"

"Yes, but you're scaring me, Harold."

187

"Here it is. What I am going to tell you is circumstantial, that means I can't prove any of it, but my years of experience with this kind of crime and criminal give me what I need to make an educated guess who did this and why.

"We know it wasn't the work of an outsider, we went over that before. For starters, there was too much water outside not to have some wet spots and soggy footprints. Also, this was a focused crime, not a random burglary. The man knew precisely what he was after, and he could afford to wait until the exact right moment to strike. No outsider could do that.

"He also had to know that Bartles had been Kinsky's servant well before they arrived at your boarding house. He learned it in all probability while he was in prison then tracked them down when he got out. My guess is, given her age, accent, regal manner, obvious paranoia, and fancy jewel box, she was Russian, probably one of the many members of the Czar's family who escaped early, taking what she could—her royal ass and box of jewels. Remember how she exploded over the word 'communist?' That seals it. She probably sold just enough of her valuables to keep herself going and support a servant. But the Russians have been very aggressive in recent years hunting down, killing, and taking back valuables they think belong to the Russian people.

"The killer is Litton, your radio pal who probably knew all about me through your chats. I'll bet he was even with you sometimes when we were talking. He was the most recent arrival, had a room perfectly situated at the top of the carpeted stairs, the closest of anyone to the victims. He knew Bartles would have the second key, so when the moment was right, he slipped down the stairs, tapped quietly on Bartles' door, and when he opened it, he shoved a fish knife into his chest. Then he got the key, probably right there in plain sight, tossed a couple of drawers, clipped his wallet, and cracked the window, all for effect.

"Then he waited for a thunder clap and opened the door to Miss Kinsky's room. He yanked her out of bed, demanded to know where the jewel box and key were, and when she wouldn't tell, he twisted her pinky finger until it broke. She told him, he strangled her, opened the box, did the window trick, left the door unlocked to make it look like it all started in her room, returned the key to Bartles' room, hid the jewels somewhere—convicts are very clever when it comes to hiding things in confined spaces—and went to bed. The police were too stupid to question anyone, so he never really needed a good hiding place.

"He did a good job of forcing the police to look outside, and they fell for it simply because the latches were easily slipped and the rooms looked like they had been tossed looking for goodies. It was such an easy explanation they were willing to overlook the lack of real evidence like wet spots on the rugs.

"And before you ask, I'll tell you how I know he was a con. You said he looked awful, pale and washed out, but at the same time, and in spite of his disability, quite strong. That's an odd combination unless you've been living in a gloomy cell for a long time defending your space from other cons. And the dislocated arm? The most common injury in jail is a dislocated shoulder. Cons get them from endlessly being handcuffed with their arms behind their backs, or from fighting. Either way, it's a simple matter to slip it in and out of the joint, quite painlessly, I might add. The great Houdini made many of his escapes because he was able to dislocate his shoulders at will.

"The others just didn't have it to pull this off. Your 'Colonel' was a fraud and a buffoon, nothing subtle about him. The banker was a possible since he could have known about Miss Kinsky and her jewels, but he lived on the third floor and had been there quite a while. It would have been very risky for him to travel up and down from your perch, and I really do think he was quite batty, a white collar criminal, as we call them, not someone willing to kill so easily. Also, he left suddenly. Too obvious. Litton stayed on, acting calm, courting Miss Dauthington, the image of innocence, waiting quietly for the right moment to leave.

"Blivens was a petty criminal, an alcoholic in all probability, and just too scattered to pull off such a calculated crime. And besides, he left, too. Again, too obvious. Mic didn't have the balls, and we can easily eliminate the landlady and her daughter.

"No, Eric, it's Litton, and he's on to you, and you have to get the hell out of there before you become his next victim.

"Come back, Eric."

Nothing came back, just silence, a long, chilling silence. Harold sent countless CQ's through the night and into the next day. There was no response.

SATURDAY, JULY 15, 1933:
At 10:00 a.m., the RMS *Olympic*, sister ship of the *Titanic* sailed from Southampton for New York City.

MONDAY, JULY 17, 1933:
9:30 a.m. RMS *Olympic* was making good time. In spite of her age, she was in fine shape and the passengers were enjoying the summer air

and smooth sailing. On the First Class deck, Thomas Litton Baxter was enjoying an after-breakfast cigar, thinking he might have a stroll around the deck to see if there were unattached ladies who might like to join him later for lunch.

Harold Newcomber continued his tireless effort to raise ZQ2ENO.

THURSDAY, JULY 20, 1933:
Harold Newcomber took the train to Portland, then a taxi to the New England Bell Telephone Building on East Water Street. After explaining his problem, he was introduced to Overseas Operator, Daniel Cushing.

"I need to contact the chief constable in Lyme Regis, England. I don't have a name or number but I assure you this is a life and death matter. I don't give a damn what it costs or how long it takes, I must reach him."

After several hours of trying, Cushing was able to reach the police department in Lyme Regis, but by then it was night and the chief constable had left for the night. Harold checked in to a local hotel, spent a sleepless night, and was back in Mr. Cushing's office the next morning at eight o'clock. This time it only took thirty minutes to reach the chief constable.

Harold had rehearsed his lines carefully so he wouldn't be instantly dismissed as a lunatic Yank. He introduced himself as a detective (omitting the retired part) with a keen interest in HAM radio then briefly described how he had been following the investigation of the recent murders at the boarding house in Lyme Regis.

"What murders, Mr. Newcomber?"

Harold quickly reminded the chief constable of the murder of Miss Kinsky and Mr. Bartles. How in the world could he pretend he didn't know?

"Kinsky and Bartles? Surely, you are joking, sir. As I recall, that happened two years ago. Who did you say told you about this?"

"Eric Obstervent."

"Obstervent? The radio fellow?"

"Yes, Obstervent."

"Well, you must be talking to ghosts, Mr. Newcomber. He was murdered shortly after the other two. Someone made off with his radio as I recall. We never did solve that one, I am ashamed to say."

"But I've been talking to Obstervent for months!" Harold protested.

"Not likely, sir. Someone is pulling your leg, I'm afraid," he said and hung up.

Harold paid $28.75 in telephone charges, returned to Coffin House, and went to bed.

FRIDAY, JULY 21, 1933:
9:00 a.m., the RMS *Olympic* docked in New York City. Customs received the first class passengers. Thomas Litton Baxter quickly passed through the inspection with nothing to declare, took a taxi to the Barkley Hotel, checked in then went for a stroll down 47th Street to Mr. Silverman's office, just past 5th Avenue.

"Mr. Baxter! How nice to see you again. It's been almost a year, sir. Have you something lovely for me today?"

"Indeed I have, Mr. Silverman, a stunning gem I have been saving up for this moment."

"A special occasion, Mr. Baxter?"

"Yes, I am not returning to England. I plan to move to Florida; I think the weather will favor my arthritis. But first a couple of errands, starting with this."

Mr. Baxter placed a red velvet bag on the counter. Mr. Silverman opened it and exclaimed, "Goodness, Mr. Baxter, you have been teasing me up to this point. What a lovely ruby!" He held it up to the light then inspected it for several minutes through his loupe.

"This is an extraordinary piece. Are you sure you want to part with it? I say that because the depression has hurt prices terribly, and if you wait a few years, I could do a lot better."

"I understand, but I have others and I do need cash right now. Give me your best price and we'll talk."

After some back and forth, they agreed on a price of $42,000.

"It will take a week for me to find a buyer and raise the money, Mr. Baxter, but if you can come back next Friday, I will have the cash. Will that be a problem, sir?"

"Not at all, Mr. Silverman. You see, I have to make a brief trip to Maine before I go to Florida."

"Maine? Goodness, you do get around. I hope you're not selling someone up there a stone from your collection."

"Oh, no, Mr. Silverman. I have to see an old friend. We have been playing a long distance game, very silly, but engaging. Unfortunately, perhaps foolishly, I gave him a few too many clues, and he solved the riddle so I am obliged to pay him off.

"Shouldn't take long. I'll see you next Friday."

TRANSCRIPT
OF THE TERRITORY COUNCIL EMERGENCY MEETING

[The following is a translation of the Territory Council minutes from the emergency session convened to deal with the threat of anarchy arising from recent reaction by some constituents to the widely perceived threat of an invasion of undesirables on the south side of the Territory. Warning: some of the language may be offensive to young or particularly sensitive readers, but in the spirit of honest reporting the editorial staff has decided to print the material as it was spoken. We apologize for any distress it may cause.]

[The meeting was held under the dishwasher, finally started at 3:55 E.H.T. (Early Human Time, also known as "a.m.") after a good deal of arguing, yelling, and threats by some members, especially the more strident roaches, to boycott the proceedings. No attempt to report those preliminaries has been attempted.]

[The Grand Speaker, silverfish Gamma, finally called the meeting to order.]

"All right! Let's get started. We haven't got all night for this. I know a lot of you are hungry, but if we don't deal with this, it could threaten our entire society. Are the guards posted for the spiders and centipedes? Good, then let's get right to it."

"What happened to prayer?" yelled several roaches scattered throughout the audience. "Are you silverfish so high and mighty you don't need to ask for protection from Devil Orkin anymore?"

[A lot of "yeahs" and leg scraping in the background.]

"And what about food? Do you think it just falls out of the toaster without heavenly guidance? How about at least a token prayer of thanks. Is that asking too much?"

[More background noise.]

"Okay, we'll ask the Council Chaplain to say a prayer. Where is the chaplain? Does anyone know?"

[It turned out the chaplain had been killed earlier in the evening, crushed in a surprise pantry door opening. An alternative was appointed, a prayer sent aloft to Entenmann, and the meeting began.]

"The Chair recognizes silverfish Mason."

"Mr. Chairman, I am not here to say there is no potential problem caused by the growing influx of workers from the sunny side of the doors, but…"

"Earwig shit!! You call them 'ants' and 'workers,' we call them 'blackheads'! We're tired of the coddling attitude of you silverfish."

"Silence!" yelled Gamma. "You roaches will have your turn, but I will not tolerate interruptions nor will we countenance pejorative terms like the 'B' word. Please continue, Mason."

[More grumbling and leg scraping.]

"As I was saying, it is clear and undeniable that we have a problem on the warmer border. But we have for countless lifetimes allowed a certain number of workers into the Territory without any problem. In fact, those very workers you now vilify with unacceptable language have been helpful to our economy. They have eaten or removed enormous amounts of waste, most of which I would point out has been created by you roaches who don't seem to be able to go anywhere without leaving a trail of odiferous material in your wake."

[More yelling and scraping. Several crickets joined in with load chirps and leg vibrations. A chant started in a silverfish group, "CU-CA-RA-CHAS!! CU-CA-RA-CHAS!!" Gamma was finally able to restore order.]

"Just as we will not tolerate the 'B' word, we will not put up with the 'C' word, either. Now calm down, show some respect, and stop mating while someone is speaking! Mason will continue."

"I propose we send a delegation to the warm wall and engage the workers in negotiations to decide how many will be allowed in."

"Second!!" yelled several silverfish.

"Okay, that's an idea, but before we vote on anything, roach Madonna would like to speak."

"I've had it with you carpet sharks and your naïve approach to problem solving."

[The silverfish erupted in a chorus of hissing and scraping.]

"What has wings and can't fly?" yelled a silverfish, answered in unison by hundreds of voices screaming, "Roaches!!!"

[Gamma finally regained control and told Madonna she would be ejected if she used the "CS" epithet again.]

"What I am saying to you naïve fools is you cannot negotiate with lawless, uneducated dark-headed workers who want to swarm in here, ravage our females, eat our helpless young, and steal our food. They breed like fruit flies, and it won't take long before we're pushed into the cellar with all the spiders and centipedes! Wake up, Territory! This is a war, and as long as I have six legs to stand on, I'm not giving in to some airy-fairy ideas about peace and love. We need to dispatch more crickets to the warm side, and, yes, you silverfish need to get your heads out of the book bindings and tune up your mandibles for the battle of your lives!"

[There were roars of approval from the roaches, boo's, hissing, and scraping from most of the silverfish. Several crickets demanded the chance to speak. Gamma finally recognized Disney, the elder statescricket.]

"We've carried your water far too long, and I'm talking not only to roaches but also to some of you silverfish who talk about equality and regret all those lifetimes of using us for work and entertainment while you continue to call us names in your private cereal boxes. We've fought in your wars with distinction even though we were excluded from command positions…"

[Low-level hissing in the background, mostly from roach sections.]

"Oh, don't deny it, you black-backs, you know what I'm talking about!"

"Oh, yeah," yelled a roach in the back row. "At least we don't eat our own dead."

[More scraping and general chaos.]

[Gamma finally got control, told Disney he couldn't use years of exploitation to justify calling roaches by the "BB" words and urged him to finish.]

"Okay, I'll cut to the chase—if you want us to continue to take the brunt of your aggressive plans, you're going to have to share the burden, improve our living conditions while we're away from our pods, and provide more support for families while we're sweating it out on the damn border protecting you—all of you—and then we'll go down there and crack some heads."

[Gamma recognized silverfish Molting Mate, a member of the minority laundry room tribe.]

"We fully support what Disney had to say about subtle attitudes based on old misfortunes and their continuing effect on policy, and, like Gamma, we deplore language that diminishes the value of any peace-loving insect. I hope I don't have to remind anyone in this group just how long we have suffered poverty, lack of opportunity, and poor food sources in the laundry area. Like Disney, we worry that we, too, will be conscripted to fight a war with a group with whom we feel some kinship."

[Cries of "Blasphemy!!" rose from the audience. At that point Gamma seemed to lose control of the entire proceeding. Unfortunately, at that very moment a guard cricket screamed, "CENTIPEDE!!!" Everyone scattered, including the recording secretary.]

[That is where the transcript ends.]

ABOUT THE AUTHOR

Like someone growing up in a bilingual home, Philip Hirsh's formative years were divided between two worlds, one in northern New Jersey and the other in the Alleghany Mountains on the western edge of Virginia. He was educated at Phillips Academy Andover, Yale University, and Jefferson Medical College. After a residency in psychiatry at Georgetown University Hospital and two years in the U.S. Army Medical Corps, he began working in forensics with both adult and child offenders.

He used that experience to write his first book, *When Evil Isn't Enough*, a New York City crime story about psychopaths flourishing on both sides of the law. Drawing from his Appalachian memories, he wrote *Voices From The Hollow*, stories about Appalachian people, their culture, and durable values. *Voices* was a finalist in *Foreword* magazine's short story Book of the Year award in 2006.

Ranging from bemused to lacerating, Hirsh's current collection of stories, *The Lost Tarpon*, takes a fanciful look at just how soft conventional wisdom and morality really are.

Dr. Hirsh is retired and living in Lexington, Virginia, patiently waiting for the return of Ambrose Bierce.

CPSIA information can be obtained at www.ICGtesting.com
Printed in the USA
LVOW051957060912

297702LV00008B/212/P